IN BAD FAITH
A Detective Loxley Nottinghamshire Crime Thriller

By
A L Fraine

The book is Copyright © to Andrew Dobell, Creative Edge Studios Ltd, 2022.
No part of this book may be reproduced without prior permission of the
copyright holder.

All locations, events, and characters within this book are either fictitious, or
have been fictionalised for the purposes of this book.

Book List

www.alfraineauthor.co.uk/books

Acknowledgements

Thank you to Crystal Wren for your amazing editing.
A big thank you to Meg Jolly and Tom Reid for allowing me to use their names in this novel. I really appreciate it.
Thank you to my family, especially my parents, children, and lovely wife Louise, for their unending love and support.

Table of Contents

Book List 3
Acknowledgements 3
Table of Contents 4
1 7
2 26
3 38
4 50
5 57
6 70
7 86
8 101
9 107
10 122
11 134
12 146
13 158
14 170
15 174
16 183
17 191
18 197
19 205
20 213
21 225
22 233
23 241
24 252
25 260
26 269
27 272
28 274
29 287
30 290
31 299
32 304
33 326

34	331
35	337
36	340
37	349
38	355
39	360
40	367
41	371
42	386
43	390
44	398
45	400
Author Note	413
Book List	414

1

"Me and the boys are gonna find yeh, and fucking kill yeh," the man said, speaking around a mouthful of chicken soup that dripped from his mouth and into his beard. "That's what they said to me."

Lorraine smiled and reached across the table, placing her hand on his. "I'm sorry you had to deal with that, Albert. I don't know what to suggest other than try and stay away from them if you can."

"I do, but it's hard. They're everywhere, and they're just fuckin' kids."

"Albert." She put a note of warning in her tone. "Language."

"Sorry, it's just habit." He seemed sheepish as he hungrily spooned the last of the soup into his mouth.

Lorraine watched and smiled, feeling a warmth inside, knowing that she was helping this poor man. He was a mess, with his long, scraggly beard and layers of worn-through, stained clothing. She'd seen worse in her time, they'd had people turn up to the soup kitchen who were literally at death's door and needed medical intervention, but this wasn't the case here. Albert was hungry but not starving and was just dealing with some local kids causing problems.

But hopefully, a problem shared was a problem halved.

"Bloody kids," Albert continued. "Why aren't they in school? Why are they out on the streets causing trouble?"

She had to agree and had encountered this kind of antisocial behaviour a few times herself. She could only imagine how much worse it might be for people like Albert, who were out in the streets the whole time, unable to escape it.

"Lorraine."

She looked up to see the Reverend standing close by, his hands behind his back, smiling at them. "Bernard."

"It's getting late. I think you should head home. I need to close up for the night."

Glancing around, Lorraine realised that Shirley and Esther had already gone, leaving just herself and Bernard with Albert in the church hall. "Oh, I'm sorry, of course."

"I'd better get goin' too," Albert said with a lopsided smile half obscured by his unkempt beard still containing flecks of soup. "Sorry I turned up at the last minute."

Lorraine nodded at the man, who seemed a lot older than his years. "That's okay. Earlier would be better, though. Then we can have a proper chat and see if we can help you, maybe find somewhere warm for you to sleep?"

Handing out steaming hot soup and bread was all very well, and she loved being able to feed these poor people, but they needed so much more than a hearty meal, and that was the part she really enjoyed. There was something so uplifting about being able to offer genuine aid to these victims of the modern world. She felt closer to God in those moments than at any other time, as if she were truly doing God's work.

"Yeah, sure, I'll be here earlier. When's the next one?"

"This time next week, from five PM, okay?" Lorraine answered.

"Got it. Thanks… I'll just take this… for later." Albert grabbed the last chunk of bread from the table with a cheeky smile before hobbling out, pulling his dirty coat closer.

Lorraine sighed, feeling shattered after such a long evening.

"You didn't have to let him in, you know," Bernard stated. "We have a finishing time for a reason. We all have homes to go to."

"I know, but I couldn't do that. I'll sleep better tonight knowing he's had a good meal."

"We don't deserve you, Lorraine."

"Thank you, Father."

"Now, go home. That's an order. Poor Graham will be wondering where you are."

She shrugged, feeling certain that Graham was likely asleep in his chair by now rather than worrying where she was. "Are you sure you're okay to close up?"

"I'm fine. I'm quite capable of washing a few dishes and locking the door." He picked up Albert's dirty bowl. "Are you okay getting home?"

"It's not far," she reassured him. The Reverend did so much for the community; she didn't want to impose on him. Besides, a brief walk and some fresh air would be just what she needed after being stuck in a hot kitchen and a smelly hall. She sympathised with the plight of these homeless men and women and realised it wasn't their fault, but some of them really did smell quite bad.

She'd get herself a bath when she got in.

"Alright, as long as you're sure."

Lorraine went about gathering her things, pulling on her coat and grabbing her bag. She'd already boxed up some of the leftover food and would enjoy eating it in the next day or so.

Saying her final goodbyes to the Reverend, she walked out of the church hall and into the surrounding housing estate of Whitemoor.

The air was cool, and the street lights were on now that darkness had fallen on the city of Nottingham. The walk home was a short one, just through the estate, over the brownfield site where the old mills and factories had once stood, and back into Bobbers Mill, the suburban area where she lived with her husband. It was just on the other side of the River Leen, maybe a ten-minute walk at most.

She'd be home before she knew it.

Stuffing her hands into her pockets, she strode along the road, passing boxy red-brick terrace houses with glowing windows and small front gardens divided by waist-high fencing.

She'd walked home this way many times and knew it well. Nothing had ever actually happened to her, but there had been a few creepy or concerning moments over the years. Whenever possible, she preferred to get a lift from Shirley, but sometimes that just wasn't possible, and with Graham suffering badly from his sciatica these days, she felt like she couldn't ask him to drive around either. It triggered the pain and would leave him in agony for days.

Whitemoor wasn't a bad neighbourhood, not really. It was like most inner-city areas where the local kids would hang around, bored out of their minds with nothing to do other than make their own entertainment.

Turning off the road, she followed a path heading east alongside a slender green with a couple of trees. As she walked, she noticed a small group of teenagers standing in the shadows. Smoke curled up from whatever they were smoking as a couple of them glanced her way. Their eyes glinted menacingly in the dark.

"Y'all right, love?" one of them called out. The young man's attention was unwelcome. She tensed as her heart rate spiked, almost expecting the worst.

"Fancy a toke?" One of them held up the roll-up cigarette they were puffing on, causing the others to laugh. Lorraine didn't join in, she found the laughter intimidating and pulled her eyes away from the youths in the hope that her lack of interest would be reciprocated, and they'd leave her be.

As she left them behind, their jokes and conversation faded. Ten metres further on, she glanced back, but they'd remained under the tree. With a deep breath, she allowed herself to relax a little as she reached the next road and marched along the path. She had a few more roads to navigate before she reached the railway footbridge and the long walk across the brownfield site back into her estate.

Reaching the next corner, she glanced back once more before the small green fell out of sight, hoping to catch the teenagers still where she'd left them. But for a moment, she couldn't see where they were.

Frowning, she turned her head more fully and noticed they'd moved and were walking this way.

Lorraine's breath caught in her throat.

Hoping she wouldn't be noticed, she focused on the road ahead and pressed on, putting on a burst of speed to try and outpace them.

Were they following her? It was possible, but it was also possible they were just locals going about their business and didn't even think that they might be freaking her out. After all, why would they be interested in her? She didn't have anything of value on her and had no interest in them. But, there was that small nagging doubt that maybe their intentions towards her were not honourable, and they were about to ruin her evening.

Or, perhaps she was just being paranoid.

As she walked, Lorriane squeezed her eyes shut for a second and offered a silent prayer to God, asking him to watch over and guide her safely home.

Blinking, she ploughed on, taking a right and making her way east again. She was close to the railway bridge up ahead and the final fork in the road before it.

With her leg muscles aching, she reached the junction. She could keep heading east, towards the bridge, or go west, back towards the main roads. It would be a much longer walk, adding maybe half an hour to her trip and taking her through several other areas she didn't fancy walking through, but she'd also be surrounded by people.

Looking back, she spotted the teens stroll out of the side road she'd exited from and grimaced. She couldn't go back that way.

Looking west, she briefly considered the longer walk, but as she gazed up the street, she saw a figure, a man by the looks of it. He seemed to turn towards her as if noticing her looking. He cocked his head to one side and set off walking, straight for her.

The tension in her chest intensified as her heart suddenly ached with fear. She needed to get home.

With renewed resolve, she turned east and walked eagerly up the path along the side of the road. She found herself at the entrance to a cul-de-sac that extended south. Before she reached the small ring of houses, she spotted the pathway on her left that led to the footbridge. She took it with a final glance behind her. The teenagers were nowhere in sight, but the man she'd seen, exited the road she'd walked up and continued to follow her.

She didn't wait to find out who they were and disappeared up the footpath. Within moments she was walking up the steps of the footbridge and crossing the twin rail lines. The bridge had seen better days and was covered in spray-painted graffiti. Tags and disgusting words had been written in marker pen, alongside crude drawings of penises and other offensive images.

Had the teens who'd followed her done some of this? Were they some of the local hooligans who'd harassed Albert, or had she misjudged them? Maybe they'd wanted nothing to do with her, and their walking behind her was just a coincidence.

She might never know.

Reaching the far side of the bridge, she hustled down the stairs and looked left as she neared the bottom.

There he was. That man.

The teenagers might not have been following her, but this man certainly was. She couldn't make out any details at this distance, but he stopped part way up the steps and eyed her.

Then he pointed at her.

Lorraine stiffened in terror as the man continued up the steps on his side of the bridge.

"Oh, no. Please no," she muttered in panic taking the last few steps, two at a time. There was no mistaking this. No mistaking it at all. This man was following her.

Reaching the bottom of the steps, she turned onto a single fenced-in pathway across a large area of scrubland between the River Leen and the railway with no one about and no way to escape.

Just a long dark path with no way out and a strange man hurrying after her.

Lorraine jogged into the night.

The darkness seemed impenetrable as it closed in around her now that she'd left the street lamps behind. Nothing lit this lonely path. Even the surrounding city with its bright, gaudy lights felt miles away.

If she screamed, no one would hear her.

Stuffing her hand in her pocket, Lorraine pulled out her phone. She'd always struggled with these new smartphones, finding them incredibly fiddly and not at all smart. Tapping at the glowing screen as best she could, she opened the gallery app.

"Aaagh." She'd been aiming for the phone icon. She tried again and this time managed to open up the settings menu. "No, not that."

She closed it by hitting the home button and tried again. This time she managed it. A list of recent contacts appeared, but she couldn't see Graham on there. Lorraine growled through gritted teeth while scrolling, the phone bouncing about in front of her as she speed-walked.

Her lungs were burning, her breath came in shallow gasps, and even her vision was blurring from budding tears.

Spotting her husband's name, she tapped the icon, and it started to place the call.

"Finally."

Putting the phone to her ear, she picked up speed now she wasn't trying to navigate through her mobile's operating system and waited for the call to connect.

Was the man close? Would he be catching her up? She felt like he'd be right behind her, about to grab her and throw her to the floor, or worse. The skin on her back crawled with fateful anticipation as she jogged along this seemingly endless, shadowed path with its tall fencing. It trapped her, giving her only one way to go and nowhere to hide.

The call placed. It started to ring.

Unable to stop herself, Lorraine turned and glanced back, praying she'd see nothing.

Out of the darkness, the man ran towards her.

Lorraine screamed and broke into a sprint.

"Hey."

"No, get away," Lorraine yelled. "I'm calling the police."

"Mrs Winslow, it's me!"

"What?" Lorraine slowed and turned back. The man had slowed to a walk, gasping for breath as much as she was, and suddenly she recognised him.

She stopped and drew in a long breath as the tension faded from her body, as she realised she'd made a mistake.

"Spencer?"

"I'm sorry, I didn't mean to scare you. I wanted to say thank you for the food tonight."

Lorraine shook her head as she regained her breath. Noticing the phone was still ringing and Graham hadn't answered, she ended the call. He was likely asleep and his phone on silent. Typical.

"My word, Spencer. Next time, just wave, maybe? You scared me half to death."

"Yeah, I realised. Sorry."

"That's okay. Oh, my giddy aunt. Well, it's good to see you again."

Like Albert, Spencer wore old, dirty clothes in layers with a couple of coats over the top to keep him warm. He also sported some impressive but messy facial hair and a woollen beany hat, the original colour of which was difficult to make out anymore.

"How about I walk you the rest of the way?" he suggested. "I'm sleeping down the end of here anyway."

"Oh, really?"

"There's a small area behind an old derelict building at the far end that a few of us use sometimes. I'll show you."

"Yeah, okay. Thank you."

"That's okay. It's the least I can do after scaring you."

"Indeed," Lorraine agreed as they continued up the long path. It widened part way along, and off to her left, she could make out the lone brick chimney in the middle of the site, reaching high into the leaden sky. A lone sentinel in the darkness, overlooking the remains of what had once been a thriving industrial site. Years ago, there'd been factories and mills here, producing soap or bleaching and dying things. A hundred years ago, they'd been powered by the waters of the Leen, and then steam engines. But the age of factories and manufacturing in the UK was well and truly over. She had little doubt that this site would one day be transformed into a housing estate, dotted with the identikit red-brick boxes they called houses, with perfect lawns and perfect roads. The history would be gone, destroyed in the greedy quest for profit, dressed up as the altruistic desire to provide affordable housing.

"I didn't get to speak to you much tonight," Lorraine said as they walked. "How are you?"

"Alright, I suppose."

"Just alright?"

Spencer sighed. "I've not seen my daughter since I saw you last if that's what you mean. Sandy's still reluctant because of this." He indicated his clothing and general appearance. "But at least she's open to the idea. It's Darren that always stops it from happening, though. He hates me. Always has."

Lorraine sighed. "I know it's hard, Spencer. I know you want to see your little girl, and you know I support you in that. I can talk to them if you want me to, that offer is still there, but you need to see things from their perspective. Sandy, and even her stepfather, believe it or not, both want to protect Elise. They're worried about how it will affect her to know that her dad is homeless."

"I know, but I don't think she cares. She just wants to see her dad, I'm sure of it. It's Darren that hates me, always has. He was at school with me, you know? A few years below. He was mates with Sandy's brother and always fancied her. He jumped in pretty quick when things went to shit between Sandy and me."

"You mean when you cheated?"

Spencer groaned and sighed once more. "I know what I did was wrong, and I accept that she couldn't trust me again. That's fine. But that was years ago, and honestly, I just want to see Elise again."

"I know you do. But you need to let go of this hate for Darren. Sandy is happy with him. They're married now, and I think you said they have a new baby?"

"Yeah, they do." He sounded sad.

"Well, they have to think of the baby too, and after that scene you made at their house, I think they're just being cautious. It's not good for your relationship with Elise to have the police called when you visit, is it?"

"No, I guess not."

"I know not. But as I said, we can help. You can come to us. Me, the Reverend, Shirley or any of the others at the kitchen, we can all help and get you reacquainted with your daughter."

"I think Sandy and Darren will want to use Social Services or something rather than the church."

"We can work with them too."

"Thanks," Spencer replied as they approached the end of the path. Ahead, along the short side road they were now on, beyond several cars parked beside a garage, Lorraine could see the light from her road's street lamps. She was moments from her home and feeling much happier.

"This is me," Spencer said, leading her over to an area behind an old derelict building on the left of the path. Some chicken wire fencing had been pulled back, and beyond it was a mountain of old mattresses, cardboard and tarpaulin beneath a dirty, rusty overhang of plastic sheeting held in place by metal struts that served as a roof.

Spencer walked in and sat with his back to the brick wall.

It looked like it could host several homeless people at once, but Spencer was the only one here for now. Seeing him alone, defeated and desperate, pulled on her heartstrings. He'd been through about as much as anyone, and although she found herself sympathising with Sandy when she thought of him cheating on her, he'd gone on to see his whole life collapse around him since.

His mistress had left him, he'd descended into gambling after Sandy left, ended up in debt to some loan sharks and before he knew it, he was living on the street.

She felt suddenly selfish taking this leftover food home with her.

"Here, I've got some food from the kitchen. You can have it." She sat beside him and opened the bag she'd been carrying. The contents had been banged about from her run, leaving something of a mess inside the bag.

"Thank you," Spencer said enthusiastically as she handed him a polystyrene container. He looked inside and grinned. "This is amazing."

Nearby, an engine approached. She turned as it drew closer, its red reversing lights casting an eerie crimson glow onto the side road. She frowned, wondering who it might be, and turned to look.

The rear of a white van backed into view and stopped.

She glanced back at Spencer, who was watching along with her and frowning in confused curiosity.

"Friends of yours?"

"Not likely."

Several men in black clothing, their faces hidden, jumped out of the van.

"Stay there, don't move," one of them shouted. "Don't you fuckin' move!"

One held a baseball bat, and another brandished a knife as the men swarmed toward them.

"What's going on?" Lorraine called out.

"Shut your fuckin' mouth."

"Hey," Spencer called out. "Don't you talk to her like—"

The man with the bat hit Spencer in the gut. With a grunt, he crumpled to the floor.

Lorraine screamed.

One of the men slammed his fist into her stomach, cutting off her scream as she doubled up in agony. For a moment, she thought she'd die. Struggling for breath, she gasped and tried desperately to suck air into her aching lungs. It felt like an age until she finally inhaled a lungful of life-giving oxygen.

Before she could get her bearings, she was hauled off her feet and slammed back into a wall. One of the men clamped his hand over her mouth, his face suddenly inches from hers.

"Shut it, bitch."

Flicking her eyes right, she saw the one with the bat swing at Spencer again before they lifted him to his feet and dragged him past her.

"Bring her too," one of the others said, his voice gruff. "Saves us doing this again in a few weeks."

Her heart skipped a beat as she stared between the masked men in abject fear. "No!" she mumbled through the man's hand.

He punched her again. Pain exploded across her face and the back of her head where it hit the wall. She could feel something warm, wet and metallic tasting in her mouth.

Blood.

"I said, fuckin' shut it."

He and another picked her up, carried her around the corner and threw her into the van. After landing in the back, she panicked and scrambled for the doors in a desperate attempt to flee. Someone grappled her and threw her back to the floor. A second later, someone kicked her in the face.

The world swam as she collapsed.

She heard the doors slam shut, the noise echoed through her garbled brain, and any hope of escape faded. Spencer lay beside her. His eyes had rolled back in their sockets, and there was blood leaking from his mouth.

"What do you want?" she gasped, somehow able to string a coherent sentence together.

"Shut her up," one of the men barked from close by. She didn't see who it was.

A shadow loomed in her blurred vision and grabbed her. He stuffed something dry and dirty into her mouth and heard the distinct sound of carpet tape being pulled off the roll.

Within moments they'd gagged her, pulled a bag over her head and bound her wrists.

2

Detective Sergeant Rob Loxley accelerated up the ridgeway that skirted the edge of the Top Valley estate in Nottingham, north of the city centre. The tan and red-brick houses that had been packed cheek by jowl into the estate raced by as the pool car's engine hummed. On the other side of the road, Southglade Park was hemmed in by scraggly bushes and green fencing slid by the window as they raced up the hill.

Rob eased off the accelerator as they approached the turnoff, but took the corner at speed. The pool car handled the turn with poise and grace, without the rear end kicking out, much to Rob's dismay. He longed to be gunning the engine of his classic Mark Three Ford Capri 2.8 injection, instead of this insipid, non-descript pool car. He wasn't even sure what model of safe, boring, modern car this was, and cared even less.

"Steady on, Rob," DS Nick Miller piped up from the passenger seat. "I'd like to get there in one piece."

"We will," Rob reassured him as he tempered his speed.

"No thanks to you," Nick quipped, a wry smile on his face. His partner on the job was still gripping the door handle with white knuckles, despite his levity.

"You could have driven," Rob countered. "You know I'm not a fan of these pool cars."

"You can long for the days of The Sweeny as much as you like, but the world's moved on, and there's no way I'm getting into that old banger of yours."

Rob scoffed. "Don't insult Belle like that."

Nick gave a shake of his head, but said nothing.

"How long until uniform get here?" Rob asked, choosing to change the subject.

"Shouldn't be long. We can get close and watch the building."

"I'm not sitting and waiting for a convoy of marked cars to arrive and spook him. After what he's done, I'm going in." Rob's mind was set. After the manhunt he and Nick had been on these last few days, he wasn't about to hold back at the moment of truth.

Nick shrugged. "Fair enough. They'll be here soon enough anyway."

"Damn right."

Rob navigated his way through several residential side roads lined with terrace housing until he reached the T-Junction where the grey, pebble dashed, three-floor block of flats was located. In an attempt to blend in, Rob pulled in behind a Fiesta and stopped. The block loomed large up ahead, like some drab grey edifice of hopelessness.

"Nice place," Nick commented.

"He's in flat 6." Rob eyed the top floor of the block. He'd be up there somewhere, kipping on his mate's sofa as he tried to wait out the storm he'd created.

"Rory Dukes's place," Nick said, checking his notes.

"Aye," Rob confirmed, keeping his eyes fixed on the dark windows, wondering if he'd see their target at them. Was he keeping a lookout? Would he see their approach? Hopefully not. But whatever the case, Rob was not going to sit here and allow this piece of scum one more minute of freedom. "Come on, let's go and pay Mr Marsh a visit."

Climbing out of the vehicle, Rob stuffed his hands in his pockets and strode towards the block, joining Nick on the pavement. Crossing the road, Rob hadn't seen any activity in the windows, but as they closed in on the communal door that led into the building, he spotted two guys standing outside. Both wore hoodies and had a threatening, brooding look to them.

As he watched, a third youth walked out of the building and moved to join the waiting pair.

"He says he's not here." When this new arrival saw Rob and Nick, he slowed and his movements became more guarded, as he regretted what he'd just said.

Rob allowed his gaze to wander over the faces of the three guys as they looked up. None of them was Brendon

Marsh, but he recognised them as members of the same crew that Brendon hung out with, the Top Valley Boyz gang. Lloyd 'Curby' Bristow, the leader of the gang, was one of the three young men standing before them. He was known as Curby because of his rumoured habit of kerb-stomping people—placing their open mouth on the corner of a kerb, as if they're biting it, and stomping on the back of their head.

Clearly a model citizen.

Brendon Marsh was part of the same gang, which was all the confirmation Rob needed that they were on the right track. It didn't confirm that Brendon was here, but it was close enough.

Rob smiled to himself and then caught the eye of Curby, who scowled at him. He held the kid's gaze, only for Curby to shift away and mutter something to his mates. He didn't hear the whole thing, but he did make out the word pigs, confirming his worst suspicions.

They'd been made.

The other two looked up, and Rob sighed at their young appearance. Curby was perhaps the oldest, but at twenty-nine, that wasn't saying much. The other two were maybe in their early twenties. They were barely adults, and had, for all intents and purposes, thrown their lives away. But Rob tempered his opinion, silently chastising himself for blaming them. These things might not be their fault.

They'd been born into and grown up with poverty and neglect that most had trouble comprehending. They lived with daily pressures that normal society couldn't even begin to wrap their heads around, and yet we blamed them for falling into an almost inescapable trap.

Still, it didn't excuse the violence and criminality that permeated these estates.

"Oi, what'cho doing 'ere?" the kid on the right asked.

Rob locked eyes with him and pushed on. "None of your business."

"Fuck that, it's my biz if I make it my biz," the kid replied, puffing his chest out and squaring up as he and Nick passed the trio.

With a grimace of frustration, he realised this was descending quickly. Rob reached for his inside pocket and watched as the kid visibly flinched. A flash of terror flashed across his face before Rob pulled out his warrant card.

Rob had worked the streets for long enough to be more than passingly aware of the gun problem that infected the inner-city gang culture of places like Nottingham. It seemed absurd in modern Britain, with its strict gun laws, that firearms were still a problem. But they were, especially within the criminal fraternity where it was unusual for a week to pass without someone being shot.

These gangs would fight over turf, drugs, and perceived slights against them, and this animosity would often boil over with one or more of the youths involved pulling a gun. A gun that had once been rendered inoperable by cutting away the firing pin, welding up the chamber mechanism and plugging the barrel with a steel ball, could be reactivated with basic engineering skills. And these guns were status symbols on the streets, with weapons like the MAC-10 and its insane rate of fire being seen as one of the ultimate guns to own. Of course, if you wanted to pay more than £100 for a reactivated gun, you could shell out perhaps a grand or more for a brand-new smuggled Berretta with no ballistic history, but these were usually reserved for the heavy hitters, the dealers and gang leaders who could afford that much for such a weapon.

The young man in the middle of the group didn't flinch and just watched Rob with a stony-faced expression as he held up his ID.

"Get lost, now, before I nick you for obstruction, and whatever else I can pin on you."

The comments that followed were predicably grotesque, but the trio continued to move away as Rob and Nick approached the main entrance to the block.

"Bloody idiots," Rob moaned.

"What do you reckon, friends of Marsh?"

"I recognise some of them, they're in the same gang, so yeah, they're friends alright." Rob looked back and spotted the familiar glow of a phone as one of the three guys used his device. "Come on, let's get up there."

Walking in through the front door, with its broken lock, they made their way up the two flights of stairs to the top floor and approached number six. Rob knocked, rapping his knuckles against the wooden door, and waited.

He glanced right and gazed through the windows as the sun set over another day in the city, casting its golden glow over the urban sprawl. Sometimes, it was hard to imagine the brutality that was all around them when the views were that spectacular.

"Who is it?" The male voice came from within the flat.

"We're looking for Rory Dukes, we'd just like to have a chat," Rob replied as Nick stood a few steps behind, watching.

"Who's we?"

"Detectives Loxley and Miller, with the Nottinghamshire Police. Open up please, Mr Dukes."

There was quiet for a moment, and then the muffled sound of muttering, or maybe whispering as Mr Dukes kept them waiting. It was hardly subtle. Moments later, Rob heard the security chain jangle, before the door opened and a man in his early twenties with wild hair and an unshaven jaw peered out at them.

"I.D?"

Rob showed him his warrant card. "Can we come in?"

The man held Rob's gaze, as if he'd suddenly bluescreened for a moment before he blinked and answered, "Urr, it's a bit of a mess."

Rob raised a disbelieving eyebrow. "Do you have anyone in there with you, Mr Dukes?"

"No." He sounded indignant, offended almost as he scoffed at the idea of someone being in there.

"Then you wouldn't mind us coming in and having a look around, right?"

Rob caught the flicker of panic that flashed behind Rory's eyes, but he pulled it back and shrugged, feigning indifference.

"Well..." He'd relaxed a little, letting the door open more, revealing the scene beyond. He wasn't lying, it was a mess.

"Rory." Rob dropped his tone and stepped closer, all business. "Step out and give him up, you don't want to get caught up in the middle of all this, believe me, you don't."

"Caught up in what? I don't know what you're on about."

"We know he's in there."

In the distance, he could hear sirens blaring, getting closer. It seemed like Rory heard them too, but he gave his head a shake before answering.

"Who? Who's in here with me?"

So, he was still going to play ignorant, Rob huffed, and chose to give him one more warning. "Last chance."

Rory grimaced, contorting his face as he considered his reply. A moment later, with a clatter of movement, a figure barrelled into the hallway, barged past Rory and slammed his shoulder into Rob. It happened so fast Rob barely had a chance to brace himself as the man hit him like a battering ram. Stumbling back, he fell into Nick, and the pair hit the floor in a heap, groaning. Rob grunted and scrambled to his feet.

"That was Brendon," Nick hissed.

"I know," Rob snapped.

"Get after him."

"Stay in there," Rob bellowed at Rory, before he took off down the stairs after Brendon, who was an entire flight of stairs ahead of him. Taking several steps at once, Rob sprinted around the corner and down the second flight, in time to see Brendon hesitating at the front door, then turning and making for the back of the building.

Rob spotted flashing blue lights out on the road and chanced a grin. He'd gained precious seconds when Brendon had hesitated on seeing the lights.

At the bottom of the steps, Rob swung himself around the corner using the bannister. "Brendon, stop. You can't escape." But the young man pushed on, banging through the back door and out into the rear car park.

Brendon stumbled as he tried to flee over a small wall, and then sprinted into the rear road way, towards two rows of garages that faced one another.

Rob charged after him, gaining ground. "Brendon, give it up." Ahead, Rob saw a fence at the back of the lot. Brendon leapt for it, but slipped and fell back. Rob grabbed him by the shirt and yanked him off the fence. He fell onto his back and rolled away.

Rob went for him again as the younger man scrambled to get back up. He wasn't big, but he was fast and scrawny. Grabbing him again, Rob pulled Brendon back to the ground and tried to pin him. "Stop resisting, you little shit."

"Get the fuck off me, piggy. I'll fuck you up." Brendon flailed around, but to little effect until Rob grabbed his arm and managed to yank it behind the kid, turning Brendon onto his front.

"Aaah, my arm," Brendon yelled in desperation. "You'll break my arm."

"After what you've done, that's the least you deserve. How does it feel to fight an adult, Huh? Someone your own size?"

"I'll kill you."

"I wouldn't go around shouting that if I were you. Not with Scott on life support."

"Piss off."

Rob jerked his arm, feeling very tempted to pull it a little further and dislocate it.

"Rob!"

He looked up to see DS Miller running over, and behind him, coming from around the side of the block, he spotted the three youths they'd seen out front.

Rob entertained the idea of breaking the man's arm for a moment, letting his personal feelings towards this brutal young man play through his head as a revenge fantasy, before relenting and pulling out a pair of cuffs. He leaned in as he worked. "Consider yourself lucky we're not like you."

"You alright?" Nick asked as he drew nearer. "You got him, okay?"

"Yeah," Rob confirmed. "He's not going anywhere."

"Oi," one of the youths called out as they approached. "You leave him alone?"

"What's he done to you?" another added.

Remaining silent and brooding, Curby stopped a few metres away and peered down at Brendon. "Found you."

Brendon grunted as he shifted beneath Rob's weight. "Get this fuck off me."

"You're staying right where you are, Mr Marsh," Rob answered. "You're under arrest for assaulting a minor. You do not have to say anything. But it may harm your defence if you do not mention when questioned something which you later rely on in court. Anything you do say may be given in evidence. Do you understand?"

"A minor?" Curby asked, attracting Rob's attention. "You mean a child?"

"I need you to back off," Rob warned, sensing anger from the youth.

"Brendon," Curby continued as Nick moved in. "What did you do?"

Brendon hissed. "I can explain."

Curby straightened and backed away a few steps, guided by Nick. He was pissed off. "You better fuckin' do." He glanced at Nick who was trying to get him to back further away. "Alright, I got it, man. I just want to know what's going on?"

Rob spotted a uniform running around the side of the building, back lit by the flashing blue lights of their pursuit cars. Removing his weight from Brendon, he hauled the young man up by the cuffs and glanced over to Curby, who was backing further away, suppressed fury boiling behind his eyes.

Rob leaned in closer to Brendon. "I don't think your mate is very happy with you. What did you do, play with his dolls?"

"Piss off."

3

Pulling into the garage at Nottingham Central Police Station, Rob manoeuvred the car into an empty spot and turned the engine off.

"Any news on the kid?" Rob glanced over at the marked car that contained Brendon, still unsettled as to why he'd taken out his anger on the boy. They'd already interviewed Tess, his girlfriend, and even she seemed to be in the dark as to why he'd exploded that night. Rob was keen to find out more and provide Tess with some answers.

"No, nothing. He's still in intensive care, as far as I know," Nick replied. "I can make some calls when we get in, see if there's been any developments."

Rob gave his partner a nod. "At least we have Brendon now."

"Aye," Nick agreed.

"Let's get the hairy bollock booked in, shall we?" Rob exited the car and walked over as one of the uniformed officers guided Brendon out of the rear seat. Brendon stared over at Rob with a look of utter contempt, as if he were contemplating all the fun ways he could kill him.

"Right then, Brendon, this way," Rob said and led him away from the car toward the door for the custody suite and the processing desk.

"This is bullshit," Brendon complained as he followed Rob, his hands in cuffs, flanked by two uniformed officers with Nick bringing up the rear. Rob ignored Brendon's protestations as he acted all tough in front of Rob's colleagues.

Inside the custody suit, the room was dominated by a tall, sturdy desk, behind which the handful of attending officers waited and chatted amongst themselves. Monitors protected by clear Perspex screens hummed in the clean, light grey room, while in the distance, the sound of someone banging against their cell door echoed through the corridors.

The moment Rob walked in, he spotted an unwelcome face across the room and rolled his eyes with a sigh. Shit. What on earth was he doing in here other than causing trouble?

Rob shot Nick a tired look. He spotted DI William Rainault across the room and mimicked Rob's eye roll before leaning into Rob.

"Go on, you deal with the Sheriff," Nick said, using their nickname for Rainault. "I'll get Brendon booked in."

"Cheers, mate," Rob replied before he wandered over to where Rainault was standing with a smug, self-important smile on his face. He dressed smartly and always seemed well turned out with his tailored suits, slicked-back dark hair, and neatly trimmed goatee. His prim and proper appearance was just one more annoying thing to add to the list. He greeted Rainault. "Bill."

"Rob," Rainault answered in stilted tones.

"What brings you down here?"

Rainault's eyebrows climbed up his forehead. "I would have thought that would be fairly obvious by now." He smirked and shrugged. "I'm just checking up on you, that's all."

"Of course, you are. And what's your excuse this time?"

"The integrity of this force and its officers is of paramount importance to me, Rob. You know that."

"Lovely." Rob felt tired of this seemingly endless dance he and Bill regularly went through. He sometimes wondered when it would end, but ultimately, Rob knew the answer to that and settled into the familiar back and forth.

"Who's this?" Bill nodded to Brendon.

Rob glanced at Bill, determining if he was serious for a moment before he answered. "This is Brendon Marsh, brought in on suspicion of assaulting a minor."

"I see. And things didn't get heated at all during the arrest?"

"Of course not," Rob replied while he glanced across at the faces of the officers he'd brought Brendon in with. Had one of them harboured concerns about Rob's treatment of Brendon and called ahead to report it in?

Internally, he had been tempted to inflict a little of the unimaginable pain that Scott must have felt upon Brendon by breaking or dislocating his arm during the struggle. But naturally, he'd resisted because that was the difference between him and people Like Brendon. He might well have thoughts about hurting people he thought deserved it, but that didn't mean he'd act on them.

He was better than that and knew the difference between right and wrong. Unfortunately, Bill and several other Anti-Corruption officers had certain ideas about him, no matter how exemplary his career was.

Had someone contacted Bill, or had he just wandered down here to show his face, and cause Rob to second guess himself?

It was all too easy to slip into thinking that there were people watching him the whole time, reporting his every move to Wild Bill here, but Rob couldn't let himself fall into that trap. That kind of paranoia was never healthy.

"Good," Rainault replied and looked over to where Brendon was giving his details to the Custody Officer who was entering them into the system. "Mr Marsh, I hope you found the actions of your arresting officers to be... satisfactory?"

Rob couldn't help another eye roll as Brendon turned to Rainault and glared at him as if he was a pile of sloppy dog shit he'd just stepped in.

"Fuck off. You pigs are all the same."

Catching Rainault's expression, Rob struggled to keep his smile under control. Stifling his amusement, Rob turned to Rainault.

"If it's okay with you, sir, I'd like to get Brendon here processed and into a cell. We have a lot of work to be getting on with."

Rainault peered at Rob through narrowed eyes, his lips twisted into a look of disgust, but Rob knew there was little for him to go on here. He was just trying to make Rob feel uncomfortable, making him aware that he was being watched by the boys and girls in the PSU, the Professional Standard Unit, that had been on his back for years now.

But Anti-Corruption had nothing because there was nothing.

They were persecuting him for things that were utterly out of his control and in the distant past. But no matter what he did, no matter how dedicated to the job he was, how clean his record, or even how many vetting tests he passed, there would forever be that fog of suspicion around him. He knew he was clean. He knew he wasn't on the take, and he'd long ago realised that he just had to accept their suspicion and get on with the job.

It was something he had to deal with.

"I'm watching you, Loxley," Rainault hissed.

"Yeah, good luck with that."

"I don't need luck. You'll screw up one day, and I'll be there to see you go down. That's a promise."

"Is it?" Rob's voice dripped with sarcasm. "Well, I am blessed. Thank you so much."

"I'll see you around."

"Aye, sir, you will. Toodle pip." Rob waved his fingers as Rainault turned and left the suite, his head held high. Once he was out of sight, Rob took a long breath and released it, letting the stress and tension fall from his body. He had enough to deal with today without Rainault stirring the pot.

"Y'all right?"

Rob turned to Nick as one of the custody officers led Brendon off into the cell block. Brendon shot Rob a brief look of contempt before he moved out of his eye line.

"Yeah, I'm okay. Just the usual shit."

"Aye. I figured. Just ignore it. He's not worth your time."

"Right then, let's get back upstairs and report in. Might as well deal with all the dickheads at once."

Nick smirked, catching Rob's reference to his commanding officer, DCI Peter Orleton. "Lead the way."

They took the back staircase, keeping away from reception and minimising the security doors they had to pass through to return to their office. Outside, night had fallen, and the city was bathed in artificial light as people drove home or hit the streets for a night of fun.

Upstairs, Rob led the way back into their office, finding DS Frank Parish and DC Tony Darby sitting at their desks, talking and smiling. There were other desks with civilian investigators and uniformed officers in the large, open-plan space, as well as doors leading to other rooms and side offices, such as the one that led to the DCI's private office.

Frank and Tony glanced up as Rob walked in followed by Nick. Rob ignored them and wandered over to his desk, where he removed his jacket.

"Successful bust, was it?" Frank asked from across the room.

"Nicked one of your own, did you?" Tony added, much to Frank's amusement.

Rob fought the urge to make an exaggerated eye roll, but it was hopeless. He followed it up with a mock frown. "What, you mean a law-abiding citizen? No, I didn't arrest one of those. That would be a little counter-productive, don't you think?"

Nick snorted.

"Don't get smart, Loxley," Frank replied, his voice losing its levity.

"I wouldn't dream of it, Frank."

The door to Peter Orleton's office opened, and the DCI leaned out. "Loxley, Miller, in you come."

Peter disappeared back into his office as Rob turned to Miller, who shrugged.

"Let's get this over with," Nick muttered.

"Aye." Rob got up, led the way over, and walked in. Behind him, Nick pulled the door closed.

The office wasn't large or opulent. Instead, it was clean and functional, very much a typical boring modern workspace with a table, chairs, some filing cabinets and a few certificates on the walls. The only personal effects in the room were a couple of framed photos on the desk that Rob couldn't see the fronts of, a collection of lanyards, a couple of trophies for archery, some policing qualifications, and a Thank You card that was the most colourful thing in here.

Apart from that, the room looked like a thousand other offices in this city where people were working into the wee hours.

"Alright, let's make this quick. I've already been late home a little too much recently, and I don't want to repeat it tonight. How'd it go?"

"We got him," Rob replied, allowing a self-satisfied smile to touch his face. "Brendon is in custody downstairs."

"He's requested a solicitor," Nick added. "So, we'll need to wait for them to arrive and talk to him once he's ready."

"Tomorrow, most likely," Rob chipped in.

"Let him stew for a bit," Peter replied with a nod. "Fair enough. And what's the latest on the case. I'm guessing Brendon's denied any involvement."

"He's not said much about it, actually. I guess we'll find out more tomorrow. But this isn't his first rodeo, and his mates usually answer everything with no comment, so…"

"Oh, he's one of *them*," Peter replied, fixing Rob with a brief wide-eyed look.

Rob sighed. Frank and Tony might harbour similar suspicions or thoughts as Rainault, but they weren't the office ring leader when it came to the prejudice against him. No, that dubious honour belonged to the man sitting before him, Peter Orleton, who seemed to relish his position as Rob's superior and often enjoyed making his life difficult.

But like Rob, he also had a job to do, so at least on that front, they were united.

"Yeah, he's a known member of the Valley Boyz gang," Rob confirmed.

"You'll have fun interviewing him tomorrow, then. What about his girlfriend and her boy?"

"I've not had an update on Scott yet," Nick replied. "I'll follow that up and see how he's doing. His mum, Tess, has been somewhat cooperative."

"Only somewhat?" Peter asked.

"She answered our questions," Rob answered, "saying that Brendon came back to the house angry, and things quickly deteriorated until he was hurting her. When Scott tried to defend his mother, Brendon turned on him and attacked the boy."

"Does she know why he was so upset?"

"No, sorry, guv. She also refused to have any police protection at her home, a Liaison officer or any counselling. She doesn't want any help at all. But, she is angry and has said on several occasions that she wants to kill Brendon."

"Good thing we have him in a cell, then."

"Aye, guv."

"We have been watching her, though," Nick added. "She might not want us babysitting her, but given her anger at the situation, we've been monitoring her to make sure she doesn't do anything stupid."

"Alright, well, I'll leave it with you. You've got a shit tonne of work left to do on this, so that'll keep you busy."

Rob bobbed his eyebrows.

And you happy with me out of the way for a while, dealing with paperwork.

Based on the years of experience working with Peter, it seemed to be the time when the DCI was the happiest.

When he could look out of his office window and see Rob in the building, Peter didn't bother him so much, even though he clearly didn't have much love for him. It was as though Peter liked to have him on hand to offload the shit jobs to.

Keep your friends close, and all that…

But this rubbed Rob up the wrong way, especially when Peter would hand off jobs to him that seemed designed to keep Rob occupied, quiet, and at his desk. He preferred to be out there, doing his job.

"We'll be busy for a little while," Rob admitted.

"I'm sure I don't need to remind you that we have a new DC joining us tomorrow, and I'll be putting her under your care, Loxley. So, show her around and get her up to speed, alright?"

Internally, Rob groaned as he remembered. He'd known about this new recruit for a while and of Peter's desire to have him show her the ropes. It wasn't Rob's idea of a good time, and he suspected it was a way for Peter to split him and Nick up. He'd been working with Nick for years, and they had a good working relationship that had started long before Peter had become DCI, back when the team was led by Jon Pilgrim.

He and Nick worked well together and knew how the other thought. They got results and had an excellent track record. He was also on his side when it came to these unfounded accusations and was very much a rock for him to lean on when he needed it.

There was little doubt in Rob's mind that this was something else that Peter hated, and it wouldn't be the first time that he'd attempted to separate them.

Still, this new DC would need someone to work with and help get her settled in. Someone had to do it, so why not him?

"I'd not forgotten," Rob lied, biting his lip in mild frustration.

"Good. She'll be in tomorrow morning."

"Excellent," Rob hissed through gritted teeth.

"Off you pop, then. I've got a few things to finish up, and then I'm heading home. I'll see you tomorrow."

"Guv," Rob replied, and they walked out of the office, leaving Peter to his final jobs of the day.

"You'd forgotten, hadn't you?" Nick asked.

"Yeah. Bollocks."

4

Bill examined himself in the tinted windows of the building, checking that his suit was lying right and this his tie was straight before taking a moment to adjust things and get them looking just as he wanted them to.

After all, appearances were important, and it was the work of mere moments to put in that little extra effort and look professional. But so many of his fellow officers didn't do this. They seemed content to look like drunks and tramps with their cheap, poorly fitted suits and wonky ties—if they even bothered with a tie. It was just laziness, and to Bill, if you looked like you were lazy in your appearance, what kind of impression did that give? Did it suggest you would be dedicated and diligent, or half-baked and useless?

He knew what he thought, and it most certainly wasn't the impression that the police should be putting out there.

He pulled at the hem of his jacket to banish some wrinkles before using his fingers to smooth out his hair. Luckily, he'd not inherited his father's genes, who had lost his hair at an early age. Instead, he had thick, lustrous hair like his mother, although he kept his short and neat, just like his perfectly trimmed goatee beard.

"Careful," said a voice to his left. "You'll crack the glass."

Bill turned to see DCI Orleton walking out the back entrance with his bag and jacket in his arms. He was the epitome of an overworked, high-ranking officer of the law.

"Peter," Bill began, turning to face the DCI and clasping his hands behind his back. "Just the person I wanted to see."

"Oh? You could have come to my office."

"No, I don't think so," Bill replied. "I wanted a private word with you, sir."

Peter raised an eyebrow but wore a knowing expression on his face. "About Loxley again, is it?"

"I appreciate your cooperation in this matter, sir. I really do. But it feels to me like we're missing something, sir. His family connections are clear, and I just cannot believe that there isn't something more going on there."

Peter sighed and shrugged. "I'm watching him, just as much as you are, Bill. If there's something amiss, we'll catch it, I'm sure. Corruption doesn't remain hidden forever."

"No, it doesn't, not without help from the powerful and influential, and the worrying thing is, we know there's that in Loxley's connections."

"That depends on who you talk to."

"You're talking to me, and our intelligence is clear on this. We know that—"

"I know the details, Bill," he snapped. "There's no need to remind me."

"Of course, sir." Bill lowered his gaze for a moment as he grimaced, deferring to his superior officer. He'd crossed a line there, so chose to change the subject. "I'll want to talk to Brendon, the gang member he's brought in tonight."

"I see." Peter gave him a curious look as if he wasn't sure of his motives for wanting to talk to this latest suspect.

"I want to make sure Loxley treated Brendon with respect and in a professional manner, that's all."

"Of course. But that's hardly going to get Loxley suspended, is it?" Peter let that remark hang in the air for a moment before continuing, "I and others like me may well sympathise with your opinion of Loxley, Bill, but he has his friends too, you know."

"You mean DCI Nailer?" Bill had several run-ins with Nailer under his belt already and was well aware of his mentor-like relationship with Rob, and how much he'd vouched for him over the years.

"I do, and Superintendent Landon. DCI Pilgrim as well, although he's down in Surrey now."

"He has friends in high places, I know. It doesn't make my investigation any easier, but he's not the only one with influential friends."

"I know, but they could be troublesome."

"Their rank doesn't scare me, Peter." He puffed up his chest, giving out as much confidence as he could. "We all serve the public trust, and when we breach that trust, justice needs to be done. Friends in high places or not, I will get to the bottom of this, one way or another."

"You're convinced of his malfeasance, are you?"

"Rob Loxley is dirty, I'm sure of it, and I will prove it, one way or another. I promise you that."

"Alright, well, you know you have my support in this."

"I know, sir," Bill replied with a smile, pleased that Rob's direct superior was on his side. It gave him excellent access to his target and his movements, which was just what he needed. Peter had given him plenty of tip-offs over the years, including the one about his arrest tonight. It was a long shot to head down to the custody suite and confront him, but he needed Rob to know he was being watched. He needed Rob to feel under pressure. If he felt pressured, then he might make a mistake and give Bill the break he needed.

He'd tried various tactics over the years, from intense, close examination, to backing off and acting as though he had no interest in Rob at all. All to see how he might react and what he might do, but so far, there was nothing concrete—no *Prima Facie* evidence—much to Bill's frustration.

He'd heard stories of other PSU officers going to less than legal lengths to get a corrupt officer, such as planting evidence or fabricating situations to flush their man or woman out. But Bill didn't subscribe to such methods, and had, on occasion, reported other PSU officers for such dodgy tactics. Those methods never really sat well with Bill, and it would be a cold day in hell before he stooped to such lows.

He would catch Rob in the act and stay within the bounds of the law in doing so or not get him at all.

"Well, Bill, if it's okay with you, I'd like to get off home. I have a family waiting for me, and I don't think Carmen would appreciate me being late again."

"Of course, sir. I didn't mean to keep you. Are you doing anything special?"

"Date night," Peter replied. "We've got a babysitter booked for the kids, and we'll be hitting the town. What about you? Any women on the scene at all?"

Bill grimaced as he remembered Francine, the last date he'd been on. The night had gone well, he thought, with a lovely meal and drinks at a restaurant in town, but she'd not called him back or responded to the messages that he'd sent to see if she'd wanted a second date.

He'd since written her off and started hunting through the dating app again to see what other fish might be in the sea, but he'd failed to find anyone. He wondered if he was being a little too judgemental or whether his standards were too high? He didn't think so. That wasn't to say he'd go for just anyone, of course. He had to have some standards, after all.

He thought back to Francine. She was good looking, in a certain light, he supposed. She looked like she carried a little extra weight on her hips, but he could live with that... maybe...

Internally, he grimaced at his thoughts. Was he being shallow?

He shook his head, banishing those thoughts and answering Peter's question. "No, no one right now. I'm on a couple of sites, but..."

"Dating apps? Ugh! I can't even imagine what that's like. Back in my day, we went out and actually met people in the real world. We didn't have mobile phones and apps and all that crap. I don't know how you do it."

"It's not that bad."

"Well, I'll thank my lucky stars that I'm happily married, if it's all the same to you. I can't think of anything worse. Anyway, I really must dash. Call me or come and see me if you need anything, alright?"

"Will do, sir. And thank you."

"My pleasure."

Bill watched the DCI stride off down the stairs, clearly in a hurry to get home to his family. He scowled and shook his head in disappointment at the state of his own barren love life before he turned and made his way back inside, keen to focus on something other than the fairer sex.

5

The vehicle juddered as it powered over uneven ground, making Spencer jump and jolt at every noise. With the black fabric bag over his head, he couldn't see much beyond shifting areas of darkness and light as they drove, and it didn't do much to keep him warm, either. Apart from the bag, he was naked and had been all day. He felt vulnerable and cold with his bound wrists resting awkwardly in his lap.

They'd been on the road for what felt like ages, mainly over smooth roads that didn't cause the car to roll and bounce, but for the past few minutes, the ground beneath the car had changed. They were off-road somewhere, and the uneven ground was making the engine work.

He had no idea what car he was in, but he felt sure it wasn't the van they'd used when he and Lorraine had been kidnapped. It sounded and felt different. For a start, he was on comfortable leather seats that sweated beneath his bare legs and not the hard wooden base of the van.

At a guess, given the light he could make out through the bag, and the length of time that he'd been locked in a room, it had been a whole day since they'd been taken. A whole day that he'd shared with Lorraine in a room somewhere.

During the day, they'd both been stripped naked, the bags removed from their heads, and left cuffed to a radiator, sitting on the dirty floor of what he could only guess was a house. They'd screamed and shouted, trying their best to alert anyone who might hear, but to no avail. Their calls for help had been drowned out by the almost constant deep bass music that was ringing through the building. He could make out voices, too, including the occasional shout or yell. There were people close by who must have heard them, but no one seemed to care.

Once during the day, a scruffy, foul-mouthed young man who'd hit both of them, and groped Lorraine, left them some food, forcing them to eat like animals with only their mouths.

The scruffy man, who can't have been much more than maybe twenty years old, didn't answer any questions. He just hurled abuse and mocked them as they struggled to eat before finally leaving them alone once more.

Lorraine had sobbed for hours, leaving her eyes bloodshot and red until she had no more tears. Afterwards, she joined him in a kind of shocked, paralysed, disbelieving silence as they contemplated their lives.

Later, Lorraine had talked about her husband, Graham, as she wondered if he'd reported her missing. By turns, she was both furious at him for letting her go out alone at night and distraught that she might never see him again.

Spencer didn't have a home life that he missed, but he did feel sad that he might never get to see his daughter again. Would she remember him? Would Sandy's new stuck-up, self-important husband, Darren, become her dad?

He bloody hoped not.

He was a piece of work, alright, a real bastard. Spencer remembered him from school. He'd been a friend of Sandy's brother, and Spencer had always known that Darren had a crush on Sandy, who was several years older than he was. And now, the little shit had the gall to restrict his access to Elise, saying that he needed to clean himself up, that he'd scare his own daughter.

Darren clearly hated him, and Spencer wouldn't put it past him to do something like this, just to get some kind of revenge.

In any case, many hours after they'd been dumped in that room, two men had entered, including the one who'd fed them earlier, and had pointed to him.

"That one," the second guy had said.

They'd put the bag over his head soon after that and led him out naked into the night to this vehicle. He was sitting in the back, flanked as he was between two unknown passengers who kept him quiet and in his seat. They weren't afraid to get violent to enforce their rules either.

Spencer felt like his sanity was slowly leaving him, waiting for whatever grisly fate might be at their ultimate destination. He'd tried to ask where they were going and what they would do with him, and the only answers he got were a fist to the face or an elbow into his ribs, often both.

So, he remained silent.

But the feeling in the vehicle had changed. There was an air of anticipation now as if they were nearing the end of their journey and whatever it was that awaited them. Spencer hated this feeling, it set his teeth on edge. Whatever it was they were going to do once they stopped, it wouldn't be good for him.

This was his endgame. He was sure of it.

Beyond his mask, he saw a new light glow between the threads before the vehicle turned.

"Here, park here," one of the men in the car said before the vehicle stopped.

Doors were opened, and suddenly hands grabbed him by the arms and dragged him out.

"Move it."

"Get out."

"What are you doing?" Spencer tried to ask. He felt grossly terrified as they yanked him out of the back of the vehicle. They weren't gentle about it either and gave him no warning about how far off the ground he was. Stepping out, he stumbled and fell, landing on his knees on soft earth and grass. Before he could appreciate the soft landing, he was gripped by both arms and marched around the vehicle for several metres before they dropped him. He landed on his knees again, doing his best to steady himself with his bound hands.

"Stay there and be quiet."

Spencer nodded.

"He's a thin one," a new voice said, also male. "Looks wiry, though. Fit. He might be a bit of a challenge for once."

"We have another one ready too, an older woman."

"Aaah, you've been busy." The man sounded impressed. "Alright, well, hold onto her. It's been a while since we had a woman. That'll be fun."

Spencer listened, trying to figure out what was going on, but felt none the wiser.

"Any trouble? Were you followed?" It was the new voice again.

"We know what we're doing."

"I hope so." He sounded patronising. "Alright, let's do it. I've been looking forward to this all day. Get his hood off."

Someone ripped the hood off, along with a few hairs from his head. Spencer squinted against the blinding glow of headlights that were pointed right at him. Two men were standing to either side of him. They looked young, teenagers maybe, or a little older. In front of him, an older man, his face in shadow, leaned closer.

"Listen up. I have high hopes for you." The man reached forward and grabbed him by the jaw in a vice-like clamp and lifted his head. Spencer met the man's wild eyes as he grinned. "Don't let me down."

They were standing in the middle of some kind of scrubland, with tall grass, low plants and bushes. In the distance, against the glow of local towns and cities, he could see woodland and forests.

They were in the middle of nowhere. Was this Sherwood or somewhere else?

There were two vehicles—including the 4x4 he'd been driven here in—and about eight people that he could make out. He noticed a couple of them held handguns by their sides. Spencer's blood turned cold.

"What are you going to do?" His throat hurt as he spoke.

The man smiled. "We're going to indulge in a little sport, my good sir."

"Sport?"

"That's right," the man replied with an easy smile. "You'll like it. I'm going to give you a chance to escape."

"What?" Spencer felt confused.

The man grinned again, but it was a predatory smile and wasn't in the least bit friendly. What was he talking about?

He glanced about as the man walked to one of the cars and reached into a long case on its bonnet.

Apart from the headlights, Spencer couldn't make out any other nearby lights, such as from other cars or buildings. There was only the distant glow of towns or villages that couldn't have been too far away. Could he be in Sherwood? Was that where they'd taken him? The Forest wasn't that big anymore, really. Not like it was back in Robin Hood's day, when it stretched for mile after mile, right across the middle of the country.

These days, however, you couldn't walk for very long before you found a road or some kind of civilisation. But did that mean he really did have a chance to escape, as the man had said?

This made no sense.

Spencer saw the man lift something from the case and turn towards him. The item's shape was distinctive and quite unmistakable, as he held it by his side.

It was a long, shaped and curved length of wood, its ends connected by a taut string.

It was a bow.

Spencer's breath caught in his throat as a hundred different scenarios raced through his head, but none were very comforting. The man walked slowly back, holding a long thin item in his other hand. As he got closer, Spencer recognised it as an arrow.

The man leaned in and waved the cruel-looking head of the arrow before him. Its metal head was large and triangular, with three blade-like cutting edges sloping away from the keen point.

It would do a lot of damage to anything it hit.

The man brushed the cool metal of the arrowhead against Spencer's cheek.

"The game is simple," he began. "We let you go, and I hunt you down. That's it. If you somehow manage to escape us, then you're free. See? Simple."

"And, if I don't lose you?"

"I think you can work that out for yourself," the man answered and stepped back, nocking the arrow. "Cut him loose."

One of the kids stepped closer and pulled out a key, which he used to unlock the cuffs before removing them entirely. His job done, the kid stepped away, watching him carefully.

Spencer flexed his hands and rubbed at his wrists, relieved to be free of the restraints.

"I'd get moving if I were you," the archer suggested, causing Spencer to look up. "But, I want this to be fun, so how about a five-second head start? Sound good?"

"Please, you don't have to do this. Just let me go. I won't tell anyone."

"Five."

Spencer jumped to his feet and started to back away. "Please, I have a family, a daughter…"

"Honestly, I'd start running. Four."

Spencer took one last look around the stony faces watching him as the man adjusted his bow, raising it but not yet pointing it at him.

"Damn it." Spencer turned and ran, sprinting away as fast as he could. A heartbeat later, he heard the man's voice slowly call out. "Three, two, one."

Spencer broke left, changing his direction, hoping to dodge any arrow shot at him. Running hard, Spencer waited for a few seconds before breaking right. He needed to make it as hard as possible for this man to hit him and hoped that running in a serpentine back and forth pattern, he might be able to dodge some of the arrows.

Several seconds later, something zipped by, cutting through the air at high speed, sending leaves and twigs falling in its wake as the arrow cut through a bush.

Spencer felt his heart bulge as he realised he'd somehow dodged the arrow. Finding a low bush, he ducked behind it and peered back through the darkness. Not too far away, he could see several figures with torches walking toward him. It was the gang, and they'd spread out, combing the area ahead of them, driving him on. He couldn't stay here, they'd find him easily enough, and that would be the end.

As he contemplated his next move and which direction he should run, Spencer glanced at his bloody feet and realised how much pain he was in. But he couldn't worry about that right now. He'd deal with that later, once he was away from here.

If he got away from here.

Pushing the pain and worry away, he focused on somehow escaping and seeing his daughter again. He needed to focus on that and not let his crippling fear get the better of him. He could do this. He could escape these psychos if he believed it hard enough.

Taking one last deep breath, Spencer closed his eyes and pictured his daughter, summoning her smiling face into his mind's eye. He could almost hear her laughter and feel the boundless life that she always had whenever he saw her. She didn't care what he looked like. She didn't care about his troubles. She just loved him, and that was everything to him.

Spencer heard a sudden 'thwip', as something whipped through the bush he was hiding behind, followed by what felt like someone punching him in the thigh. The pain was sudden and intense. A burning heat poured through his leg, making him hiss and grunt.

For a moment, he almost didn't look, but the temptation was just too great.

Looking down, it was almost surreal. Blood was everywhere, and one of the man's arrows was buried in his thigh. The head had ripped right through his flesh, tearing it open, leaving the arrow's shaft halfway through his flesh.

For what felt like forever, he could only stare at it, not quite believing what he was seeing with his own two eyes. How could this happen?

The sound of approaching voices soon snapped him out of this trance.

"I'd get running if I were you."

Adrenaline surged as he realised they were close, and suddenly the pain seemed to dull as if it were at arm's length. There might still be a chance. He could still escape this and see Elise again.

Without another thought, Spencer broke from cover and ran. He charged off, veering right to where there seemed to be more vegetation that he hoped to use to his advantage. But he couldn't keep it up. Within seconds he started to feel his energy reserves fade, and the searing pain in his leg clawed his attention back.

Pushing on as hard as he could, he tried to dig deep and find those last reserves and somehow keep going, but it was just too hard. As he limped, he could feel his strength fading as if it flowed out of him along with his blood.

Reaching a low tree, he leaned against it, gripping the trunk with his hand, he looked down again. His left leg was red and slick with blood, but the pain seemed to be fading as if he was somehow growing numb to it.

With a thud, an arrow slammed into the tree, just inches from his hand, showering him with bark. Jumping away, he turned to run, only for another arrow to hit his upper right arm. This one didn't pass all the way through. The pain was intense. Shockingly intense. Had it hit the bone?

He tried to look, but his arm didn't seem to get the message and wouldn't move as it should. He felt a kind of grinding deep inside where the arrow hit.

He couldn't die like this. He just couldn't. He had to live, to see his daughter again. She needed her father. She needed him to be there and tried again to picture her face.

He wasn't sure when he'd dropped to his knees. He couldn't remember doing it and did his best to pick himself up and stagger on. There was a thicker grouping of trees in the distance, not too far away. If he could just reach them, and disappear into the forest, maybe he could get away.

Something hit him in the back, right between his shoulder blades, and sent him straight to his hands and knees. His grip on reality and life loosened. There was nothing left for him now. No more reserves of strength, no more energy. Only the growing, inviting nothingness of oblivion and eternal rest.

For a moment, it was almost as if he could hear his daughter's voice. She seemed to be calling out to him, reassuring him that everything would be okay. But as he tried to focus on it, she retreated, and soon there was nothing.

6

Pressure or tightness filled Rob's chest, pressing down on it and restricting his breathing.

He rose from his slumber, gasping for breath in a mild panic, wondering why he found it difficult to breathe. Opening his gunky eyes, he was greeted by a furry face just inches from his own.

Muffin, his black tom cat, lay on his chest, purring. The vibrating cat locked eyes with him but didn't move, content to just lie there as he stared at Rob with his yellow eyes. Muffin closed them, looking regal in his reclined aspect, showing no signs that he might actually get off, just like every morning. It was a sign of affection, so Rob supposed he should be grateful, but he did wonder if he might ever get a lie in one of these days.

Rob relaxed and gave his cat a little fuss, scratching him behind the ears and at the back of his head. The feline's tail rose high in the air as he leaned into Rob's petting, enjoying the attention. Glancing out the window, Rob noticed it was still dark and sighed.

"Couldn't leave me alone, could you?" Reaching for his phone, Rob checked the time and groaned. It was early, not quite five AM yet, but Rob felt wide awake. He took a moment to relax a little while longer, but it soon became clear that there was nothing for it. He was awake now, and he wouldn't be getting back to sleep any time soon. Especially not with his lordship using him as his throne.

Apologising to his cat, Rob surrendered to the morning and accepted his fate.

In the shower, he concluded that he might as well head in and see what was going on. He had an interview to conduct with Brendon at some point today and a whole mountain of paperwork. Plus, now that Brendon was in their hands, he felt keen to find a new case, something that would get him out of the office and away from the other officers.

Oh yeah, and there was that new recruit coming in today as well.

Wonderful.

His day would clearly be filled with joy, he mused sarcastically.

Remembering that he was babysitting the new girl served only to spur him on, to get in early, so he could see what he could get done before he was inevitably saddled with her, whoever she was.

He couldn't remember the woman's name, now he thought about it. Peter *had* told him, he was sure of it, but he was having difficulty putting a pin in it. Was it Sarah, or Sabrina, or… What was it?

He mused on that for a few more moments before giving up and getting out of the house as quickly as he could, making sure to refill Muffin's bowls and grabbing a slice of buttered toast before leaving.

He decided to take the steps outside his apartment, enjoying the feeling of movement as it slowly banished the tiredness from his limbs.

Rounding the corner to take the first flight down, he saw a woman halfway up who seemed to be having a little difficulty.

"Morning, Erika," he said, greeting his young neighbour. She was in her early twenties and lived in the small flat next door. His voice seemed to surprise her as she jumped and clutched the bannister with a grimace.

"Not so loud." She took in a deep breath and steadied herself before looking up, her piercing blue eyes standing in stark contrast to her olive skin and black hair. "Oh, hi, Mr Loxley."

"You look a little worse for wear." The weak smell of stale beer and cigarettes wafted up the stairs. She wore a sparkly dress that showed off her legs, strappy heels and the only concession to the cool weather, a jacket that was currently barely clinging to her. She wobbled as she smiled up at him, some of her makeup was smudged. "The walk of shame, huh?"

Rolling her eyes, she attempted a few more steps, still with a white-knuckle grip on the bannister. Rob offered his hand.

Erika glared at it suspiciously but took it and allowed him to walk her up the remaining few steps. "Thanks."

"My pleasure." Rob smiled at her. "Get some rest."

"I will, thanks, Dad." Sarcasm dripped from her reply.

Rob frowned. It didn't feel right for her to be calling him her dad, even if it was in jest. "I'm not sure how to take that, but I'm willing to bet your dad doesn't know you were out all night, right?"

Erika raised an eyebrow and gave him an incredulous look.

Realising he'd crossed a line, he turned to go. "Sorry. None of my business. Lock your door, have a big drink of water, and get some rest. I hope you feel better soon." She was a grown woman, after all, and what she did with her life was nothing to do with him.

"Hey, wait," she called after him. "I started it, so I'm the one who should be apologising. I'm sorry. It's just... it's been a long night." She rolled her eyes and gave a half-smile. "Thanks for the helping hand."

"Any time," he replied. "See you later."

"You will."

Rob walked down the stairs, leaving her to recover in whatever way she felt best. He'd crossed paths with Erika a few times since she'd moved in a few months ago, and she seemed like a typical young woman, enjoying the city's nightlife and the freedom of living away from home for the first time. She was young and energetic, and Rob felt somewhat protective over her, especially when he saw her after a few drinks. He might not be her actual father—and had never met the man—but he certainly had that paternal instinct somewhere deep inside. That alone had come as something of a shock when he'd recognised it for what it was, especially as he didn't have any children and had little desire to have any.

Within moments, Rob was downstairs and outside, approaching his pride and joy. She was waiting for him just where he'd left her, looking as gorgeous as always in the early morning haze.

She always managed to put a smile on his face in the morning, making him feel like a kid again, getting away with pinching sweets or something even though he knew his mother would object and chastise him.

"Morning, Belle." Rob ran his fingers along her sleek curves, catching his reflection in her polished black paintwork. Pulling out his key, Rob unlocked the door the old-fashioned way by using the key hole, climbed into his 1985

Mark Three Ford Capri, 2.8 Injection Special, and enjoyed the creak of the Recaro leather seats as he settled his weight into them.

A few changes had been made over the years, but he wasn't a purist about these things. He just enjoyed the car for what it was and the memories it conjured.

Inserting the key, he gave it a twist and fired up the 157 Brake Horse Power, V6 engine, hoping he didn't wake up half the neighbourhood in the process. Backing out of the parking space, he set off north, away from his riverside apartment block, towards Nottingham Central Police Station.

He'd be in early, before the night shift finished, but it didn't bother him. There'd be work of some kind to do. He felt sure of that.

The winding city streets didn't really allow him to use all five gears like Jackie Stewart used to do on the track. But the car handled the city street with ease, its power steering making light work of the corners.

When he reached the station, Rob parked up and made his way upstairs into the office. Several of the night shift were at their desks. They greeted him as he walked in and settled at his PC, feeling his heart sink at the prospect of the paperwork that had yet to be done on the Brendon Marsh case. This was his least favourite part of the job, and it only made him desperate to be out there on a new case rather than tapping keys on a keyboard.

As the machine fired up, he settled into the typical sounds of the office. Around him, people talked, phones rang, and radios chirped. It was almost hypnotic in its rhythms.

"...roger that control, is there anyone from Nottingham CID available to come out to Sherwood for this one, instead?" Rob heard on a nearby officer's radio.

He looked over at PC Craig Cooper standing in the doorway talking to one of the night shift. "Hey, Craig, what was that?"

"Um, I think there's a crime scene up in Sherwood. They're having difficulty getting someone in from Mansfield."

Eager to get out, Rob jumped up. "Tell them I'll take it. I'm on my way."

"If you say so, Sarge. I'll let them know." The PC grabbed his radio and did just that as Rob dashed out of the office, grateful that his luck was holding up this morning and he'd be out of the office when the DCI got in.

Of course, that would probably mean he'd bust his balls when he got back for taking the new case, but it wouldn't be the first time, and what was he going to do? Reprimand him for being proactive?

Within moments, Rob was back downstairs and faced with the choice of using either a pool car or his Capri. But of course, it wasn't even close to a contest in Rob's mind. Besides, Belle could do with stretching her legs, he rationalised and got into his own car.

He took the A60 and then the A614 north out of Nottingham, relishing the feeling of letting those 157 horses off the leash as he raced towards the crime scene.

He passed the Sherwood Pines Forest Park, and the Center Parcs resort, driving north of Edwinstowe along lush tree-lined roads to the remains of the once massive Sherwood Forest, home to the Major Oak and the legend of the hooded outlaw, Robin. He'd heard somewhere that the Forest used to be the size of greater London, once upon a time.

Using his phone hands-free, he soon found a side road guarded by a single marked car and a couple of officers in high-viz vests. There were a few news vans close by, too, with reporters doing bits to cameras or photographers taking photos.

Rob pulled in and as he approached the nearest officer, wound down his window.

"Can we help?" one of the officers called out, mistaking him for a member of the public.

"You can't come through here," the other joined in.

Rob raised his warrant card. "DS Loxley, from Nottingham CID."

A look of surprise appeared on the man's face. "You came out of your way."

"I think there was a shortage of available detectives on your patch, so we got the call."

The first officer turned to his mate and asked him to check before he cast an appraising look over Rob's car. "Not really police issue, is it?"

Rob shrugged. "It was this or catch the bus." That wasn't strictly true today, but a shortage of available pool cars was a recurring problem, and he knew of several detectives who'd been reduced to using public transport on more than one occasion. Besides, he was hardly involved in a high-speed pursuit.

"He checks out," the second officer said, walking back after a brief chat on his radio. "He can head on up there."

Rob smiled.

"Alright, follow the road and just keep going. You can't miss it."

"Will do."

Rob set off, driving up the dirt track. A grassy field stretched to a tree line on his left, but on his right, the oak and birch were right beside the track, their gnarled trunks holding a canopy of verdant emerald leaves aloft. Leaves fluttered in the breeze as Rob delved deeper into the ancient woodland.

The scene was peaceful and relaxing, hardly the feeling you'd associate with a crime scene, and yet, like many areas of wilderness, it was bound to conceal countless secrets, many of which it would continue to hold for centuries to come.

Further up, as the forest closed in on both sides of the track, a collection of police vehicles had been parked up to one side in an attempt to leave the road passable. Officers in high viz or the distinctive white forensic all-in-ones were going about their business, but the main hive of activity was through the trees, on the edge of a wide-open area of scrubland.

Rob parked up, got out, and was immediately assaulted by the almost raucous sound of early morning birdsong and the unique but calming aroma of the flittering leaves, ancient trees, decaying fungus, and fresh grassland. It felt jarring but served to put Rob's mind at rest.

Leaving his car, he flashed his ID at the first few officers, who directed him to a nearby Sergeant.

"You're Detective Loxley?" the woman asked. "From Nottingham?"

"Good morning, yes," Rob replied, and offered his hand. "DS Rob Loxley."

"Sergeant Megan Jolly, good to meet you. Thanks for coming out."

"I heard you were having a shortage of local CID?"

She bobbed her eyebrows. "Busy night, I think."

"No worries. Do you have a forensic suit for me? I didn't bring mine."

"In the van," Megan replied, waving towards a nearby white van where he soon found what he was looking for.

"So, what do we have?" Rob started to pull the coverall on.

"The body of a male, found half-buried this morning by a group of women on their morning dog jog."

Rob glanced up with a single raised brow. "Dog jog?"

Megan shrugged. "They were out jogging with their dogs, so..."

Rob took a moment to consider this. "I mean, of course, it's so obvious. I don't know why I questioned it."

"Me neither. It's quite self-explanatory," Megan replied. "It's right there in the name. Anyway, it seems like they scared off whoever was burying the body, as they claim they saw two people drive off in a four-by-four."

"And where are they now?"

"We sent them to Nottingham Central, given that's where you were coming from. They live in Arnold anyway, so it makes sense."

"Excellent, thank you. Let's take a look at the body."

Sergeant Jolly nodded and led off the track, through the trees, towards the scene a few hundred metres away. As they walked, Rob wondered if this would turn out to be a murder, because if it did, then the case might be taken away from him, anyway. The thought of coming all the way out here, only for it to be ripped away from him, was annoying. The statements of the women who found the body, and saw people driving off, suggested this was anything but innocent, but it was best not to jump to any conclusions yet.

"Are you with Mansfield Police?" Rob asked, in an effort to focus on something else.

"That's right," Megan confirmed. "I think we have things a little easier than you do down there."

"Perhaps a touch. Still, you seem happy enough."

"That's me, jolly Mrs Jolly."

"Err, yeah."

"Beat you to it, didn't I?" She glanced at him with mischief in her eyes.

"Absolutely not. I wouldn't dare make light of your name, officer."

Megan snorted. "Yeah, right."

They pressed on through the well-trodden pathway to the taped-off section of scrubland on the other side of the trees. There had been less than thirty metres of woodland before the oak had ended, and beyond was a huge open area of rural land, dotted with bushes and ferns amongst the long grass.

Ahead, a tent had been erected over the immediate scene, with one side left open as the attending team worked.

"An FME has already been and gone to declare life extinct, and we have Pathologist May Shephard from Queen's Medical Centre in Nottingham coming out too. Figured we'd keep it local to you."

"Thanks, I know May." Again, Rob wondered if this effort to make life easier for him would be pointless if this turned into a murder enquiry.

"Great. In the meantime, I'll hand you over to our CSM, Officer Saunders."

The woman walked over, dressed in the same white jumpsuit that everyone close to the scene was wearing.

"Detective Sergeant?" Saunders asked.

"That's right," Rob confirmed but didn't offer one of his latex-gloved hands in order to keep them clean, and neither did the Crime Scene Manager. "DS Rob Loxley. Sorry, I'm a little late, Officer Saunders."

"Don't worry, you're good. Thanks for coming and call me Ava. We were beginning to wonder if we'd *ever* find a free detective."

"That's alright. So, what can you ascertain so far? Is this an accidental death, natural causes, or are we looking at a murder?"

"Well," Ava began and turned back to the tent, indicating that Rob should follow her. "It looks like this was a body disposal that got interrupted. We have a male victim in his mid to late thirties, who was found naked and partially buried."

That sounded like a murder to Rob, causing a grimace of annoyance to creep onto his face.

They stepped into the box-like white tent with yellow detailing, where a shallow grave had been dug. In it, a naked man lay in the dirt as Scene of Crime officers slowly uncovered his almost completely buried legs. If you ignored the bruises and dried blood, the man looked almost asleep and half covered by a muddy blanket. The man's hair was long and scraggly, much like his beard. But his extensive and wild hair couldn't hide the trauma he'd clearly undergone.

Lurid purple bruises peppered his torso and arms, along with raw red marks around his wrists. But apart from that, there were no other obvious signs of attack.

There was no way this was accidental or natural causes. This was malicious, which meant that the East Midlands Special Operations Unit would likely take over. Rob felt annoyed, but despite this setback, he still had a job to do, and he'd do it to the best of his ability. "How did he die? Was he beaten?"

"That was our first guess, but then we noticed this." Ava led Rob around to the other side of the grave and crouched next to the victim. Reaching out, she lifted the man's upper right arm, twisting it to show the back. There was a deep ragged wound with angry discolouration around it.

"One of the team spotted the lesions creeping around the arm, and that's what we found."

"Nasty," Rob remarked as he crouched to get a better look. "It looks like a stab wound, but there's a lot more tearing of flesh than I'd expect."

"I agree. We did manage to have a quick peek at the victim's back as well, and although we've not yet had a proper look, there seems to be a similar wound between his shoulder blades. The pathologist will have a better look later, and there might be more wounds that we've not found yet."

"Okay. Any clothes?"

"We've not found any, no. But we have found tyre tracks and footprints, which we're in the process of documenting."

Rob scanned along the body again, appraising him. "He looks thin, maybe even malnourished. I don't think he was looking after himself very well."

"Couldn't, or wouldn't?" Ava asked.

Rob shrugged. "Good question. We need to find out who he is. I'm guessing there was no ID found?"

"No, none," Ava confirmed.

"Wonderful." Rob turned back to the corpse and frowned. "So, who are you, sir?"

7

"There you are," Nick commented as Rob wandered back into the office, where the scene was quite different to this morning. The night shift had long since made their way home, to be replaced with Nick and his fellow team members.

He spotted DCI Orleton in his office, pacing back and forth, holding his phone to his ear while gesticulating wildly. As Rob walked towards his desk, the DCI spotted him and scowled, but that was nothing new and kind of expected. Rob ignored him and continued towards his desk.

Just outside Peter's office, three people were sitting on chairs or desks, talking. Frank and Tony were familiar faces, but they both had their backs to Rob and were talking to a new face sitting and waiting for the DCI. The young blonde woman wore a sharp suit to match her equally sharp features. With her hair tied up, she smiled serenely at the two men and their attentions. The pair seemed to be crowding around, giving her their undivided attention. The scene caused Rob to wrinkle his nose uncomfortably.

Two men fixated on an attractive young woman?

Rob sighed and gave his head a brief shake. If asked, they'd likely deny there was anything untoward going on. They were just being friendly and welcoming the new officer to the group, and if Rob were feeling particularly pessimistic, he'd guess they were likely trying to poison her against him.

Nick followed his gaze and sighed. "Yeah, I know," he muttered. "Like moths to a flame."

"I was thinking of flies on shit," Rob whispered, "but that would be unkind to her."

"Frank'll be up to his usual," Nick added.

"You mean recruiting to the anti-Rob club?"

Nick smirked. "Something like that. It worked on Tony."

"No shit. He lets me know most days."

A grin split Nick's face. "So, where have you been? You're not moonlighting with another detective, are you? Cheating on me?" There was mirth in his voice.

"Just visited a crime scene up in Sherwood as no one else was around to take it."

"Sherwood? Mansfield were forced to scrape the bottom of the proverbial then, were they?"

"I know. I felt bad for them. But beggars can't be choosers. Doubt I'll get to keep it, though. It looks like a murder."

"Aaah, shame. We're stuck with the almost murders then."

"Aye." Rob nodded towards the DCI's office. "Any idea what's going on in there? He looks pissed."

"At you?"

"Obviously."

"Christ knows. Probably. So, what did you find in the woods?"

"A body, male, half-buried," Rob answered. "Looks like it was being disposed of, but they got interrupted and scarpered. The body was covered in bruises and had at least two stab wounds."

"Damn, sounds like it would have been a juicy one. The Special Ops guys get all the big cases."

"Jealous?" Rob asked.

"Damn right. Instead, we're going to be stuck babysitting the new girl."

Rob shrugged. "I'm sure that'll be fun, too." He looked over to where Frank and Tony were talking to the woman and briefly locked eyes with her. She smiled nervously at him.

Noticing her expression, Frank turned to look, followed by Tony. Neither smiled and returned to their discussion.

He'd seen this enough times to know what the pair were doing. Rob felt his chest tighten in annoyance and frustration, feeling powerless to do much about it.

"So, when did she get here?"

Nick shrugged. "She was here when I got in and already talking to Tony. Or Tony was talking *at* her. Frank joined in when he got here."

"Poor girl. We should rescue her."

The door to the DCI's office burst open, and Peter leaned out.

"Rob, Nick, in here."

"Sir," Nick replied.

"Guv," Rob said as the DCI retreated back into his office.

Nick leaned in. "Looks like she'll have to wait for you to ride in wearing your shining armour, oh gallant knight."

Rob grunted and walked towards the office door. He kept his eyes forward but listened to Frank and Tony as he passed by.

"…Yeah, just, really dodgy, you need to be careful…" Rob could guess what they were discussing, but gritted his teeth and forced himself to ignore them as he walked into the office. A moment later, the door closed behind them, cutting off Frank's voice.

"Sit," Peter snapped.

Rob did as the man asked and sat alongside Nick, feeling very much like a naughty schoolboy who'd been called into the headmaster's office. Peter paced side to side behind his desk until they were settled, then came to a stop behind his chair and turned to face them.

Peter glared at Rob. "So then, care to tell me where you've been?"

"I attended a crime scene. Mansfield were short-staffed and needed someone from CID in Sherwood Forest. I was in early because I couldn't sleep, so I took it."

Peter grunted and walked around his chair.

Rob tensed as he watched the DCI's face. It was quite obvious he wasn't surprised by the news. "But, I suspect you know all this?"

"What were you thinking?" Peter snapped. "You already have Brendon downstairs, who needs to be interviewed. You have enough going on."

"I was just doing my duty, sir." The comment caused Peter to press his lips into a thin line. Rob imagined he was wrestling with his personal annoyance at him and the fact that he was actually doing nothing wrong. In fact, he was helping Mansfield CID out.

"I know that," Peter barked, annoyed. He sat down.

"Surely the issue is with Mansfield?" Nick added.

Peter gave Nick a dirty look, betraying his annoyance at Nick's comment. "Don't you worry, I'll be having words with them soon too," he replied, wagging his finger at Nick. "But that's not the end of it, is it? Because it's a bloody murder, meaning you wouldn't be investigating it anyway. East Midlands Special Operations would take it."

"I am aware, sir," Rob wondered why Peter was so annoyed and angry. He figured he was working up to something and decided to stand his ground and see what the DCI revealed to them. "But they needed someone, and I was available. I'm sure Special Operations will take it off my hands soon enough, and I'll be back to the Marsh case."

"Wouldn't that be lovely," the DCI ranted, making Rob frown. Something was different and bothering him. Peter continued, "If only it were that simple. But no, it isn't, because guess what? I've just been talking to the Special Operations Unit, and they want *you* to run the case."

"They what?" Rob wasn't sure he'd heard Peter right and decided to clarify the point. "They want me?"

"I know. I'm as shocked as you are. But this comes from higher up than me, and they were quite clear about it. They—for some god-forsaken reason—would like you to run the case." Peter sat back and muttered to himself. "As if you haven't got enough on, as it is."

"That's great—" Nick said, smiling. He sounded thrilled by the idea.

"Not you," Peter cut in, wiping the smile from Nick's face.

"What?" Nick sounded shocked and confused.

"Why not? We can work on this together," Rob added, equally lost as to what Peter was talking about.

Peter addressed Nick. "Knowing that we had DC Stutely joining us," Peter pointed out the window to the back of the blonde woman's head, "I agreed to let DCI Nailer have you for a while over at Sherwood Lodge. They're short-staffed, and they need more bodies."

"So are we," Rob protested.

"So's everyone," Peter countered.

"But, what about us and this case?"

"It wouldn't have been our case, would it, if you hadn't got all keen. Besides, the deal's been done," Peter said in a matter-of-fact tone. "It's not permanent, but that's what's been agreed. So, you're heading up there today, leaving you," he pointed to Rob, "with the Brendon case and this Sherwood murder."

"This is insane," Nick replied.

"You know what things are like these days," the DCI argued. "I'm sure I don't need to explain it, given what's happened today. We're stretched thin, and we have to make do with the resources we have." Peter turned back to Rob. "As for you, I don't know who's been talking to the brass in the Special Operations Unit because it ain't me, but someone thinks you can handle this."

"I'll take that as a compliment, sir."

"Take it however you like. But you report back here to me with everything, and I'll liaise with the unit. Got it?"

"Of course, sir."

"You better not mess this up."

"Wouldn't dream of it, sir."

Peter turned back to Nick, wearing an expectant expression. "Well, what are you waiting for? Get yourself over to Sherwood Lodge and report to DCI Nailer."

Nick got up, looking like he was grinding his teeth in annoyance. "Sir." Rob caught Nick's eye as he got out of his seat. He shrugged as he turned to go.

"And send DC Stutely in on your way out, will you?"

"Will do, guv."

"See ya, matey," Rob said. "Say hi to Nailer for me."

"Yeah, catch you later."

Rob turned back to Peter as Nick left the room. The anger rolling off the DCI in waves battered against Rob as they waited for the DC.

"I know you think you're doing the right thing by helping out, Rob," Peter said, "but I've made it clear in the past that there needs to be a back and forth between us. It's your blatant disregard for my orders that I dislike. I think you sometimes forget that this isn't Jon Pilgrim's unit anymore. I run a tight ship, and I won't have this shit from you." He paused for a moment, as if mulling something over. "You know I had the Sheriff poking around last night, asking about you? He wanted to know what you're up to."

"I didn't know that, sir, no."

"Mmm," Peter mumbled in a huff as he waited for the DC to join them.

Rob knew he'd done nothing wrong and felt sure that any other DCI would be happy for their officers to be as proactive and helpful as he tried to be, but then, there wasn't much that was rational about Peter when it came to him. Peter didn't like him. It tainted all their interactions and had done for years. It wasn't likely to change any time soon, either.

He was probably just pissed that the EMSOU had gone over his head and seconded him to the unit to take on the case. Peter had always been a control freak, and ever since Pilgrim had left and Peter had taken over, he'd never quite seemed confident in the role. It was as if he believed that someone would take it away from him if he wasn't careful, so he put on this tough, overbearing persona to make up for it. It reminded Rob of a supply teacher who'd take the class when the usual teacher was off ill or something, and to make up for the lack of rapport they had with the students, they'd always take things a little too far. They'd overcompensate for what they lacked in other areas by being strict.

Of course, where Rob was concerned there were other issues at play, meaning he got the brunt of the DCI's ire, and now with the EMSOU undermining his authority—which wasn't true, of course, but that was probably how Peter saw it—the DCI was making sure Rob got it in the neck.

But this wasn't the first time that Peter had given him a dressing down, not by a long way, and he was used to it by now. Plus, he was still on a high from the revelation that the EMSOU were handing him the Sherwood case.

Rob would have preferred to report to someone within the unit directly, but he'd settle for dealing with Peter for now in the hope that things might change further down the line.

He could just imagine Peter throwing his weight around on the call to whoever it was from EMSOU, insisting that everything was routed through him.

It was an amusing thought.

The door sounded again, and Rob heard the woman walk in.

"Morning, DC Stutely."

"Good morning, sir. Thank you for the opportunity." She offered her hand, and the DCI gave it a brief shake. She turned to Rob and smiled. Jesus, he thought, she could cut wood with those cheekbones.

"DC Scarlett Stutely, this is Detective Sergeant Robert Loxley. You'll be working with him."

"It's a pleasure to meet you." She offered him her hand. Rob took it and returned the smile as she continued her greeting. "I'm looking forward to working with you."

"That's a first," Rob muttered.

"Sorry?" Scarlett replied, frowning. "I didn't…"

"I'm pleased to meet you, too." Rob let go of her hand. She seemed unbearably bright and happy, which was already starting to grate on him. He wondered what Frank and Tony had told her.

"Right," the DCI cut in. "Now you're acquainted, off you go. You've got a busy day ahead of you. And remember, I want regular updates."

"Of course, guv."

"Absolutely, sir," Scarlett replied and smiled at Rob before gesturing that he should lead the way. He did. Leaving the office with Scarlett close on his heels. The DCI followed them to the door.

"Frank?" Peter yelled from his office door. "Get in here."

Frank got up from his desk and made for the DCI's office, sending daggers Rob's way as he walked. Tony watched them both, sneering at Rob.

He ignored them and made for his desk. Nick had already gone, leaving his workstation vacant and the office feeling a little less friendly.

"Sorry about him," Rob said as he reached his desk and dropped into his chair. He turned to see that Scarlett had picked up a bag that she'd left outside of the DCI's office, and after seeing Rob drop into his chair, she scanned around for one of her own.

"Oh, that's okay. Sound like you guys have a lot going on." She found a chair and placed herself in it.

"You could say that. You could also call it a shit show." Leaning back in his chair, he noticed how alert and full of life she seemed.

Scarlett smirked at his comment.

"I hope my two colleagues didn't annoy you or say anything that might…"

"Oh, no. Not at all. Don't worry, I can handle them, and I'll make my own judgements on people, thank you very much."

Rob gave her a brief nod, pleased with her answer. He found himself warming to her. "So, what brings you to Nottinghamshire? I noticed that's not a local accent you have."

"No, it's not. I'm from Surrey."

"Surrey? What is this, some kind of cultural exchange?"

"Excuse me?" She clearly didn't understand.

Rob smiled. "My previous DCI, Jon Pilgrim, moved down to Surrey a year or so back. Did they send you up to return the favour?"

"Oh, um, no. I don't know any Jon Pilgrim, I'm afraid. My fiancé recently got posted up here for his work, so I put in for a transfer, and here I am."

"You're engaged?"

"We are, yes." The smile that appeared on Scarlett's face was dazzling in its intensity.

"Congratulations."

"Thank you. His name's Chris. Chris Williams. He works for an investment company with offices all over, but their HQ is here, in Nottingham."

"I see. Well, I hope we don't disappoint you. I've no idea how they work down in Surrey, but we've got a fairly full plate in front of us."

"Of course, I'm keen to get stuck in," she confirmed, still ridiculously bright and breezy as she pulled out her notebook. "What have we got on today?"

"Well, we've got two open cases to work on. Firstly, we brought in a young man called Brendon Marsh yesterday who, for reasons we're not yet certain of, is suspected of beating up his girlfriend and her ten-year-old son, putting him in intensive care. We have door cam footage of Brendon's girlfriend running out the house after him, blood all over both of them, shouting that he'd killed her son. Luckily, he hadn't killed Scott, the son, but he came close. Brendon is in our cells downstairs with his solicitor, so we'll need to talk to him. Secondly, there's the new case that I attended the scene of this morning. We have a dead body in Sherwood Forest, found half-buried in the mud by a bunch of dog walkers who, it seems, interrupted the disposal of the body. We have no

ID, so we don't know who the victim is yet, but based on the extensive bruising and the two stab wounds we found, we're fairly sure it's a murder."

"I see." Scarlett was busy scribbling away in her pocketbook as he spoke, noting down what he was saying in her own unique shorthand.

"Murder isn't usually our thing. The East Midlands Special Operations Unit usually takes on murder cases in Derbyshire, Leicestershire, Lincolnshire, Northamptonshire and Nottinghamshire, but I've been informed that they've handed this one to us. I'm not sure why, but I'm not one to look a gift horse in the mouth, so I'm running with it."

"Of course, yes. I take it identifying the victim is a priority?"

"That's right. We'll have fingerprints soon, DNA and maybe dental later once the pathologist gets them back to the lab."

"Gotcha."

"In the meantime, the dog walkers who interrupted the disposal of the body are apparently downstairs, waiting to be interviewed, and I think there's no time like the present."

"Absolutely."

"So, you're ready to jump in?"

Scarlett grinned enthusiastically, which caused Rob to warm to her a bit more, despite her overly shiny disposition.

"With both feet," she confirmed.

8

Curby strode through the estate, hands stuffed into pockets, his hood up and head down, flanked by Gary and Rory. They weren't far from where they were going, which was in the heart of their territory, where he felt safest. The Bulwell Crew wouldn't dare venture this deep into Top Valley, not unless they wanted all-out war. But if they ever decided they wanted that, Curby was more than willing to bring it.

He was ready. He was *always* ready.

The bulky, cool metal of his gun was stuffed reassuringly into the back of his jeans, ready for him to use if the need arose.

But he felt sure there would be little danger here, this early in the morning.

Instead, his troubled mind was on something, or rather, *someone* else, and he wanted answers. He hoped that Rigby would be the one who could give him those answers.

As they meandered through the estate, the few locals that saw them coming crossed the road to keep out of their way. Curby's reputation preceded him, just as he liked it. There were times when he felt like royalty, here on the estate, as random strangers recognised him and kept a respectful distance.

Now that was power, and it was something that could not be bought.

It was earned, and he'd spent years building it, working these streets and even serving hard time on a couple of occasions. He was never inside for long, though. He knew enough of just the right people to make sure it wasn't long before he was back out on the streets, back in Top Valley.

This was his home, his territory, his manor!

Reaching Rigby's house, he turned in, walked up the front path, and banged on the door. Taking a step back, he turned to look at his two followers. Both wore the hoody and puffer jacket uniform of the crew, with their hoods up, dropping their faces into shadow. Gary stared over at Rory, giving him a dead eye, while Rory kept his eyes fixed firmly on the ground. Curby could still see the cuts and bruises on his face and nodded approvingly at his handywork.

No one defies him and gets away with it, not even members of his own crew.

The click and scrape of the front door unlocking refocused Curby's attention. As it opened, Curby kicked it and stepped inside. The young woman on the other side yelped. She seemed like she was about to scream until she saw who it was.

Curby stared at Kay as she bit her lip in frustration, holding herself back before regaining control and finally speaking.

"Oh, it's you. He's out back," Kay said, guessing his reason for being here without him saying a word. She backed up quickly, getting out of his way, but kept reproachful eyes on them as Curby strode into her house. Respecting her deference to him, Curby gave her a quick nod before moving through the house into the kitchen at the back, to the rear door.

Walking through it, he found Jordan Rigby holding his recurve bow at full draw, aiming the arrow at the foam target at the bottom of the garden. Curby noticed the print off of a cartoon policeman pinned to the board and smiled.

"Don't miss, bruv," Curby barked, trying to get Rigby to jump and miss. But he didn't flinch at all and loosed the arrow with confidence and finesse. It slammed into the target, skewering the police officer right in his chest. "Nice shot."

"No thanks to you," Rigby replied deadpan as he walked over. Curby grabbed his raised hand and pulled him in for a brief back-slapping embrace. "You're up early."

"Can't sleep, innit." Curby ambled over to one of the nearby deck chairs and almost collapsed into it. "Fuckin' Brendon. He's fucked everythin' up. I ain't got enough gear now, and I'm down a few grand. If he gets out, I'll fuck 'im up."

Rigby nodded as he took a spare seat, resting his bow across the arms of the chair. "Yeah, that sucks."

Curby bit his lip in frustration. "Did he do it? Did he do what the police nicked him for?"

"Yeah, I think he did. That's what I heard, anyway."

"He killed his girl's kid?"

"He didn't kill him. He just fucked him up," Rigby answered. "Really fucked him up. He's in Queen's Hospital, on life support. Did a number on Tess too, broke her nose, split her lip. She's black and blue."

"Christ," Curby hissed in frustration, annoyed by Brendon's idiocy. He had no idea what the little shit was playing at, but it was extra attention from the feds that he did not need. And to add insult to injury, the drugs buy he'd sent Brendon on, seemed not to have happened, and he had no idea where the money was. "Why the fuck did he do that, and where's my gear and green?"

"I'm looking into it, but it's unclear what happened. I know he didn't make it to the buy, though."

"No shit," Curby replied. "If he did, I'd 'ave my fuckin' drugs and I wouldn't have the lads from Liverpool asking me where my man is, would I? He's crossed a fuckin' line, Rigs. Crossed it big time. He knows that, and that's why he was hiding at Rory's." Curby waved to somewhere behind him, where he guessed Rory might be.

Rigby looked up at the bruised young man. "And he didn't tell you nuthin' when he was hidin' out at yours?"

"Nah, man. Nothing." Curby could hear the wobble in Rory's voice as he spoke. "I didn't know he was hiding out. I thought he was jus' visitin', didn't I."

"You tell the filth that, did you?" Rigby pressed.

"I didn't tell the cops nuthin'," Rory snapped, referring to the statement he'd given them on the night of Brendon's arrest.

"Good, and make sure it stays that way."

"What the fuck was he doing, Rigs? Why dis me like that? Is he working for someone else? The Bulwell Crew? Is he settin' up on his own and making a play? It makes no fuckin' sense."

"Fuck knows," Rigby said. "I can try to find out, though. Are there any other loose ends?"

"Just Tess," Curby replied. "She went to the police rather than come to me. I can't have that. She could be saying anything. These bitches need to know that if they have a problem, they come to me. They don't go to the filth."

"Fuckin' aye. How do you wanna go about this? What do you want to do?"

"I want to speak to Tess. We need to discuss how things are done in Top Valley."

"She might also know why Brendon went crazy," Rigby noted.

Curby nodded, agreeing with his most trusted ally within the gang. "That she might. Lamar?" He turned to Gary.

"What's up?" Gary Lamar replied, stepping forward.

"Find Tess for me. I want to see her. Me and her need to have a little chat."

9

Walking into the interview room on one of the lower floors of the building, Rob found the three women still in their running gear, sitting behind a desk, looking a little shaken.

He guessed they were all in their forties, or there abouts, as they sat with blankets that had been provided by the station draped over their shoulders or legs. They'd long since lost the internal heat they'd built up from the run, and their running outfits weren't doing much to keep them warm in the cool interview room.

"Sorry to keep you waiting. I hope you're not too cold."

"We're okay," one of them replied.

"It is a little cold," another added.

Rob noticed the empty plastic cups on the table. "Can I get you another hot drink?"

They all confirmed they'd like another, so Rob asked the officer in the hallway to sort that out before he closed the door and settled into one of the chairs, with Scarlett taking a seat beside him. She pulled out her pocketbook and pencil, ready to take notes.

"Thank you for helping with this."

"That's okay," one of the women replied.

Rob smiled, and then glanced down at his notes. "So, we have Ella Aaron..."

One of the women nodded in confirmation. "That's me."

"Sam Merchant, and Mary Wakefield, right?" The other two women indicated who they were. "Excellent. My names Detective Sergeant Rob Loxley, and this is Detective Constable Scarlett Stutely."

"Hello," Scarlett added.

"May I ask, why were you out running so early in Sherwood Forest?" Rob asked. "It was about five AM, wasn't it?"

"We all like to exercise," Mary replied. "But we have very little time these days, what with work, school runs, housework, shopping and all that. So, we get up early and have an hour in Sherwood. We live fairly local, so it's easy."

"And you always go as a group?"

"You never know what you're going to come across out there. I'm just glad we were in a group this time," Ella replied.

"So, it's for safety?"

"That's right."

There was a knock at the door, and moments later, the three ladies were clutching steaming disposable cups of coffee, with a fresh scattering of used milk and sugar sachets on the table before them. Their mood seemed to brighten a little.

"Alright, run me through this morning's events," Rob suggested. "What happened, and what did you see?"

"We went for a run, as always," Mary began. "We took one of our usual routes, and all was going fine. That's when we saw the lights."

"When was that, do you think?" Rob pressed.

"I don't know, maybe fifteen minutes in," Sam confirmed.

"And is that unusual?"

"It's not unheard of," Mary replied.

"We've seen cars and motorbikes out there before," Ella added.

"Oh yeah," Sam said. "I hate those bikes. They ride around like they own the place. It's dangerous."

"But, no bikes today?" Rob asked, keen to get them back on track.

"No," Mary replied. "Just the four-by-four."

"Tell me what you saw after the lights," Rob asked, keen to find out more, as Scarlett scribbled notes into her pad.

"We were running up the track that skirts the edge of the scrubland area, near the road, when we saw the red rear lights from a car. I spotted people nearby too. We'd only just seen them when Max started barking like crazy."

"Bailey, too," Ella cut in.

"These are your dogs, I take it," Rob clarified.

"Yeah," Mary confirmed, "they all joined in. It must have spooked them because the people ran to the car, got in, and drove off."

"How much could you see?" Scarlett asked, speaking up for the first time. Rob smiled at her question, pleased to see her joining in. "Were they men, women? Could you see what they were wearing?"

"Not really, no," Mary replied. "The sun wasn't up, but it wasn't pitch dark either. The sky was getting lighter, and I could see two people, I think. I guess there might have been more in the car, but I didn't see them. I think they were men, but I can't be sure. They were wearing dark clothing, though."

"And the car?" Scarlett continued. "What could you make out? Could you see a number plate?"

"It had one, but I didn't pay much attention to it," Mary answered. "I'm pretty sure it was a Land Rover, or some kind of four-by-four, and dark in colour, but don't quote me on that."

"That's what I saw," Ella added. "It was a big, off-road vehicle, for sure. But yeah, I didn't see the number plate."

"Me neither," Sam added. "I thought it was black, but I could be wrong."

"We didn't realise they were criminals. It was just a car and two people out in Sherwood. It's not an everyday occurrence, but it does happen, and I didn't think much of it until we found the body."

"Yeah, that's right," Mary agreed. "It's not as if we expected to interrupt someone burying a body. I would have paid more attention if we had."

"So, tell me about that. When did you find the body?"

"It was the dogs that found it," Ella answered. "That's probably why they were barking. They could smell it."

"We wouldn't have found it if it wasn't for the dogs," Mary said. "The men had been digging a short distance away from the track, and all the dogs, all four of them, were desperate to get to the body. We didn't know it was a body though, until we investigated what the dogs were so excited about."

"Ella saw it first," Sam added.

"I'm too much of a softy when it comes to Bailey," Ella confirmed. "She's always dragging me around, here and there, finding dead animals or chasing after squirrels."

"And that's when you called 999?" Scarlett asked.

"It was," Mary confirmed.

Rob nodded and leaned back into his seat as he thought through what they'd just told him.

Over the next half an hour, he drilled down into their account, asking specific questions about the various details, pushing them to try and remember more about what they saw, but ultimately there was nothing new to discover.

They finished up by checking their personal details were correct before finally sending them home and returning to the office.

"There wasn't much to learn from them, really, was there?" Scarlett commented. "So far, we have an unidentified body, two unknown people disposing of it, and a car, which was probably an off-road, four-wheel-drive style vehicle, but could be something else."

"Yeah, I know. That's not much. We can work with what we've got until identification comes in from the body's fingerprints or DNA, but let's start with the dog walkers."

"Do you think they had something to do with it?" Scarlett asked.

"Probably not, but it never hurts to check these things out. The devil is in the details. So, see what you can find on those three ladies, check their families and see if there's anything there at all we should be concerned about. I don't think there will be, but let's give it a try."

"Sure thing. Shall I use this computer?"

She pointed to Nick's PC, and the idea of someone else taking over Nick's desk caused Rob's insides to knot. As much as he'd warmed to Scarlett, he didn't like that the years of working with Nick had just been brushed under the table as if it were nothing. But, they weren't going to get far if she couldn't access the HOLMES 2 system.

With a nod, Rob confirmed that she should settle herself at Nick's desk.

"Sure, go ahead."

"Thanks," Scarlett replied, the cheerfulness in her voice matched the smile on her face. "We should hunt through local CCTV from that morning to see if we can pick up a car that matches the one the women described."

"I was just thinking the same thing," Rob confirmed. "It's a long and thankless task, but needs must. The CCTV coverage isn't great around there, and if the gang is intelligent about this, they'll know where those cameras are."

"Worth a shot, though."

"Absolutely, but we're going to need help. We can't do all this on our own. I'll see what investigators can be assigned to us."

"DCI Orleton will authorise that, surely."

Rob took a deep breath as he pondered his answer. Ideally, the answer to that question would be an unequivocal yes, but Rob had learned never to assume these things. "Let's hope so."

"Right," Scarlett replied. "I'll get started. What are you going to do?"

"I was thinking of hunting through recent missing person reports to see if anyone reported our man as missing. Another long shot, I can only search based on physical description for now. If nothing turns up, we'll run it again once we get an ID."

"Not bad if it turns up someone of interest." Her eyes twinkled with the anticipation of the hunt.

"Damn right," Rob confirmed and turned to his monitor and started to hunt through the system, seeing what it had to offer.

It didn't take long to bring up a list of recent local missing person reports. There was an endless list of them as there seemed to be a new report most days, but on closer inspection, many of those could be discounted with a little investigation, and some were likely hoaxes.

The most recent report came from inside Nottingham City, where a woman called Lorraine Winslow, age fifty-two, a resident of the Bobbers Mill area of the city with no previous record, had been reported missing by her husband Graham yesterday. Rob dismissed it as irrelevant to the case and was about to click away when he noticed that the case had been referred to DCI Nailer at Sherwood Lodge.

It had been weeks since he'd seen Nailer, and they really were overdue for a drink and a catch up, if only their busy work lives would allow them to have a spare evening. He wondered if Nailer had assigned Nick to the case.

Out of curiosity, he scanned through the notes on the case. Lorraine had been at the local church, helping with a soup kitchen for the homeless and had left there without issue according to the Reverend Bernard Sharpe. But she had failed to return home. So far, there didn't seem to be any solid leads.

Rob shrugged and closed the case, resolving to get in touch with Nailer as soon as he had a spare moment.

"Missing persons?" said a voice from behind him.

Rob jumped and turned to see DCI Orleton standing there, peering over his shoulder.

"Just a hunch," Rob explained.

"Of course. It's always worth checking everything," Peter replied. "How did the interview with the runners who found the body go?"

"They don't know much," Rob explained. "They saw two people, they think, and an off-road vehicle. Some kind of four-by-four. But that's it. There's nothing concrete there, so we're looking for corroborating evidence. CCTV, missing persons, that kind of thing. I know there were footprints and tyre tracks, so those might throw something up. It's too early to know yet." Rob took a breath, feeling very much like he was being monitored, which given this case was basically under the auspices of the EMSOU, wasn't surprising. They'd want to know everything that was going on and were likely putting pressure on Peter to follow Rob's every move.

With that in mind—and despite the animosity between them—he tried to cut Peter some slack.

"Alright. And the Brendon case?"

Rob grimaced, realising he'd not checked up on the latest developments. "I'll need to check that."

Peters glared hardened. "No need. I checked it for you." Rob could hear judgement in the DCI's tone. "We've had word that Brendon and his solicitor are done talking, and they're ready for him to be interviewed."

"Very good, sir, I'll get on that."

"See that you do."

"I will," Rob confirmed.

"Mmm. Are you sure you've not taken on too much, Loxley? Dealing with Brendon and this murder inquiry is no small task. Why not let *me* handle the murder, and you finish off with Brendon?"

And let you get all the glory from the Special Operation Unit, Rob thought, hell no! This was his case, he would see it through and maybe, just maybe, he'd impress the right person. If Peter really wanted to lighten the load, he'd offer to take the Brendon case but that wasn't likely to happen.

"No, sir, but thank you. I'm more than capable of dealing with both, and with Scarlett helping me, I'm positive we'll be fine." Rob was aware of Scarlett watching the exchange in the periphery of his vision.

Peter held Rob's gaze for a moment, seeming to assess him and his answer before he replied. "As long as you're sure."

"Positive." Rob made sure to sound as confident as possible in his answer.

"Alright, but the offer is still there, and if things get too much for you to handle, there's no shame in asking me to take it off your hands. I wouldn't want to see you drown under the workload, what with the PSU sniffing around."

Rob bit his lip at the mention of the Professional Standards Unit. Peter was no doubt referring to Bill Rainault and his personal vendetta. "Noted, sir, and have no fear on that account."

The DCI turned to leave. "Alright, I'll leave you be…"

"There is *one* thing, however," Rob added, causing the DCI to pause and look back.

"Hmm?"

"We have a lot of CCTV to go through, so I'd like to bring some civilian investigators in to help us. I presume that's okay?"

Peter sighed, but after a moment's thought, he shrugged. "Of course. Speak to the office manager and see who you can get."

"Will do, thanks. We'll need all the help we can get. Don't want to disappoint Special Operations."

Peter screwed his lips up and shrugged, before he turned and looked across the office. "Tony," he called out. "Give Loxley a hand with the CCTV, will you."

Across the way, Tony looked up from his monitor, his eyes flicking between Rob and the DCI. "I've got the Harris case to work on," he complained.

"Then make time, Mr Darby."

Rob could hear the groan from where he sat, but Peter didn't respond and returned to his office without a backward glance.

Half a minute later, Tony ambled sullenly over, looking like a kid who'd been forced to play with someone he hated. He sighed. "Go on then. What do you want me to do?"

"Scarlett will give you the details when she's ready, but it's basically watching CCTV looking for cars that match our description and making a note of their plates."

"Ugh. Alright, fine. I'll be over there, under my own mountain of casework, when you need me."

"Cheers," Rob replied dismissively as Tony rolled his eyes before leaving.

"Thank you, Tony," Scarlett added sweetly. Rob watched Tony glance at her and smile. His whole demeanour seemed to lighten as she showered him with her attention.

As Tony walked away, Rob glanced over at Scarlett, who winked knowingly at him. She then leaned over and whispered, "Being a woman in a mainly male environment can occasionally have its advantages."

"Noted," Rob replied as his phone chimed, alerting him about a new email. He pulled his device out and read through the message. "Okay, interesting."

"What's up?" Scarlett asked.

Rob scanned the message for a second time. "The body's fingerprints came through with a match. We have a name now, Spencer Lawson. He's apparently in the system with a photo, which is a visual match for the body we retrieved. There's also a tattoo that matches our records. They're going to run DNA and dental when they do the post-mortem, but this is about as definitive as it gets."

As he spoke, he heard Scarlett tapping away at her keyboard.

"Lawson is spelt as it sounds, I guess?"

"Aye," he confirmed.

Scarlett hit return and clicked into the file.

"Okay, Spencer Lawson…" she mused as Rob scooted his chair over to peer at her screen. He spotted the photo at the top of the page, and images of the body he'd seen at the crime scene flashed in his mind. It was him. It was Spencer.

"Age thirty-eight, of no fixed abode, with a single listing here for disturbing the peace earlier this year while visiting his ex-wife's house to see his daughter. It seems that he got into a scuffle with her new husband."

"Sandy and Darren Pierson," Rob read the names of Spencer's former wife, and her new husband aloud.

"And Spencer's daughter with Sandy is called Elise," Scarlett added.

"Any next of kin apart from his ex-wife?"

"Yeah, we have a listing and address for his parents."

Rob pondered this for a moment, as he considered their next moves. Both Sandy and Spencer's parents needed to know about Spencer's death as soon as possible, and they needed to speak to both parties to find out what they knew. Of the two, given the divorce, Rob thought it best to inform Spencer's parents first.

"Right then, I've got to get ready and interview Brendon downstairs."

"Of course."

"How do you feel about visiting Spencer's parents and conducting that interview? Have you ever notified a family of a tragedy before?"

"I've been through the training, and done it a few times, yes. I can do this."

"In that case, get some CCTV details to Tony, see if you can arrange a Family Liaison Officer and then head over to Spencer's parents. They might know something that will help. With any luck, once you've done that, I'll be done with Brendon, and we can pay a visit to his ex-wife."

"On it, Sarge."

10

Scarlett smiled to herself. Leaving the office for the first time in one of the force's pool cars felt a little more nerve-wracking than it had any right to. Despite the tight feeling in her chest and the slight shakiness, she felt amused by her nervousness while navigating out of the building.

Using her phone to find her way through the unfamiliar city, she soon settled and let her mind wander through the day's events so far.

Rob seemed pleasant enough. A little gruff and rough around the edges now that he'd spent years in the trenches, but she could already tell he was a dedicated officer.

The opinions and attitudes of some of his colleagues, however, didn't quite seem to match with what she'd experienced. They seemed to think he was dangerous and toxic for her career and had warned her about getting too close to him. She'd picked up on the mention of the Nottinghamshire Anti-Corruption Unit, the PSU, a couple of times, as well as some kind of issue with his family, but didn't know much more beyond that.

Was he as bad as the others made out, or was all this manufactured to fit with someone's agenda? It felt like there were some office politics at play here, but if it was a family issue, she could certainly relate.

One thing was for sure, she wasn't about to take someone's word for it just because they had an opinion. She'd make her own judgement and go from there, but it was a little too early for her to come to any conclusions about Rob and who he was. She'd only known him for a few hours.

Still, apart from the staffing issues they were dealing with, which were a country-wide problem, the team seemed to be fairly typical for an inner-city police force, and she was already settling in and feeling more comfortable.

Having checked her phone before setting off, she'd seen the string of messages from Chris waiting for her, asking how her day was going several times over. His concern was adorable, and she'd taken a moment to send him a quick, reassuring answer that everything was okay and she was enjoying her first day. He was probably worried that she hated it given that he was the one who'd been asked to move up north by his work, and she'd chosen to follow.

What other choice was there? They were engaged to be married, and she had no intention of calling everything off because of a promotion opportunity that Chris had got. Besides, putting some distance between her and her parents was well overdue.

As it turned out, the force had been very understanding and accommodating, leading to a transition that was about as smooth as she could have hoped for.

Now she just had to make a good impression.

The drive out to the suburbs of Hyson Green didn't take long, and she soon turned into a T-shaped cul-de-sac of semi-detached houses made from sandy-coloured bricks with small sections of grass scattered here and there for the local kids to play on. The area was quiet and perhaps one step up from the rows of tiny terrace houses that were a stone's throw away in neighbouring streets. Cars were parked up, a few locals were walking to the shops, and a labourer was grabbing tools from his white van.

Scarlett spied the house of Spencer's parents and took a moment to mentally prepare for the discussion that was to come. It was never easy telling anyone that someone they loved had died, especially when it was a parent, doubly so for a murder. You never knew how they might react, and although she'd only done this a few times during her career, it never seemed to get any easier.

After less than a minute, she realised she was just wasting time and climbed out of the car. These things were often better done quickly rather than prolonging the agony.

She'd put in the call for a liaison officer to meet her at the house, but they seemed to be running a little late and a glance up the street didn't reveal their approach. She'd wait with the family until they arrived, though.

The file for Spencer's parents had listed them as Vanessa and Roger Lawson. He was a retired fireman, and as far as she could tell, they were living on his pension, meaning it was likely that at least one of them would be at home.

Approaching the front door, she rang the bell and waited. But she didn't need to wait long.

"Hello," a woman in her sixties said as she opened the door.

Scarlett held up her leather-clad warrant card with her ID in it, the chrome on the Nottinghamshire Police badge glinting in the late morning light. "Good morning. I'm Detective Stutely, and I'm looking for Vanessa and Roger Lawson?"

"I'm Vanessa," the woman replied. "What's this about?"

"Is your husband at home?"

"He is," she confirmed.

"Might I come in and speak with you both?"

Vanessa frowned. "Is this about Spencer?" She sighed. "What kind of trouble has he got himself into now?"

"I'd really rather not discuss it on the doorstep, Mrs Lawson."

She narrowed her eyes and stepped back. "Of course, come in."

"Thank you." Scarlett followed the woman into the modest house, where she called up the stairs. "Roger? The police are here. They'd like to talk to us."

"What?" a male voice yelled back. "The police?"

At the same moment, a woman in her thirties stepped out of the kitchen with a look of curiosity on her face. "What's going on?"

"This woman's with the police," Vanessa said. "She wants to talk to me and Roger. I think it's about Spencer again."

"Spencer? Then I should be in there too," the woman added.

"I'm sorry," Scarlett cut in, "I don't mean to be rude, but who might you be?"

"I'm Spencer's sister, Vickie."

"I see. Okay, yes, then you need to hear this too."

Within moments, Roger, a tall, barrel of a man with a grey beard, had joined his much thinner wife on the sofa while Vickie took a seat nearby. She was the spitting image of Vanessa, tall and thin but with darker, longer hair.

"Thank you," Scarlett began once they were all settled. "Okay. I'm sorry to be the bearer of bad news, and there really is no easy way to say this, but Spencer is no longer with us. I'm sorry to say that he was found dead in Sherwood Forest in the early hours. You have my condolences."

"What," Roger asked, disbelieving.

"Oh god," Vanessa gasped. "Are you sure?"

"We're certain, yes. It's him. His fingerprints match those in our system. I'm sorry."

The reality hit home, and Vanessa sobbed.

Vickie went to her mother's side and hugged her. Scarlett looked down at her hands as she let the moment play out. There was no need to rush things. She needed their help, after all.

"How did it happen?" Vickie asked finally.

"We, unfortunately, believe he was murdered." Scarlett watched as another body-shaking cry escaped Vanessa's lips.

"Murdered?"

"Why would someone murder him," Roger asked. "He doesn't have anything."

"We would very much like to know that too," Scarlett replied. "We have a Family Liaison Officer coming over to help and guide you through this, but in the meantime, I'd like to ask you a few questions, if that's okay?"

"Of course," Roger confirmed. There was a look of vacant shock on his face that betrayed the pain he was feeling at this moment, even though he was controlling his tears. "Anything we can do to help."

"Thank you. We had your address on file, but we didn't have one for Spencer. Did he not live with you or…?"

"No. He didn't." Roger sighed and clenched his fist, before calming down again. "Damn it. He... He was married... Used to be married..."

"To Sandy, right?"

"That's right. Yes, of course, you'd know, what with the incident. So, he, um, he had an affair with a woman from work. Sandy found out he was cheating, so she left him and got custody of their child, Elise. That's when it all went to shit—"

"Language," Vanessa hissed.

"It's okay," Scarlett reassured her.

Roger continued, "Thank you. The woman he'd been seeing quickly dumped him, and he wasn't left with much after that. Most of his wages went to Sandy for child support, and he sank into a pit of depression."

Vanessa sobbed again. Roger gripped her hand and rubbed it with his other before continuing. On her other side, Vickie stared into the middle distance, no doubt still processing this shock, with her arm around her mother.

"He started drinking and gambling and ended up in deep debt. He couldn't pay his bills, so he borrowed money from people he shouldn't, and things spiralled out of control from there. We helped him as much as we could in those early days, giving him money. But we're not rich, we can't spare much, and the money we did give him ended up at the bookies anyway. Shit. He was such a bloody idiot."

"Roger!" Vanessa scolded him.

"I'm sorry, but if he'd just listened, none of this would have happened."

Vanessa scowled at him and looked away.

Spencer's father turned back to Scarlett. "He ended up losing the house and everything else to try and pay off the debt, but it wasn't enough. He ended up staying with us for a little while, but—"

"You kicked him out!" Vanessa's voice was hot with rage. "Go on, tell her. Tell her what you did. You threw him out into the street, and now look what's happened."

"He was stealing from us." Roger's face dropped, a look of guilt added to his grey pallor and shock. Continuing, his voice began to shake and crack, "He took money, the TV, even some of Vanessa's jewellery. Some of which had sentimental value. He would have sold the house out from under us if we'd given him the chance. I had no choice… No choice…"

Roger leaned back in the chair and put his hand to his face as tears finally fell. While it might have been the pragmatic choice back then, it was surely one he was now regretting.

Scarlett gave them a moment before continuing her questioning. "Do you know who he owed money to?"

"No," Vanessa replied.

"No idea," Vickie added. "He didn't want us to know. He was worried they'd find him. I don't think they were nice people."

"So could this have been them taking what was owed?" Scarlett asked, wondering if the gang he owed money to was behind all this.

"I guess that's possible," Vickie replied. "He'd not seen them in well over a year, though. I don't think they were looking for him anymore."

"So, where did he live?"

"He was homeless," Vanessa snapped, her venom aimed at Roger rather than Scarlett. "He didn't dare come home after being thrown out. He was scared of his dad, scared of what he'd do and terrified of who might come to find him. He was living in fear of both himself and others."

"I see." Scarlett noted the details in her pocketbook. "He didn't want to drag you into it."

"I think that was his biggest fear."

"What about Sandy and his daughter, Elise?"

"Elise was pretty much the only thing that kept him going," Vickie replied. "He loves his little girl, and it broke his heart when he couldn't see her, all because of Darren."

"Sandy's new husband," Scarlett clarified.

"Piece of bloody work, that one," Vickie spat. "Sandy wasn't much better either, though."

"All he wanted to do was sort himself out and see Elise, that's it," Vanessa added. "I honestly think he would have ended it himself much sooner if it wasn't for his daughter. She's so sweet, and I've not seen her in months." She broke down again as her emotions crashed over her once more.

"This is why I don't like her very much," Vickie added. "I'm her aunt. We're her family, and we just don't see her. It's not right. And it's all because Spencer is homeless... oh... was homeless... They were worried about her seeing her dad looking like a tramp." Vickie using the last of her immediate energy dropped her head on her mother's shoulder and tightened her hold around her.

"Which led to the confrontation and the police being called, right?"

"Yeah," Vanessa said, bringing her tears under control. "He went to see her after a few drinks. God only knows where he got those from, but it didn't help matters. He caused a scene, got into a fight with Darren, and the police were called. It's all just one big mess."

"I see," Scarlett replied, making notes. "Had you seen him recently?"

"No," Roger said. "It's been months."

"I've seen him," Vanessa admitted.

"Me too," Vickie whispered.

"What? When?"

"You scared him, Roger," Vanessa continued. "You'd washed your hands of the whole thing, so he didn't want to see you. But I kept meeting him in town, buying him food and giving him money. Not much, just enough to buy something to eat. I'm his mother. I couldn't just sit by and do nothing."

"So, when was the last time you saw him?" Scarlett asked.

"Last week," Vanessa said.

"Mine was a few weeks ago," Vickie added.

"Bloody hell," Roger hissed.

"And I take it you talked?" Scarlett asked. "Did he say anything that concerned you? Did he seem scared or worried about anything unusual? Was there anything he said that might help me?"

"There was nothing out of the ordinary, no," Vanessa answered.

"Vickie?"

With renewed vigour and anger Vickie replied, "No, nothing. But if I had to pin the blame on anyone, it would be Darren. He's always hated Spencer for stealing his girl. Darren fancied Sandy at school, but was several years younger, so she didn't look twice at him. When Spencer found out that Sandy had started dating Darren, after the break-up, it ruined him. He'd brought it on himself, though, I suppose. But, if you ask me, if I had to pick who I think did it, I'd say it was Darren."

"Not the people he owed money to?"

"No, it's not them. It's Darren."

11

With his notes properly organised and his questions jotted down, Rob finally felt ready to take on Brendon one-on-one in the interview room to see what he could get out of him.

It was likely too much to ask for a quick and unreserved admission of guilt from the young man, especially given his association with a street gang. But he could hope, he thought optimistically.

This wasn't Brendon's first brush with the law, either. He'd spent several nights in the cells in various stations around the city, as well as doing a little time on a couple of occasions, but it didn't seem to change things. He never learned his lesson and always returned to the life of crime he had obviously become accustomed to.

In some ways, Rob could just about understand it. The drug trade was a lucrative one, and the draw of that easy money was too much for many to resist, including Brendon.

And like many of his mates involved in the same criminal activity, the money seemed to burn a hole in their pockets. To a one, they wore pristine white sneakers, branded baggy jeans and hoodies and as much bling as they could carry.

It made them easier to pick out, but there was more to policing than keeping an eye on the fashion trends.

As he gathered his notes, Rob wondered how Scarlett was getting on and cursed his luck that he had to deal with this slime ball and miss out on what could be a critical interview with the Sherwood victim's parents. But, there was little choice, and he wasn't about to let Brendon slip through the cracks just because he'd rather be out there.

He felt sure that Scarlett could handle it. She'd impressed him over the short time that they had worked together this morning, which boded well for the rest of the case. She got on, was proactive, and didn't seem to have taken Frank and Tony's poisonous words to heart.

He missed working with Nick, but the early indications were that Scarlett would give him a run for his money.

Rob made his way downstairs into the custody suite and the corridor with the interview rooms. Rounding the corner into the hallway, he spied a woman leave Brendon's room and wander into the corridor.

He recognised the tailored business suit, with its knee-length skirt and white blouse as the woman's heels clicked on the slick flooring. She turned, recognised him and smiled.

"Aaah, so it's you I'm dealing with, is it?"

"Mornin' Matilda," he said.

Matilda placed her hand on her hips and cocked her head to one side. "That's Mrs Greenwood to you, Detective Loxley."

Rob deferred to her. "Of course, we should keep this formal."

"I think that's best," Matilda confirmed. She wore her hair up in a tight bun at the back of her head, giving her a severe appearance that suited her position, but it was a world away from the softer look he'd seen when he'd run into her at the Dragon pub a short while ago, and got chatting over a drink.

"Have you been back to the Dragon recently?"

Her eyebrows climbed up her forehead, and then she chuckled. "Um, no. Not since...." She paused and coughed. "I think we should head inside, don't you?"

Rob smiled. "Of course, wouldn't want to keep the little toerag waiting, would we?"

"I'm not sure my client would appreciate being referred to as toerag, Detective." She lowered her voice to a whisper. "Despite my personal opinions... a-hem."

"Mmm," Rob agreed. "Sorry, you have to represent such a shining star of the local community."

Matilda's lips drew back into a thin hard line as she listened to him. "It's the job."

She opened the door and strode inside, quickly taking a seat beside her client and opening her folder. Beside her, a dark-haired, tall young man stared at Rob as he entered. The cold stare was chilling to be the subject of. There didn't seem to be much life or soul behind his eyes, as if he were dead inside. They were the eyes of an uncaring, brutal man, who thought nothing of beating a boy half his size to within an inch of his life.

"Mr Marsh," Rob began. "Let's get this started, shall we?"

Brendon shrugged but made no sound as Rob set up the DIR and hit record.

"This is Detective Sergeant Robert Loxley, interviewing Mr Brendon Marsh under caution. He was arrested for violent behaviour against a minor last night. Solicitor Matilda Greenwood is in attendance representing Mr Marsh." Rob got them to state their names for the recording before he sat back and gave Brendon a long look.

"Why did you do it?"

"Do what?" Brendon shrugged.

"You know what."

"I don't think I do."

"Okay, just to be clear, I'm giving you a chance to own up to this. A young boy, an innocent boy, is in hospital today, recovering from a brutal attack. He was on life support, having very nearly died from the injuries he sustained in the attack. It's frankly a miracle that he's still alive. And this is something that will live with him for the rest of his life. From what I hear, he's already suffering from nightmares, and I suspect he will have them for a long time to come, all because of the beating he sustained. So, in light of that, why not make it easy on yourself. We know you did it, so just admit to us that it was you and save us the hassle of this stupid game?"

"But what if I didn't do it?"

"You did it, Mr Marsh. I know you did. So why not save us, and yourself, the pain and anguish?"

"No comment."

Rob's heart sank at the mention of those two words. "Alright, fine. You want to do this? We can do this. So, let's remind ourselves of the evening in question. Firstly, where were you a week ago, on the evening of the eighth, at about nine-thirty in the evening?"

"No comment."

Rob grimaced. "You were at Tess Dyer's, weren't you Mr Marsh?"

"No comment." The words were dull and without emotion as he stared into the middle distance, just off to Rob's right.

"Well, we have witnesses who say they saw you arrive at the house of Tess Dyer, shortly after nine PM."

"No comment."

"We also have personal security cameras and door cams that show you arriving at that time and entering the Dyer household. Neighbours say they heard raised voices a short time later, and then screams."

"No comment."

"Screams, Mr Marsh. The screams of a woman and also those of a child not long after. Did you not hear them?"

"No comment."

Rob sighed at the repetitive answers and his bullish refusal to engage in the process at any level. He glanced across at Matilda, who briefly met his gaze. He saw a flicker of emotion flash across her face, and then it was gone as she returned to concentrating on her note taking.

"The screams were quite loud, Mr Marsh. But, let's continue, shall we?" Rob didn't wait for an answer. "Not long after that, the same cameras recorded you storming out of the house, with Tess running after you, shouting…" Rob consulted his notes. "She was yelling 'You bastard. You've killed him. You've fucking killed him.' That's what she was shouting. Do you remember that?"

Rob paused and looked up, searching for any hint that he'd broken through Brendon's granite-like exterior, and for a moment, he thought he could see the stirrings of emotion behind Brendon's eyes. Tears glistened briefly, before Brendon blinked, and the emotion was suddenly gone, wiped away before it overcame him.

"Does that stir any memories, Brendon?"

"No comment."

Rob sighed. He could see where this interview was going, and yet, there was little else he could do. "Why were you so angry that night, Brendon? It's not like you to go beating up kids, is it? That's not how you usually act."

"No comment."

"No comment? No bloody comment to that question?" The anger rose inside him as he thought of that innocent boy, that child, who'd been mentally and physically scarred for the rest of his life, because this monster before him had a bad day. Slamming his hands onto the table, Rob stood and leaned in. "Stop with this 'no comment' bull, Brendon. You could've killed him. You could've killed a child. It's damn lucky you didn't, but I promise you this, he will never forget what you did to him. So why don't you grow a pair and admit it?"

Matilda had already raised her hand, urging him to stop. "There's no need to get so aggressive, detective."

Rob glanced at Matilda, whose expression gave him a clear warning.

With a sigh, he relaxed back into his chair. "We have you, Brendon. We can place you at the scene. We have the door cams, we have the eyewitnesses, and we have your phone GPS, which you picked up from Tess's during that visit." Rob frowned as if a new thought had occurred to him. "Now, why would you have left your phone at Tess's place? Were you perhaps out doing something that you shouldn't?"

"No comment," he snapped, and this time his voice had an edge to it. Rob narrowed his eyes. He didn't like being asked about what had happened before the beating. Interesting.

"Had someone annoyed you, Brendon, before you visited Tess? Is that why you exploded at hers? What happened? What went wrong?"

"Nothing." He seemed a little flustered, but quickly pulled it together. "No comment."

So, he cared more about what had happened before than he did about the attack, or so it seemed. Rob was curious about what that might be, but it wasn't exactly critical to the case against him. All he had to do was prove that Brendon was, without a doubt, the one who had attacked and beaten young Scott, so he decided to go back over the whole thing in a little more detail.

But it made little difference as the interview continued.

No matter what Rob asked or how he asked it, Brendon showed little or no emotion and answered almost exclusively with the words, no comment.

After what felt like an age and a thousand pointless questions, but with more information than what he went in with, Rob called a halt to the interview and turned off the recorder.

"You'd better watch your back, Pig," Brendon muttered as Rob stood to leave.

"Brendon," Matilda hissed at him.

Rob turned back and met the young man's shark-eye stare. "And what's that supposed to mean?"

"My boys will want to have a word, like."

"That's enough," Matilda barked, raising her voice. "One more word, and I walk."

Brendon pulled a face and sat back, saying nothing more.

"Good." She looked up at Rob. "Thank you, officer. I'd like to have a word with my client, please."

"With pleasure," Rob answered, noting her apologetic smile. He gave her a nod before looking back at Brendon. "I'll look forward to this 'chat'." He turned and walked out, leaving Matilda glaring with frustration after him.

Standing outside the door to the interview room, Rob took a long, deep breath and let it go, allowing the anger and emotion to fall away. Breathing in through his nose and out through his mouth, Rob heard a door go up the corridor and turned to look.

DI Bill Rainault, the 'Sheriff' and Rob's personal pain in the arse, walked out of the monitoring room and turned towards him.

Rob sighed. Had he been in there for the whole interview, watching in on him to see how he performed? For a moment, Rob found himself thinking back through the interrogation and remembered the little outburst he'd had early on when his emotions got the better of him. Had Bill seen that?

Walking up the corridor, the Inspector turned and gave him a polite smile that didn't touch his eyes. "Good interview?"

"Not really."

"Mmm. I hear you have a new partner."

"News travels fast around here." Did Rainault and his Anti-Corruption guys have anything to do with Nick being transferred and him getting a new partner? For a brief moment, he wondered if Scarlett might be somehow in league with the PSU, or even be a Professional Standards officer herself?

But after a moment's thought, Rob decided that he must not allow himself to get too paranoid about these things. Was it possible that Scarlett was actually an undercover PSU officer? Sure, it was possible, but it was also unlikely.

This wasn't some corny police show, after all.

That being said, it would be easy for him to do a quick check on Scarlett and see if there was anything suspicious in her background.

"Will I get to meet her?" Bill asked.

"Oh, I'm sure of it," Rob replied and noticed DC Stutely walk into the corridor and stop a short distance away when she spotted him talking to Bill. "But not today. I'll see you later."

"Oh, undoubtedly," Bill replied with a smug smile.

Without another word, Rob walked up the corridor and met with Scarlett, who eyed Rainault with suspicion as they set off.

"How'd it go," he asked.

"They're upset, obviously," Scarlett replied. "But they're cooperative. I've left a Family Liaison Officer with them."

"Okay. That's good. Did you learn anything new?"

"They confirmed a lot of things we already knew or suspected, such as the confrontation with Darren. There's also some animosity between the father and son related to him getting into financial trouble. But I don't think it was anything more than a few arguments a long time ago. Spencer's mother and sister have been seeing him, giving him food, but he refused to go home because of his father."

"I see," Rob replied. "So, where was he living?"

"Nowhere. He was homeless."

12

"You can drive," Scarlett suggested as they walked into the garage. She tossed him the keys to the pool car, which he caught. "I'm still getting to know the city."

"Sure thing, duck." He grimaced at the modern car with all its mod cons. They practically drove themselves these days. They weren't like they used to be…

Oh god, did he just think that? Well, it had finally happened. He was turning into an old man. At least he'd not said it out loud in front of Scarlett. She'd probably wonder what kind of grandad she'd been paired with.

Giving his head a quick shake, he switched mental tracks. "You said Spencer was homeless, right? How long for?"

"The best part of a year, by the sounds of things. He was scared of going home, partly because of his dad who'd thrown him out for stealing from them, and partly because of the loan sharks he owed money to."

"Bleedin' idiot. When will people learn not to borrow money, especially not from criminals."

"If you're desperate, and you can't borrow it from a bank or whatever, then you're going to go elsewhere, aren't you."

"And get yourself in trouble," Rob hit back. "Well, that adds a new dimension to this. Do you think it was the loan sharks who killed him?"

"Seems like an obvious option right now, doesn't it," Scarlett agreed. "But Spencer's family didn't think so. They seem to think he'd successfully dodged them."

"No way. They wouldn't let him off the hook so easily. Hiding on the streets is a good way to stay hidden, but he'd only need to pop his head up once, and they'd be all over him like flies on shit."

"Sadly, I agree."

"So, who were these people who loaned him the money?"

"Well, that's where we hit a problem," she answered. "No one seems to know."

"Really?"

"Yep."

"Bugger."

Scarlett gazed out the window as they made their way north out of the city's centre and into the sprawling suburbia that surrounded it, leaving Rob to his thoughts. How would they find out who these loaners were if the only person who knew them, was dead? They needed some leads before Orleton ripped him a new one.

"How did the interview go?"

"As expected," Rob confirmed. "The hairy bollock answered no comment to just about everything and didn't seem to care about the boy. The only time I got anything out of him was when I asked him what he'd done before he attacked the kid. He didn't like that, but he didn't tell me anything either. Whatever it was that upset him, I doubt it was a stubbed toe."

"What are you thinking?"

"He's a gang member, part of the Top Valley Boyz, north of here. So, I'm betting it was something to do with them. Lost some drugs, maybe? I don't know. A couple of his mates were there when we picked him up, and they didn't seem best pleased with 'im."

"Well, whatever it was, how do things stand with the evidence against him for putting that kid in hospital?"

"He'll go down, for sure."

"Then it's a job well done, don't fret about it," Scarlett suggested.

"I'll try."

Scarlett said nothing and returned to watching the world pass them by for a moment, before finally asking another question. "So… Who was that officer outside the interview room you were talking to?"

Rob gave Scarlett side-eye, but she wasn't looking at him.

"That was William Rainault, but we all call him Bill. He's just a pain in my arse, don't worry about him."

"Oh, okay." She didn't pursue the line of questioning any further, although he sensed that she very much wanted to. She wasn't daft. She'd had a chat with Frank and Tony, she'd seen how the DCI was with him, and now she'd seen him with Bill. She had to have suspicions and was probably wondering why all these officers had issues with him.

He'd need to talk to her about it at some point if they continued to work with each other, but he wasn't in a rush to divulge that particular aspect of his sordid history. Not just yet.

All in good time.

He didn't want to scare her off, after all. Not when they were starting to gel as a team.

"What's the plan for this interview then?" she asked.

"Sandy and Darren," Rob muttered.

"Vickie, Spencer's sister, suggested that Darren should be our main suspect. They've never liked one another, and there was that confrontation between them not too long ago."

"Did she now. Well, keep your eyes and ears open while we're in there, and if you think of a question, don't hesitate to ask it."

"Will do, Sarge."

The semi-detached house they parked outside hinted at an upwardly mobile family doing okay for themselves. The road was quiet and clean, and a homeless person would certainly stand out here. If the couple were interested in keeping up appearances, Rob could see why they might resent Spencer walking up their driveway.

A pretty blonde woman with a baby on her hip answered the door quickly and looked between Rob and Scarlett with a slightly startled expression on her face. Rob guessed the baby was a boy from all the powder blue he was wearing.

"Hello, yes?" The woman, who Rob guessed was likely Sandy, looked shattered. She sported dark rings beneath her eyes, roughly tied up hair with strands falling about her sallow, make-up-free skin, and loose-fitting jogger bottoms, vest top, and unzipped hoodie. A pair of fluffy bunny slippers finished off the look, and for a moment, Rob was jealous of her footwear. They looked damn comfortable.

"Sandy Pierson?" Rob asked.

"Yeah?" She sounded like she didn't have time for this. "What is this? If you're Jehovah's Witnesses, I'm not interested." She went to shut the door.

"No, no." Rob held up his ID, and so did Scarlett. "We're with the police."

"Oh." She pulled the door wider. "Sorry. Just been getting a lot of them recently. It's been a while since we've spoken to anyone from the police. Is this about the thing with Spencer?"

"Kind of," Rob confirmed. "Can we come in?"

"As long as you don't mind the mess."

"Is your husband home?"

She shot a reproachful look back at them, betraying her annoyance. "Yeah. He's supposed to be on paternity leave, but you wouldn't know it. He's out in his office, working. I'll just call him. Come in."

She led them into the lounge at the front of the house and then left them there. A moment later, Rob heard her in another room speaking briefly to someone on the phone.

The lounge looked like a bomb filled with baby toys, nappies, blankets and baby bottles had exploded in here. Finding patches of carpet to walk on was something of a challenge, and he kicked or stepped on a couple of things as he crossed the room. A toy squeaked as he stood on it, making him jump.

"I told you to leave your clown shoes at home," Scarlett quipped.

"Har-di-har." Rob walked around part of the room, casting his gaze over some of the photos on display, most of which showed Sandy, a man with short-cropped dark hair and a slim physique that he guessed was Darren, and a young girl of maybe six or seven. That was likely Elise, who was probably at school right now. There were also a few brand new, just printed off, baby photos propped up here and there, filled with smiling faces.

Further up on a shelf, Rob noticed several ornaments, including a couple of small trophies for a number of sports, such as football, archery and golf, all with Darren's name on them.

A moment later, the back door banged, and he heard muffled voices before Darren walked in, followed by Sandy, who was dealing with a now slightly grisly baby.

"Afternoon, I'm Darren. How can I help you?"

Rob introduced himself and shook the man's hand. Scarlett did the same. "Thank you for seeing us. We'd just like to have a chat, I'm afraid, and I think you should take a seat."

Sandy frowned. "What's going on?"

"Is it Spencer again?" Darren asked.

"It is, yes. It's bad news, I'm afraid. I'm sorry to inform you that he was found dead this morning up in Sherwood Forest. We think he was murdered."

"What?" Sandy gasped as the baby continued to try and get her attention, his little head wobbling about on his still-developing neck muscles. "You're kidding."

"Damn," Darren whispered and sat back on the sofa, staring into the middle distance.

"I'm sorry," Rob said again.

"Oh, shit. What do we tell Elise? Oh god. Oh Christ. I can't..." She sank into the seat and hugged the baby close, with one hand on her forehead. "This is crazy. How... What happened?"

"We're still not sure, Mrs Pierson. We're still working that out, but as his former wife and mother of his child, we needed to come and speak to you."

"Aww, no. This isn't about the fight, is it?"

"We do need to talk to you about that."

Darren sighed. "I knew it would come up again."

"What?! You don't think..." Sandy asked. "You think Darren did this?"

"We're just following up all the leads, that's all, and looking for anyone who might have cause or reason to do something like this. It's routine, that's all. This won't be your only visit either, we'll have support officers coming to see you too, and help you through this difficult time."

"Oh, okay. Thank you."

"Well, go on then, ask your questions," Darren replied, sounding annoyed.

"He didn't do it," Sandy cut in. "When did this happen? Last night? We were both in all night and up for half of it with this one. He needs feeding during the night, so I know when Darren goes for a piss, let alone heading up to Sherwood to murder someone."

"So, you were both in all last night," Rob asked.

"Yeah."

"We were," both confirmed.

"Okay. So, tell me about the fight. What happened?"

"He was drunk," Darren replied. "That's what happened. Look, we were never against Spencer seeing Elise. She needs to see her father, but it needs to be at scheduled times in an agreed location so we can prepare her for it. But he's missed most of them or turned up drunk or high, or just stinking to high heaven. He's a mess, but we never stopped him seeing her."

"That's not what Spencer's family believes," Scarlett countered.

Darren shrugged. "I'd expect nothing less. He'll have lied to them, no doubt telling them what a terrible man I am, right?"

There are always two sides to any story, Rob thought before returning to the incident. "And he just turned up on your doorstep?"

"Yeah, he did. Out of the blue, he just appears, clearly pissed, ranting that he wants to see Elise. Making a scene. So, I tell him to get lost and come to the next agreed meeting, which he missed, by the way."

"And you had a fight?"

"The idiot attacked me. He just went for me as he tried to get into the house. I defended myself. We both got a couple of hits in before I pinned him down and waited for the plod... Um, police to turn up. They took him away, and we gave statements. I think he got a warning for it, but that's all."

"He'd just had a few too many drinks," Sandy added, her tone pleading. "We didn't want him in prison or anything, but he needed to know that he couldn't just turn up. It upset Elise for weeks, and she's already sensitive about all this."

"About the break-up?" Scarlett asked.

"Yeah. He was her dad, so I get it. But after what he did... I couldn't stay with him."

"He had an affair, right?"

"That's right. Shagging some bimbo from work. I don't know how long it had been going on, but I'd suspected him of something like this before. I just didn't have proof until two years ago. I was heartbroken."

"So, you ended it?"

"Of course," she confirmed, trying to pacify the baby, but his cries were only growing more insistent. "Look, I'm sorry, but do you mind if I feed him? He just needs some milk."

"Sure, go ahead," Scarlett confirmed. Rob noticed she went to lift her shirt and averted his eyes. Moments later, the cries from the baby stopped, and a serene silence fell over the room.

Sandy broke the silence. "Sorry."

"It's okay," Rob answered, brushing off her concern.

"So, you ended it," Scarlett pressed.

"I did. I couldn't trust him anymore. Our marriage was shattered from that moment on. Whenever I saw him, all I could think of was him shagging this other woman, and who knows how many others. I know some people can move on and rebuild, but I just couldn't do that. I didn't believe it would set a good example for Elise, and I just couldn't forgive him. Anyway, I ended up getting custody and the house." She waved at the room around them.

"We met not long after that," Darren cut in. "It was a bit of a whirlwind romance, and when we realised that we were pregnant, we knew we had to make it official."

"We never wanted this to happen to him," Sandy said. "I feel terrible for what happened after we split. I know he's had it tough and lost basically everything. I hate that I seemed to have been the catalyst for that, and this... This makes it worse. He didn't deserve to die." She sighed and swallowed back her tears. "Elise is going to be devastated. She never cared that he smelled or looked a state. He was her dad, and she just wanted to spend time with him. What upset her was when he didn't turn up for his sessions. That killed her. It was like a part of her died each time he didn't show. I hated it."

Sandy took a moment and gasped back a quiet sob before she continued, "But, I guess he can't disappoint her anymore."

Rob clenched his jaw. "I guess not."

13

"I'm about to get off," Rob announced as he walked into the DCI's office, stretching his back as he went. Several hours sitting at his desk, staring at a monitor hadn't done him any favours at all. "The Brendon Marsh case is about done, and I'll be handing it over to the CPS. I'd expect him to be sent down over this. The evidence we have is pretty damning."

"Right you are," Peter said as he leaned back in his chair, the end of his pen in his mouth as he looked up. "That's some good work then, well done."

"Took up most of the afternoon."

"And how did the Pierson meeting go?"

"As always, there's two sides to every story. Spencer's family make out that Sandy and Darren were making Spencer's life hell and restricting his access to his daughter. The Pierson's say that's not the case. They said they wanted Spencer to see his daughter but to stick to the arranged meetings. But according to them, he couldn't do that. He missed most of the meetings, which upset Elise and would just turn up drunk on their doorstep at random times, which led to the confrontation."

"And who do you believe?"

"I suspect the truth is somewhere in the middle, to be honest."

"Okay, and does this bring us any closer to finding his killer? The East Midlands Special Operations Unit will expect an update in the morning, and all you've told me is there's some family drama. Which is all very fascinating, but I'm not sure it moves things forward."

"Well, right now, we have two possibilities. We know that Spencer and Darren don't get along, and Spencer's sister, in particular, thinks that Darren might be to blame. It's certainly possible, so we'll keep that in mind. However, he does have a fairly rock-solid alibi. The other option, and the more likely one, I believe, is that the loan sharks who lent Spencer money found him and came to collect."

"Do we have a lead on these people?"

"Right now, no. Spencer was cagy about it, but we'll find them. I expect the post-mortem to be done tomorrow, and we may well get DNA or other evidence from the scene, such as details about footprints and tyre tracks and the like. Then there's all the CCTV we're going through. Background checks on the dog walkers, and so on. We've got a long way to go yet."

"Alright, Loxley, keep me posted."

"Will do, guv."

Rob walked back to his desk, pleased with the way the meeting had gone. It was quick and relatively pain-free, although he did pick up on the hint Peter dropped about how the EMSOU might react to the progress on the case so far.

Peter couldn't resist getting a dig in whenever possible.

"That was quick," Scarlett said as he returned to their corner of the office, where she was gathering up her things.

"In and out, quick and painless," Rob replied, feeling chuffed with it. If only all the meetings he had with Peter went like that.

"Indeed," Scarlett replied with a knowing look. "So, where are you taking me tonight?"

"Just over the road," Rob replied. "We'll meet up with Nick and see how his day at the Lodge went."

"And what's over the road?"

"The Bar and Block Steak House. The grub's lovely, but we can just have a drink if you like."

"You're kidding, right? Just a drink? No way, I'll eat. I've told Chris I'll be back later and to eat without me, so I'm good. I'm starving anyway, so a steak will do nicely."

Rob gave her an approving look. "You like steak?"

"Sure, why not? That and a side of chips? Yum. Come on, you've got my tummy rumbling now. Don't you know not to keep a girl waiting?"

"I'm coming, I'm coming. Keep your hair on, duck." He gathered the last of his things before making their way out of the station.

"I'm not sure I'll get used to this 'duck' thing you all say up here. I don't know if I should be offended or…"

"It's a term of affection. It's a nice thing to say."

"Are you sure?"

"Positive."

"Okay then, duck."

Rob's jaw clenched. "Mmm, not sure it sounds the same with your southern accent. It sounds wrong."

"Yeah, I'm not common enough, clearly."

"Oooh, hark at you."

Scarlett smirked.

The Bar and Block was just a short walk across the junction from Nottingham Central and already seemed to be doing a brisk trade from what Rob could see beneath the red and white striped awnings across its front.

Inside, the restaurant and bar were decked out with wooden flooring, comfortable seating and modern décor as serving staff weaved between tables and customers ate and drank. The smells of cooking meat wafted through the air, joined by popular music played on a low volume. He spotted Nick sitting at a table alone, with empty chairs waiting for them.

"Evening," Rob said as he approached. "Eyeing up the menu already?"

"I'm famished, mate. Need to get some grub down me."

"I was just saying the same thing," Scarlett joined in. She offered her hand. "Scarlett Stutely. I don't think we got to properly meet earlier."

"Nick Miller. Nice to actually say hello. Have you been keeping him in line?"

Rob sighed as they took their seats. Waiting for the inevitable roasting they were about to embark on, he started to look over the menu.

"He needs a babysitter, does he?" She shot him a cheeky look.

"Oh, for sure. He'd be lost without someone to look after him."

"I'll keep that in mind."

"If he gets upset, his dummy's in my drawer."

"Alright," Rob cut in. "That's enough. No need to bring my pacifiers into this. I like the look of the burger."

The other two started to examine the menus as they talked.

"How was your day at Sherwood Lodge?" Rob asked.

"Not too bad, actually. Nailer got me onto a new case nice and quick, so I've been kept busy all day."

"How is he?"

"Nailer?" Nick asked. "He's alright. He asked after you. Wondered how you were getting on working for Orleton."

"As well as can be expected," Rob muttered.

"That's what I said. Needs must, and all that."

"Aye, something like that."

A waiter appeared, and they soon picked out their drinks and meal, with Rob opting for a succulent-sounding burger, Scarlett going for the steak and chips she'd mentioned, and Nick choosing a mixed grill.

"Steak and chips, nice one," Nick commented to Scarlett.

She raised an eyebrow. "What is it with a woman ordering steak? We can enjoy meat too, you know."

"You tell him," Rob joined in.

"Don't you start. You're just as bad," she countered, good-naturedly.

Rob raised his hands. "Sorry."

Scarlett sighed and gave them an exaggerated roll of her eyes.

"Did you finish up the Brendon case?" Nick asked, changing the subject.

Grateful for the new line of conversation, Rob answered eagerly, "Yep, it'll get handed over to the CPS tomorrow, most likely. He'll go down, for sure. Shame you weren't there for the interview."

Nick shrugged. "At least we got the ending we hoped for."

"Aye."

"So, you're on this Sherwood case now? Seconded to the East Midlands Special Ops Unit?"

"Aye. I've not met anyone from the unit yet, they seem to be dealing with Peter mainly, and then he's dealing with me."

"It's a murder case, so they need a DCI leading it, I guess."

"Don't know why they asked for me, though," Rob admitted, still a little bemused and unsure why they had gone over Peter's head.

"Aaah, well, I think I might know a little more about that," Nick replied. "I was chatting to Nailer about it, and he said that the Nottinghamshire unit was involved in a big organised crime sting in north Notts which went wrong..."

"Oh, shit, yes. I remember that. Wasn't that long ago, was it?"

"No. Just a few weeks back. They've kept it fairly quiet, though, as it's still an ongoing situation with the gang."

"They got their asses handed to them," Rob mused, recalling some of the details. "Some of them died, didn't they?"

"Yep. Which means they're down a few men..." Nick glanced at Scarlett, "...and women, which would explain why they gave you this case."

"Do you think they're looking for new people?"

"No idea. But here's another thing. Superintendent Landon's part of the unit now. She's running things in Nottinghamshire for them. So, I bet that's why they asked you."

"Shorty's part of the Special Ops Unit?"

"Aye."

"Bloody hell. I knew she'd been transferred, but I didn't know where."

"Friends in high places, and all that."

"Who's Landon?" Scarlett asked.

"Evelyn Landon," Rob explained. "She was my boss a few years back. She helped me get promoted to Sergeant, along with DCI Nailer and DCI Pilgrim." He thought about it for a moment longer before addressing Nick again. "She must have heard that I went to the crime scene and decided to hand me the case."

"That would be my guess, too," Nick added.

"Did they ever find out who killed the Special Ops officers?" Scarlett asked.

"No," Nick replied. "The case remains open, as far as I'm aware."

A waiter brought their drinks over, and Rob sipped his cold beer, savouring its cool, crisp taste.

"Speaking of cases," Nick said, "how's the Sherwood case going?"

"Slow, for now. The post-mortem will happen tomorrow and hopefully generate a few more leads for us. We don't know much about the victim. We've got his name and spoken to his family and his ex-wife, who are basically blaming each other. The victim was homeless but had a daughter with his former wife and hated her new husband. He could be a suspect but has an alibi. It's the usual family politics."

Nick frowned at him. Something had struck a chord. "Homeless? You said he was homeless?"

"Yeah, why?"

"Hmm. Well, it's just that the case I'm working on is of a missing woman, and before she disappeared, she was working in a soup kitchen, feeding the homeless. She was quite active in helping people who found themselves on the street."

"Oh, okay." Rob narrowed his eyes as he considered this new information. "Do you think they could be linked?"

Nick shrugged. "I think it's worth finding out, don't you?"

"Yeah."

"Why don't you pop up to the Lodge first thing, early, and speak to Nailer? We can see what we've got."

"Sounds good. I'll do that."

It wasn't long before their meals were delivered to their table, and as Rob started eating, he realised how hungry he'd been. The chips were to die for, and the burger smelled intoxicating.

"This is good food," Scarlett exclaimed, sounding impressed. "I'll come here again."

"It's one of our regular haunts," Rob said between mouthfuls.

"So, how was your first day?" Nick asked her.

"Good, thanks."

"What did you think of the DCI?"

"Um…" She paused, thinking about her reply. "He seems a little stressy, I suppose. I think he wants results and expects a lot from his team, but there's nothing wrong with that."

"That's very diplomatic," Nick said with a smirk.

"Generous, too," Rob added, deadpan.

"I've only spoken to him a couple of times, so I don't want to judge a book by its cover. But I'll admit, he does seem to have it in for Rob." She nodded to him.

"That's because he does," Rob replied.

"Did you see the Sheriff?" Nick pressed.

"The who?"

"He means Bill Rainault," Rob clarified and side-eyed Nick, wondering where he was going with this.

"That man you were talking to after Brendon's interview?" she clarified. "Why? Who is he?"

"A pain in my arse," Rob mumbled.

"You said that earlier," Scarlett countered, skewering another offcut of steak. Rob picked up his burger and took a bite. The flavours of the beef, cheese, salad and sources mixed with the toasted bun in the most delicious way.

"He's Anti-Corruption," Nick explained. "He's been after Rob for ages."

"Anti-corruption." She sounded surprised. "I take it this is related to what Frank and Tony were saying to me while I was waiting outside the DCI's office?"

"It's all related," Rob confirmed.

"So, what's the deal? Should I be worried?"

"No," Rob replied, still not keen on getting into all this yet. "it's just…"

"It's prejudice. That's all it is," Nick explained.

"About what?" Scarlett asked.

"It's been going on so long, I'm not sure I even remember anymore," Rob lied. He knew exactly the reasons behind it all, but the whole thing was just tedious by now and had been going on for far too long.

He'd tell Scarlett the truth of it one day, but not tonight. Tonight, he just wanted to chill out with his friends and enjoy some good food.

"Really?" Scarlett asked, incredulous. She didn't believe him, and rightfully so.

"He knows," Nick said. "It's just old news, right?"

"Right," Rob confirmed. Scarlett watched him for a moment, and then seemed to accept that explanation. "Whatever. How's your mixed grill?"

"Nice," Nick replied. "I'll never eat it all."

"Really?" Scarlett replied.

"They always give too much."

Quick as a flash, Scarlett reached over and plucked a sausage from his plate, and before Nick could say anything, she'd taken a bite.

"Oh, you didn't just do that," Rob said, making sure to sound suitably horrified.

"It's tasty. I like a good sausage."

"That's what she said," Nick quipped with a smirk.

Scarlett giggled. "Nice one."

Rob laughed.

14

Lorraine shifted on the hard chair as she tried to ease the painful cramp in her bum. She'd been in this chair for hours. Everything hurt. Her arms and wrists hurt from being tied to the back of the chair, her neck ached, and the backs of her legs were sore from sitting naked in her own mess. The sock in her mouth and the gag that held it there made her feel sick, but she didn't dare throw up in case she choked.

At a guess, she'd been in the same room for maybe two days now. The first day she'd been with Spencer, tied to the radiator against the wall until several of the gang appeared and took him away. He screamed and struggled, but it was pointless to fight them. It didn't help or achieve anything other than making them angry, which invited retaliation.

It wasn't too long after that they'd moved her to the chair and tied her to it. She hated the way they manhandled her, the way they touched and hurt her. It was gross.

She'd spent hours praying, asking for God to help her, to save her from this hell on Earth. But so far, her prayers had not been heard. In her weaker moments, she wondered what she'd done to deserve this. Had she not followed God's path and spread his word? She did more than most, surely!

The Lord worked in mysterious ways. Perhaps he was teaching her some kind of lesson?

Around her, she could hear voices and music in other parts of the house, and no matter how much she tried to scream through the gag or make noise, no one came to help her.

She was alone, and no one was going to help her.

The lock on the door sounded. In the next moment, it opened, and a teenager walked in with a plate of food and some water. He stopped just inside the door and looked her up and down in disgust. With a sigh, he closed the door behind him and wandered over.

"You gotta eat, ain't it." He placed the plate and glass down, reached up, ripped the tape off her mouth, and removed the sock. "I've gotta give you this to keep your strength up."

"Thank you," she rasped before he held up the glass and helped her to drink. The water was room temperature and stale, but right now, it might as well have been the nectar of the gods, as it instantly soothed her throat. "That's better."

The kid grunted and pointedly avoided looking into her eyes. She started feeling a little more aware of her own nakedness and vulnerability as he reached down to what looked like a cheese sandwich.

"Eat," he said and stuffed the bread into her mouth. She did as he asked and hungrily took a bite. As she chewed and swallowed, she wondered if he might be able to tell her anything and decided to chance her luck.

"Where did they take Spencer?"

The kid stiffened and looked up, meeting her eyes for the first time.

"Where is he?"

"Dunno," he answered.

"He's not..." Her voice caught in her throat. She swallowed. "They didn't kill him, did they?"

"Shut up."

She sighed, aware she was pissing him off, but she had to know. Why was she here? What did they want with her? The agony of not knowing was killing her inside as she waited to find out her fate. She gratefully took another couple of bites of the sandwich and another sip of water before she tried again.

"What do you want with me? Are you going to kill me, or...?" She didn't want to finish that statement. She didn't want to even think about what horrors they might subject her to.

"I said, shut up." He shoved the remains of the sandwich at her mouth. She didn't dare refuse in case he left, but a couple more mouthfuls later, she found she needed to know, consequences be damned.

"Please. Can you help me? You look like a good kid. Do you have a mum? Someone my age?"

"Shut it," he snapped.

"I've not done anything wrong. Please help me."

He slapped her. Pain flashed across her cheek as her head rang from the impact. "I said shut the fuck up, bitch."

The kid threw the remains of the sandwich across the room and kicked the glass, smashing it and spilling the water across the floor. Grabbing the sock, he forced it into her mouth and used some fresh duct tape to secure it.

Seconds later, he slammed the door and left her alone with her thoughts.

Quietly, Lorraine started to cry.

15

Scarlett wandered back to the station garage with Rob and Nick and approached her car feeling comfortably full and tired.

Pulling out her keys, she turned to her fellow officers. "Thanks for introducing me to the culinary delights of the steakhouse, guys. That was lovely."

"Our pleasure," Nick replied.

"Absolutely," Rob added. "I'll see you tomorrow, but I'll probably be late in. I'm going to pop over to the Lodge and have a chat with DCI Nailer."

"I don't mind tagging along," Scarlett offered, keen to help out and show her enthusiasm for the case. "We could head up there together."

"No, no, don't worry. There's no need. Besides, I'd like you to keep going through the CCTV and the background of the dog walkers."

"There's not much where the dog walkers are concerned, honestly."

"Alright, but it's worth being sure."

Scarlett shrugged, dismayed that he wanted to visit the Notts HQ without her, but it didn't take both of them, and they certainly had a mountain of CCTV to trawl through, along with a small but growing list of numberplates to check. "Okay, I'll see you when you get in, then."

"You will. Hopefully, we'll dig up a few more leads tomorrow."

"Here's hoping," Scarlett agreed as Rob made his way across the underground garage. As she neared her car, she noticed where Rob was walking and couldn't help a quick double-take. "Is that *your* car?"

Drawing up short, Rob turned back with a victimised look on his face. "Yeah."

"That old thing?" It looked ancient. Well maintained, but extremely dated. It was some kind of British muscle car with its large bonnet, swept-back driving position and low profile.

"Oh, no," Nick mumbled.

Rob placed his hands protectively on his car's bodywork. "Hey, don't be so cruel." Rob turned towards the car. "Don't listen to the mean lady. She doesn't appreciate you like I do."

"Seriously," Scarlett said, bewildered at the scene before her. "You talk to your car?"

"Belle. Her name's Belle, I'll have you know." His offended voice sounded a little melodramatic.

"You talk to your car, and you've named your car?" She'd seen it all. "Oh, dear god."

"You wouldn't understand," Rob said dismissively.

"Yeah, clearly."

"That's his pride and joy you're talking about," Nick commented.

She ignored the warning. "Let me guess, you're single, aren't you?"

"Daaamn girl," Nick exclaimed. "You went there?"

Rob shook his head, placed his hands on his hips, and sighed. "This is a 1985 Ford Capri. A classic, I'll have you know, and there's nothing wrong with enjoying classic cars." He winked at her.

He was defiant, and she realised she might have overstepped her mark. "Sorry, I didn't mean to offend."

"I'll tell you what, this right here," Rob pointed to his Capri, "has way more character than that ever will." He pointed to Scarlett's Fiat.

She raised her hands up and out to her sides in defeat. "I'll concede that one. Fair point."

"Perhaps if you apologise to Belle one day and say nice things about her, I'll take you out for a spin. I think you'll change your opinion after that."

"He has a point," Nick agreed. "She's got some welly, what's for sure."

"Okay, okay. I've clearly touched on a sore point. Rob, I'm sorry, and Belle…" She sighed, and muttered under her breath. "Oh my days, I can't believe I'm talking to a car, but, whatever." She raised her voice. "Belle, I'm sorry." She looked back to Rob. "Better?"

He rubbed the bonnet of his car. "We'll discuss it and get back to you."

She rolled her eyes but knew he was messing about with her. "You do that."

"Are we all friends again?" Nick asked.

"For the moment," Rob quipped conspiratorially. "See you tomorrow."

She laughed. "You might," Scarlett grizzled good-naturedly with a smile on her lips as she opened up her car. "See ya."

She drove out and headed south on Maid Marian Way before taking a right onto Friar Lane and driving past Nottingham castle, or what was left of it. It was mainly just a pair of gates. Impressive gates, sure, but gates all the same. When they'd first moved up, a little over a week ago, before she started work, she made sure to visit several of the local landmarks, including the castle, to take in some of the local history. She'd even visited the Major Oak in Sherwood Forest, the legendary tree Robin Hood had supposedly hidden inside, to escape the Sheriff's men.

Pushing west, she made her way into the Park Estate, a haven of large detached houses surrounded by lush lawns and emerald trees. It was a large gated private estate that served the wealthy of the city with its own tennis and racket ball clubs, all of which were quite exclusive in their membership.

The drive home was a short one, and within five minutes, she was pulling into the entrance of her house on Clumber Crescent and clicking her key fob to open the electric gates. She parked on the pea gravel. Her fiance's car was close by, meaning he was already home. It was late, and there were lights on in the house.

Walking into the house, she closed the door behind her and relished the feeling of taking off her shoes after a long day.

"You in, babe?" she called out.

"In here," he answered.

She wandered through to the front room to find Chris sprawled out on the sofa, his feet up, watching TV.

"What's on?"

"Not much," he replied. "How was your first day?"

"Yeah," she replied, flopping down onto the sofa beside him and draping her arm over his chest. "Not too bad. I've been partnered with a guy called Rob Loxley."

"Loxley? As in...?"

"I know. I've not asked him about that actually, but I guess there are people with that surname."

"Apparently so. And he's alright, is he?"

"A little rough around the edges, but he seems like a good man."

"You like a little rough from time to time, don't you?"

She play-punched his arm. "Oi!"

He laughed and pulled her in for a hug. "So, you're happy working with him?"

"I think so. Rob seems to have some issues with a few of the other officers, but I don't think it's anything too serious."

"I should hope not. He's a serving police officer."

"Exactly my thinking," Scarlett agreed as she thought back over the vetting she'd been through, on joining the police and since, as she continued through her career. Rob would have been through the same vetting procedures to ensure he wasn't compromised and could fulfil his duties as an officer of the law. It was a key part of what they did, and if there were any serious concerns about Rob or any serving officer, they would have been flagged and reviewed. Rob himself seemed cagy about whatever the issue was, saying it was in the past and nothing to worry about, and she felt inclined to agree with him.

She didn't get the feeling that he was being dishonest with her or that he was using the job for personal gain. Instead, the feeling she got was that whatever the issue was, it was in the past. It wasn't a big part of his life, no matter what his colleagues said, and he wished they'd just forget about it and move on. He seemed exasperated and fed up with their prejudice rather than dishonest and untrustworthy.

Frank and Tony's little chat at the start of the day only served to creep her out rather than plant any kind of distrust or dislike of Rob into her. The pair were overbearing and too interested in turning her against Rob, which felt wrong. In a small way, it reminded her of her parents.

She wondered what her mum and dad would make of her up here, enjoying the job they were so against her doing. It might not be as prestigious as they'd like, but she'd be making a difference to people's lives, and that's all that mattered.

At least she was in a house they would approve of. It was kind of ironic that she'd left one gated community and ended up in another.

"What are you thinking about?" Chris asked as he kissed her forehead.

She realised she'd been quiet for a while, lost in her thoughts. "Oh, nothing, really. You?"

"Not much. Work. The usual."

"You mean to tell me you've not been thinking about the wedding?"

"Erm...should I have?"

"Chris!" She swotted at his chest. "Yes, you should. We need a date and a venue. We need to work out who's coming. We have so much to arrange."

"You need to pick out a dress, too."

Scarlett grinned, perhaps a little too wildly. "I know. I can't wait to go dress shopping!"

"Who will you go with?"

"No idea. I don't exactly know anyone up here."

A mischievous look appeared on his face. "How about this, Rob?"

Scarlett felt her face twist and contort in disbelief and shock. "Errr, no. I don't think so. Besides, he drives some kind of ancient car, so I don't think I really trust his taste."

"Ancient car?"

"Yeah. What did he call it?" she mused, thinking back. "Was it a Capri or something?"

"Oh, wow. Yeah, that's an old car. Hmm."

"What?"

"The Capri's a cool car, in a retro kind of way. I think I like this guy."

"Ugh!" Scarlett got up. "I'm going for a bath, and while I'm washing off today's stink, why don't you put some thought into our wedding."

"Yeah, I'll do that," Chris called after her as she walked out.

"No, you won't."

"Probably not. I'll fall asleep instead. Love you."

Scarlett rolled her eyes and made her way upstairs.

16

Rob rolled in through the security gate of the Nottinghamshire Police headquarters early and parked up in the expansive and—compared to the one at Central—spacious car park before walking inside. The drive up had taken a little over half an hour as he navigated north through the city and into the surrounding countryside and farmers' fields. He was still well south of Mansfield and Sherwood Forest, but the surroundings were pleasingly rural and picturesque.

It was good just to get out of the city and put some distance between him and some of the people he was less than keen on back at Central.

Within a few minutes, he was walking into an open-plan office space with several desks spaced around, monitors and files atop them, and plain clothes officers working alongside their uniformed colleagues. Having visited Nailer many times, he was familiar with many of his core team and recognised DCs Ellen Dale, Tucker Stafford and Guy Gibson. A couple of them nodded or waved at him as he walked in. Rob returned the gesture.

He spotted Nick at a desk to one side and wandered over. "Mornin'."

"Hey," Nick greeted him. "How you doing?"

"Not too bad. You? Did you sleep okay after that monster of a meal?"

"Like a log, mate. Like a log." He scooped up a few files from his desk. "Come on. Nailer's already in."

"Perfect," Rob commented and followed Nick across the work space to a side office, which sported the name Detective Chief Inspector John Nailer, stuck to the door on a shiny rectangle of metal. Nick rapped gently on the glass.

"Come in," came a voice from inside.

Rob followed Nick into the office, which was a little more lived-in than Orleton's back at Central. The desk was covered in paperwork, boxes of files were placed along the left wall, and Rob noticed several personal items on the desk, several of which had a golf theme.

Behind the desk, DCI Nailer looked up, smiled broadly, and got to his feet. He offered his hand. "Rob, it's good to see you. How's things?"

"Alright, thanks." Rob gripped Nailer's hand. Rob wasn't short, but he always felt it standing next to John Nailer. At well over six feet, he towered over both him and Nick. But despite his intimidating size, Rob knew him to be jovial and friendly to the people he liked, and he counted himself lucky to be one of them. But Nailer was no pushover and had a core of steel buried deep inside.

He'd been a part of the force for years now, rising up the ranks through hard work and graft. Rob felt a kind of kinship with the DCI for several reasons, one of the main ones being the prejudice that Nailer had encountered in the force. The reasons for Nailer's prejudice couldn't have been much more different to Rob's, however. He couldn't pretend to know what it felt like to be a black man in the force these days and wouldn't presume to, but he knew that both Nailer and himself had been forced to deal with issues because of something that was out of their control.

Nailer had said on several occasions that he saw something of himself in Rob, and that's why he'd helped all those years ago. Nailer had urged him to join the police and had been something of a mentor to Rob ever since.

"Good. That's great to hear. It's been a few weeks. We should grab a beer sometime."

"I was thinking the same thing," Rob admitted as they took their seats.

"Sorry for stealing your man."

Rob smiled. "That's okay. Hopefully, he's making himself useful."

Nailer shrugged and made a weighing motion with this hands. "Mmm."

"Hey, I'm right here," Nick groaned.

Rob smiled, matching the grin on Nailer's face. "When I put in the request for more manpower, I didn't know they'd contact Orleton, or that he'd send Nick over."

"Of course," Rob replied. "But this is Peter we're talking about, and if he can get one over on me, he will."

"Naturally," Nailer agreed. "Is Bill still sniffing around?"

"Oh, aye. When is he ever not?"

"That guy needs to change the record," Nailer muttered. "Peter too. It's ridiculous at this point."

"Tell me about it."

"But I hear you have a new partner now? Some pretty blonde, according to Nick."

"Oi!" Nick exclaimed.

Nailer grinned. "Between you and me, I think he's scared of being permanently replaced."

"Have I got punching bag written on my forehead?" Nick asked.

"Her names, Scarlett," Rob replied to Nailer. "She's alright, for a southerner."

"And you didn't bring her with you today?" Nailer made a show of looking out into the office beyond.

"She'll be working the case... I hope."

Nailer relaxed into his chair again. "So, she's a southerner?"

"Yup. Surrey."

"Surrey? That's Pilgrim's neck of the woods."

"I know, but she doesn't know him."

"Shame," Nailer said with a sigh. "It's been ages since I've spoken to him. I wonder how he's doing down there?"

"Dunno," Rob replied.

"Mmm. Okay, so what's on your mind? What can I help you with? Nick said it was something to do with your latest case."

"Aye. We found a body up in Sherwood."

"I heard. And the East Midlands Special Ops Unit are letting you run the case, right?"

"Under Peter's supervision, yeah."

"That's a vote of confidence, right there, mate." Nailer leaned in. "You should be happy about that. Who knows where it'll lead."

"I know, I am. So we got the body's fingerprints in, and the guy's name is Spencer Lawson. He's a local homeless man who has no right to be up Sherwood way."

"Rob was telling me about this last night over a drink," Nick added, "and when he said Spencer was a homeless man, something clicked."

"Lorraine Winslow," Nailer replied.

Nick nodded. "I thought it was because Lorraine went missing after working in a soup kitchen, serving food to the homeless. This is true and maybe connection enough, but I came in this morning with something nagging at the back of me head that I couldn't place until I looked back through the statement Lorraine's husband, Graham Winslow, had given to the attending officers. He said that Lorraine spent time helping these people, getting to know them, and she'd talk to Graham about them. He happened to mention several of them in his statement, including one called Spencer. No surname, just Spencer."

"You think that's the same, Spencer?" Nailer asked.

"That's a damn coincidence," Rob commented. "Spencer isn't that common a name."

"My thoughts exactly," Nick replied. "For that name to crop up in both cases at the same time, it can't be a coincidence."

"Alright," Rob said. "Tell me about your case."

"Lorraine Winslow. She's fifty-two, married to Graham, and lives in Bobber's Mill. She's a church-going woman and is actively involved with her local Baptist Church, with a particular passion for helping the homeless. According to Father Bernard Sharpe, she was instrumental in helping set up a soup kitchen they run and several other initiatives. She was helping at the kitchen two nights ago and stayed late before walking home after dark. She left Bernard shortly after nine-thirty in the evening, and that was the last anybody saw of her."

Having listened carefully, taking notes in his pocketbook, Rob looked up. He wanted to clarify what Nick had just explained. "So Lorraine, who we know is somewhat friendly with a homeless man called Spencer, went missing the night before Spencer turned up dead in Sherwood."

"Right," Nick confirmed.

Rob leaned back and scanned his notes. "I think these two Spencers are the same person."

"I agree," Nailer said.

"So where are you with the case?"

"We've taken statements from all those who knew her and who saw her before she went missing, we've been looking at the likely routes she might have taken home, and we've started going through CCTV, looking for anything suspicious. But it's hard to know for sure what we're looking for, and there's so much traffic around there."

A thought occurred to Rob. "I think you should look for a dark-coloured four-wheel-drive, off-road vehicle," Rob said. "The group of dog walkers who found Spencer, interrupted the disposal of his body, and they think they saw a four-by-four style vehicle drive away with at least two people in it. We're running our own search through CCTV for that vehicle, but we've got nothing so far."

"Dark-coloured four-by-four?" Nailer asked. "They'll be hundreds of them."

"Don't I know it. But if we can cross-reference numberplates…" Rob gave Nailer a meaningful look.

"We might just get lucky," Nailer finished. "We'll see what ANPR records throw up against what you've found so far."

"Excellent," Rob agreed, consulting his notes. "Also, would you mind if I went to see Graham Winslow? I'd like to ask him a few questions."

"Not at all. Go ahead."

17

Walking into the office, Scarlett scanned the room, picking out DC Tony Darby sitting at his computer at the back while a couple of civilian investigators worked nearby. They looked up and smiled at her. Tony did the same, but without a smile.

As Rob had warned her the previous night, he wasn't in, and his desk sat vacant and unused with his monitor still on a lock screen. The eyes of people she didn't know seemed to follow her across the room, examining the new girl as she came in for her second day on the job with the unit's pariah Sergeant as her partner.

She was probably imagining things, but Tony and Frank had said that associating with Rob would be a bad idea. Had they been right or was this all in her head? In reality, was it just the nerves of walking in on her second day as the untested newbie? Glancing into the corner office that turned the room into a blocky L shape, she spotted DCI Peter Orleton talking to DS Frank Parish. They were deep in conversation and didn't notice her arrival.

Grateful, she moved to her desk and settled in, logging into her PC and checking her messages. She'd only just had her email set up, and there wasn't much on the system yet to distract her from the job at hand.

Hoping that Rob wouldn't be too long up at Sherwood Lodge, she dived into her research on the three dog walkers who'd found the body, but there wasn't much to go on. She'd done most of it the day before and come up with zero solid leads on any of them, and she doubted that deeper checks into ever more tenuous links would bring up anything useful.

These women were innocent bystanders who'd stumbled across the work of a local criminal gang… she just had to figure out which one it was.

With a sigh, she leaned back and stretched, annoyed by the lack of leads.

"Late night?"

Surprised by the voice, Scarlett turned. The officer she'd seen talking to Rob outside the interview rooms the day before was standing right there. Tall and slim, he seemed to Scarlett someone who took great pride in his appearance with his almost flawless tanned skin, neatly trimmed goatee beard and styled hair covered in plenty of product.

"Late night? No, not really," Scarlett replied. "Can I help you?"

He offered his hand. Scarlett noticed the silver glint from his cufflinks, peeking out from beneath his tailored suit's sleeve. Hesitantly, she took his hand and gave it a shake. "I'm DI William Rainault from the PSU—that's the Professional Standards Unit. But you can call me Bill."

She listened while looking at him through narrowed eyes, having learned a little about him from Nick and Rob last night. He was Anti-Corruption, and apparently had a bone to pick with Rob. He'd made her jump, but she wasn't surprised by the visit. Although, as he moved to sit in Rob's office chair and swivelled it around to face her wearing a shit-eating grin, she couldn't help but feel a little nervous.

"How can I help you, DI Rainault?" She purposefully didn't use his first name, preferring to keep things formal and not get too friendly. It was a petty slight, but she spotted the brief grimace on Bill's face.

"Oh, it's nothing really. I just came to see how you were getting along and how you were finding the people in this unit?"

"You mean Rob. You want to know how I'm finding Rob, right?" She saw little point in being vague.

Bill shrugged and seemed to accept her reply. "Why not."

"I find him to be a competent and driven police officer, and I enjoyed my first day with him."

"I see. So, you didn't see anything untoward?"

"You mean corrupt? No."

He forced a smile. "But of course, why would you? You've only been here a day, so you don't know the way of things around here. You don't know the history of things. That's only to be expected, but you should really think carefully about your career and what you want to do with your life. You don't want to find opportunities closed off for you for reasons entirely out of your control?"

Already fed up with his pontificating, Scarlett sighed and didn't hide it. "What are you talking about?"

Bill held up his hands. "I'm not going to sit here and bad mouth anyone..."

Scarlett could hear the 'but' coming and decided she'd heard just about enough of this kind of crap. "You just did."

Bill frowned. "You seem like a nice girl—"

"Woman," she snapped as he bit his lip and shifted in his chair.

"You seem like a nice woman, Scarlett Stutely. You're early in your career with what could be a great future ahead of you. So if I were you, I'd be careful who I chose as my friends."

"I'll bear that in mind," she sneered at him. "Now, if you don't mind, I have a murder to solve."

"You can come and talk to me any time you like. My door's always open." But Scarlett had already turned away, paying him no more mind as she pointedly ignored him. She heard him grumbling beneath his breath as he got up and walked out.

Once she was sure he'd gone, she looked over her shoulder to double-check. Closing her eyes, she let out a long slow breath, allowing the anger Bill had caused to drain away.

He seemed like a slimeball of a man, in her opinion, and shuddered at the thought of him. Rob had the restraint of a saint if he'd been dealing with that for years without knocking him out. Worse still, Bill's attitude towards women seemed a little off and made her skin crawl. She'd encountered this kind of thing before and could spot it a mile off.

Speaking of slimeballs, she thought mockingly as Tony walked over from his desk, looking smug.

"I've been going through CCTV again. I've got a bunch of numberplates to look into, but nothing concrete."

"Okay, great, thank you. Are you done for now then?"

"I've got other cases to work on, so I'll need to cycle back round to it. You've got a couple of investigators hunting through the footage as well, though, right?"

"We have, thanks. Good luck with your case."

"Cheers." He nodded to the door, where Bill had just disappeared. "What did Rainault want?"

She felt her expression tighten. "Oh, nothing. Don't worry about it."

"He's just concerned about you partnering up with Rob, that's all. Same as Frank and me, we think—"

Scarlett quickly raised her hand, cutting him off. "Stop right there. I've heard enough of this crap, Tony. I don't want to make enemies, but unless you have any evidence, then that's all it is, crap. I'll form my own opinions and make my own choices. Thank you very much. I don't need you harassing me about it, got it?"

Tony brought his hands up in a gesture of surrender.

"Come away, Tony."

It was Frank who'd just walked out of the DCI's office. Scarlett gave him a hard stare too.

"Sir," Tony confirmed and turned away from her.

"She'll learn who to listen to, soon enough." She heard Frank say in a voice that wasn't as quiet as it perhaps should have been.

She did her best to shut them out and refocus on the screen before her.

18

"You went to see DCI Nailer?" Orleton asked from his leather throne. Rob nodded to his superior officer, having run through the morning's events and updated him on the investigation, including the link to the missing woman, Lorraine Winslow and his desire to speak to her husband, Graham.

Lorraine going missing one day apart from Spencer's death was just too much of a coincidence, and he hoped that even Peter could see that. But he sounded annoyed as the DCI stared back at him from behind his desk.

"I did." Rob saw Scarlett glance at him out the corner of his eye from where she was standing beside him.

"I would have preferred that you had come to me first before you went gallivanting off to the Lodge. There's proper channels for this kind of thing, Loxley."

"Apologies, sir, but I believe that time is now of the essence."

"In what way? Spencer's dead."

"And Lorraine is missing. I think they're linked, and I think that this could be the first killing of several if we don't find Lorraine soon."

"You think this is the same person? You think they kidnapped and killed Spencer, and they're doing the same to Mrs Winslow?"

"That is my assumption, sir. I could be wrong. I hope I am, but I just have a feeling…"

"Feelings aren't facts, Loxley." Peter sighed, sounding like he didn't believe his own words and was hopefully siding with Rob on this one. "Alright, fine. Go and speak to Graham. See what you can dig up. What about everything else? The CCTV? The post-mortem?" His eyes flicked between him and Scarlett.

"Nothing solid on the CCTV, sir," Scarlett replied.

"And the post-mortem is scheduled for later today," Rob added. "I've had an email for someone to attend."

"Right you are then," Peter said. "Looks like you have a packed day ahead. Get to it."

"Sir," they both replied and left the DCI's office and their unit's room, making their way down to the garage.

"So it was a successful meeting this morning then?" Scarlett asked as they booked out a pool car and hit the streets.

"I wanted a stronger link, but this is still good. I can't believe these two incidents aren't linked."

"I'm inclined to agree," Scarlett replied. As they drove west, Rob had the feeling that she was holding something back, that she wanted to tell him something, but she never spoke up, as if biting her tongue. He didn't push her on it, though, in case he was reading things wrong.

It led to a quieter car journey than they'd previously had, but it wasn't an uncomfortable one. Rob let his mind wander over what could have happened to Lorraine. There was so much they didn't know yet, so many details they had yet to uncover, that the whole thing felt overwhelming with no clear way forward, apart from speaking to Graham. But Rob honestly wasn't sure what help he could be if he'd been at home when his wife had been taken.

But maybe there was something to do with Spencer that had yet to be revealed, some detail that might open a whole new avenue of inquiry.

The estate in Bobber's Mill that the Winslows lived on was one of the newer developments and had a lovely if slightly manufactured feel. The semi-detached properties were each set just a few metres back from the road, separated by black tarmac and tiny sections of grass or woodchip with young trees planted in the beds. The houses themselves were typically modern and crammed into the space, all so that the developers could make as much money as possible.

Its location right next to a large stretch of wasteland that had once been home to the factories and mills that had given the area its name felt slightly amusing to Rob. Abject desolation sitting beside a comfortable, manicured little estate.

Rob and Scarlett were greeted at the door by a Family Liaison Officer who welcomed them in before disappearing into the kitchen while they settled into the front room, where Mr Winslow was waiting for them. Worry lines were etched across his face, and there was an air of low-key panic behind his eyes as he contemplated what his life might be like after this.

He was scared, and rightfully so.

"Mr Winslow," Rob began. "Thank you for seeing us. I'm Sergeant Rob Loxley, and this is Detective Scarlett Stutely. We're aware that you have been through this several times already, and I'm sure you don't want to relive this over and over, but we do have a few questions for you."

"I know, it's fine. You ask your questions, son. Do you have any leads on her yet?"

"Nothing new yet, I don't think. But, we're actually working on another case, which we think might be linked to Lorraine going missing, and we were wondering if you might know the name, Spencer? I believe you mentioned the name in her statement to the police in regards to a homeless man that Lorraine knew, is that right?"

Graham's eyes flicked between them as his mind seemed to race. "You mean? Did he do this? Did Spencer take her?

God damn it! I knew she shouldn't have been helping those bloody tramps. They're dangerous. I knew this would happen."

"Sir," Rob cut in. "It's not what you think. Spencer was found dead recently, and we were wondering if Lorraine's disappearance was linked to his. His full name is Spencer Lawson. You didn't provide a surname for him in your statement but…"

"That's him," Graham confirmed. "Lawson. Spencer Lawson. I remember now. I'm positive. That's him. But… What do you mean he was found dead? Do you think…?"

"We don't think anything yet. All we know is that Lorraine is missing. But we need to know if Lorraine spoke about him at all? Did she say anything about him that might help us? Did she mention anyone who was causing him trouble? Was he afraid of anyone?"

"I… I don't know. She'd tell me about them sometimes and the troubles they were going through, but… I'm sorry, I just wasn't that interested. I didn't listen to what she was telling me."

Rob grimaced at the admission, annoyed that this could be a dead-end because Graham didn't listen to his wife. "So, you don't remember anything?"

"Not really."

"Nothing about Spencer getting into a fight with anyone?"

"Oh, hang on, now that you mention it, yeah. He had some family trouble, I think. The police were involved. I can't remember the details but I remember that."

"Okay. And you said to the other officers that Lorraine would often walk home?"

"That's right. She sometimes got lifts from her friends, but she walked home too."

"Do you know which way?"

"It varied, sometimes along the streets around that stretch of wasteland out there, sometimes through it along the path. It's quite safe."

Apparently not as safe as it could be.

"Okay, thank you, Mr Winslow, and if you remember anything else, would you give me a call?" Rob handed Graham his business card.

"Yeah, of course. Thank you."

Rob and Scarlett thanked him and left the house.

"You see, if men would just listen to their wives, this kind of thing wouldn't happen, would it," Scarlett commented wistfully.

Rob frowned. "Perhaps not."

"So, what do you want to do now?"

"Well, I might see if we can go and speak to the priest at Lorraine's Baptist Church, see if he knew anything about this Spencer, maybe? But we're running short on leads."

"We could walk around the area, see if we can see anything?" Scarlett suggested.

Rob's phone buzzed in his pocket and played the tune to Genesis's Invisible Touch. He answered it, spotting the name Nailer on the screen.

"Aye up."

"Rob. Where are you?"

"We've just walked out of Mr Winslow's. Unfortunately, he wasn't able to give us anything new."

"Alright, good."

"Good?" Rob frowned, confused.

"Good that you're in Bobber's Mill, I mean," Nailer clarified. "We've just had some GPS data come in from Lorraine's phone. It was last detected very close to where you are now. I'll send over the location, so you can check it out and report back."

"Alright, sounds good, thanks." He ended the call.

"What was that?"

"That was Nailer. He's got the last known location of Lorraine's phone, and apparently, it's close."

"That's awesome, but I was asking about your ringtone."

"Oh."

"What was that song?" She asked the question with a wrinkled nose, and he got the impression she wasn't impressed.

"Genesis. Invisible Touch. It's a classic. You can't beat a bit of Prog Rock."

Scarlett slowly raised an eyebrow as he spoke. "If you say so, old man."

19

Leaning back against the car, its doors and boot wide open, Curby listened as its custom sound system blasted the latest track from NoBiz out across the estate. NoBiz himself, one of the members of Curby's crew, was stalking around in front of him, freestylin' along to his own track.

He was a skilled rapper and was by far the best in the crew, with only Gaz approaching NoBiz's level with his rhymes and tunes.

Curby nodded to the music, bobbing his head in time to the beat while some of the guys danced around, smoked, or live-streamed the rap across TikTok or Instagram to NoBiz's followers.

That was another area where NoBiz had Gaz beat. His social media following had exploded in recent months, with some of his tracks and vids going viral. He was actually starting to make some good money from them and even had a small urban record label talking to him.

Nearby, one of his crew spun a twocked BMW, burning out its tyres in a cloud of grey smoke across the wide-open stretch of concrete in the middle of the estate. Black skidmarks across the grey concrete marked the countless doughnut's the guy had been turning, while laughing and whooping.

This was a favourite haunt of the crew, and somewhere they often came to hang out.

Occasionally, Curby became aware of a local resident walking by at a distance, staring at them with open hatred. But no one dared say anything or call the cops because one way or another, Curby and his crew would find out who it was, and they'd pay them a little visit. This was their territory, and they made sure everyone knew it.

Closing his eyes, Curby lost himself to the music, letting the deep bass thrum through his body with each beat while his crew enjoyed the moment.

One of his phones vibrated twice in quick succession, alerting him to a text message. Taking his time, as he didn't want anything to ruin this moment, he removed the burner from his pocket and waited for the track to end before he held it up to check his notifications.

It was from Archer. Curby grimaced before he unlocked the device and opened the message.

Get rid of the 4x4.

That was it, short and to the point. Curby raised an eyebrow and scoffed at the order. Who the fuck did he think he was to give him orders? He couldn't boss him around like that.

A new screech of tyres made Curby look across concrete. By rights, it should be an area for children to play ball games on, but there were no kids around here that weren't affiliated to his crew in one way or another.

Curby watched a car he recognised drive onto the concrete and power towards them before it slowed and turned, presenting its side face to the group. Several of the younger kids on bikes rode in closer and stopped, keen to watch what was about to unfold.

Gaz climbed out of the driver's seat and walked around as Curby glared into the back passenger side window. Terrified, angry eyes stared back from the shadows.

Nodding once to Curby, Gaz yanked the door open and reached inside.

A young woman, her wrists wrapped in grey carpet tape, with another strip over her mouth, was hauled out with little regard for her safety. This was Tess, Brendon's girlfriend. The music drowned her muffled yelps as Gaz and Rigby, who'd been in the back seat, threw her from the vehicle.

"Get out, bitch," Gaz grunted.

Tess hit the ground on her hands and knees. She crumpled to the floor with a cry as tears streamed down her face. Blood welled up from fresh cuts on her hands as she looked up.

"She's a feisty one," Rigby muttered, sporting a couple of scratches on his arms and face.

Curby smirked. Looking down at Tess, he could hear her muffled voice but couldn't make much out. He didn't care what pain she was in, he had questions, and wanted answers.

"Bitch put up a fight. Nearly crashed the car because of her shit," Gaz added.

Curby glanced once at Gaz before he reached down, grabbed Tess by her jacket, and lifted her up. "You and I need to talk."

Face to face, with tears streaming down her cheeks, Curby saw fire behind her eyes. She wasn't broken yet. He threw her back against the car before coming in close again. She struggled, fighting him, getting blood on him from her cut-up hands.

"Fuckin' whore," he spat. Pissed off, Curby pulled back and slapped her across the face. She yelped. "Shut the fuck up."

Her wet eyes glared at him in defiance.

"Keep fighting. Next time I'll break your nose," he warned.

She remained tense but stopped struggling and seemed to process his words. After a moment, she nodded. He held her for a moment longer, trying to work out if she was having him on, but it was difficult to get a read on her. Reaching up, he pulled on one corner of the tape across her mouth, getting a good purchase between thumb and forefinger.

"I'm gonna take this off, and you're gonna answer some questions, got it?"

She narrowed her eyes but made little indication that she'd understood him, or would do as he asked.

"I said, got it?" He forced her back again, shaking her by the scruff of her neck.

She cried out and nodded vigorously.

It was about as good as he could expect, so he yanked the tape off in one quick motion.

She hissed, turned to him, and then spat in his face.

The saliva splatted against his cheek and eye. On instinct, he lashed out and thumped her in the face, hard. She screamed and started to sob as she hung from his grip. Curby pulled her back up to look at him. She had a cut on her cheek and blood in her mouth.

"Wipe it off," he barked at her.

Tess glared at him, sniffed, but said nothing.

"WIPE IT OFF!"

She flinched. A moment later, she reached up with trembling hands and wiped his cheek with bloodied fingers.

"You're a fuckin' grass, bitch. A fuckin grass. Why the fuck did you get the bastard pigs involved? Huh? Why? You know fuckin' better. This is Top Valley and I'm boss around here. So if you've got a fuckin' problem, you come to me. Got it!"

"Yeah, I got it." Her voice was weak and strained. A trickle of blood leaked out from her nose.

"Tell me what Brendon did."

Tess bit her lip. "He nearly killed Scott. Put him in hospital, in intensive care. He's still there, I don't know... I hope..."

The kid was barely ten years old and not yet involved in any of this shit. He was an innocent, and while they didn't have many rules, killing or nearly killing a kid that young was most certainly something Curby didn't agree with. "Brendon attacked him?"

Tess nodded.

"Why?"

"He got robbed. Lost your money, and didn't go to the thing you sent him to."

The drugs buy. Curby rolled his eyes at the idiot's stupidity, guessing he was scared of returning empty-handed, worried about what would happen to him. So he returned home, stressed and upset, and obviously lashed out.

"Fuckin' idiot. Now we've got fuckin' Five-Oh all up in our arses because of him. Shit-for-brains."

"I won't speak to the pigs again," Tess stammered. "I promise."

"No, you won't." Curby smiled as he reached into his pocket. He held up the small, four-inch-long metal item and pressed a catch on it. A blade snapped out and glinted in the light.

Tess gasped and started to struggle.

"Hold her," he ordered. Gaz and Rigby grabbed her.

"Hold still, missy," Gaz purred.

"This'll be easier if you don't struggle," Rigby added.

Her eyes wide with terror, Tess stared at the gleaming blade. "Wha... what are... Please, don't. What about Scott. Please."

Grabbing her arm in his steely grip, Curby cut the tape wrapped around her wrists. "Let her go."

Tess stumbled and staggered to one side, gasping for breath, stunned. Releasing her wrists, she looked back up as Curby closed the blade and put it away.

"Get the fuck out of here."

"Are... Are you sure?"

He looked at her as if she was some kind of dump child.

"Thank... Thank you." She turned and hobbled away, stumbling once to her knees before continuing on her way.

Curby laughed, and some of the others joined in as she limped away, picking up speed as she went.

"Was that a good idea?" Rigby asked, leaning in.

"She won't be any more trouble."

"You hope," Rigby scoffed.

"I know." Curby gave his friend an assertive look. "She won't fuck with me again."

"Fair enough, bruv."

"Gaz," Curby said, turning to him and waving for him to come closer. "Do me a favour and get rid of the four-by-four, will yeh?"

"Get rid?"

"You heard me. Burn it."

20

"I'm not sure I've heard much of Genesis's music before," Scarlett stated as they walked along the street, away from Graham and Lorraine's house. "I don't think I'd recognise any. Who's in the band?"

"Have you heard of Phil Collins?" Rob asked.

"Oh, yeah. I think I've heard him on the radio. Isn't there that one that goes, du-dun, du-dun, du-dun, du-dun, dun, dun." She mimed playing the drums as she made the staccato sound.

"It's called 'In The Air Tonight', and yeah, that's a very famous drum solo."

"Cadburys used it, didn't they? With that gorilla."

"Aye, that they did," Rob confirmed. "He wrote the song after splitting from his wife, I think. I'll have to play you some of their tracks. I'll turn you into a fan, don't you worry."

"Can't wait."

They walked along the road until they reached a junction with a side road leading off to their left. It was short and came to a dead-end, where it transformed into a path running out across overgrown wasteland. It was only metres away from the picturesque little cul-de-sac that Lorraine lived on, but it seemed worlds away from that almost picture-postcard street. There was a run-down-looking car garage on the corner, with several vehicles looking worse for wear parked on the side road. Including one that was up on bricks, and another hidden beneath a tarp, lashed into place with ropes. The road was bordered on the left by a fence of hedgerows, while the right deteriorated into derelict buildings covered in graffiti. Towards the end, a seemingly abandoned food truck stood to one side, its wheels overgrown with weeds. Just beyond that, massive blocks of concrete blocked any vehicles hoping to reach the path and wasteland beyond.

As they watched, a pedestrian walked out of the fenced-off path over the brown site, and nodded hello as he walked up the street. It seemed to be in regular use.

"Nailer said the phone was last picked up around here," Rob said as they reached the enormous chunks of concrete at the end of the sideroad. "Have a look around and see if you can see anything."

Finding a long stick, Rob picked it up and used it to pick through the litter that was scattered everywhere. Ripped black bin liners spilt their contents. Food and drinks wrappers, cartons or containers lay discarded, the leftovers they once contained long since scavenged by the local wildlife.

The area needed a damn good clean up.

"What are you hoping to find?" Scarlett asked as they scanned the area.

"I'm not sure, really," Rob replied. "The phone, maybe? If it was dropped around here. Just see what you can see. Anything that relates to homelessness would be useful too."

After a few minutes of hunting around, Scarlett called out, "Rob, over here."

He walked over and found Scarlett standing towards the back of the final derelict building and looking into the space behind it. He saw a partially walled-off area, blocked by a ragged and broken chicken wire fence. Inside, Rob could see boxes, cardboard, and an old mattress, all covered in litter and grime. A condemned-looking metal and PVC roof filled with holes would shield anyone in here from the rain, making it a perfect little bolt hole.

"What do you make of this?"

"Looks like somewhere people could sleep rough," Rob said, giving voice to what he felt sure Scarlett was thinking.

"I was thinking the same thing." She reached down, pulled the fencing back, and stepped through. Rob followed, and after a couple of steps, spotted what looked like a discarded, broken smartphone, its screen badly cracked.

"Huh, look here." Rob crouched down and pulled out a fresh pair of blue latex gloves. He snapped them on and reached for the phone. Nothing on it announced it belonged to Lorraine or anyone else, but it was just too much of a coincidence for Rob to leave it here.

"Well, I'll be. What are you betting that it's Lorraine's phone?"

"I'm not betting anything, but I'll be damned if it's not. Got any bags?"

"No, you'll just have to hold onto it until you get to the car," Scarlett replied. She turned and surveyed the detritus. "Broken phone, rough sleeper's paradise," she looked back, "this must be where they took her, and Spencer too, maybe."

"Damn right," Rob replied as Scarlett took another few steps across the mess.

A woman screamed and jumped up from her hiding place amongst the cardboard. "Get away." She hefted a length of wood and held it like a baseball bat, ready to swing. Rob guessed she was probably in her thirties, maybe, but years on the street, mixed with god only knows what cocktail of drugs, had aged her.

"Whoa, hold on there," Scarlett exclaimed, who was in easy reach of the woman.

Rob raised his free hand. "Calm down. We're not going to hurt you."

"Like hell you're not," the woman yelled. "Go on, piss off. I'll scream this place down. I'm warning you!"

"I believe you," Scarlett said, holding her hands up in surrender. "We won't hurt you. We're police officers. I have my ID in my pocket. I can show you if you like."

"A likely story. What else have you got in there? A gun?"

With her attention on Scarlett, Rob reached into his jacket pocket with his free hand. He held his warrant card up to show her. "Look, here. I'm Rob. This is Scarlett. We're detectives with the Nottingham Police."

"Hi," Scarlett said, brightly, and gave the woman a little wave.

The woman tick-tocked back and forth between them, seemingly unsure. "What are you doing here?"

"We're working on a case," Rob replied, then narrowed his eyes in thought. "In fact, you might be able to help us."

"Help you?" She sounded bemused. "Yeah, right."

"I mean it. Look, we're not going to move you on or anything. I'd just like to talk to you, actually."

"About what?"

She seemed curious, so Rob pressed on. "Do you by any chance know Spencer Lawson?"

She frowned, giving him a suspicious look. "Why?"

"Well, I'm afraid he was found the other day, up in Sherwood. He'd been killed."

"Oh, shit." The woman sighed, and the fight left her utterly as she finally let go of the length of wood and dropped it to the ground. "Not again."

"I'm sorry," Scarlett asked.

Rob wasn't sure he'd heard her right either. "Do you know something? Do you know what happened?"

"To Spencer? Yeah. I think so. I was here when they took him."

"You were here?" He couldn't quite believe what he was hearing.

"I was sleeping, back there beneath the cardboard to keep warm. Spencer had gone out earlier, and I didn't hear him return. But I heard him when they took him. Hard not to. I'm just glad they didn't hear me."

Realising the enormity of what she was saying, Rob took a few steps closer to make sure he heard everything. "What did you see?"

Scarlett pulled out her pocketbook and readied her pencil.

The woman sighed. "I heard sounds of struggle and people shouting orders, so I peeked out from under the cardboard. There were several men in dark clothes. They had Spencer and Lorraine."

Rob gaped at her in shock. "You know Lorraine?"

"Spencer knew her better. She was helping him with his family, wanted him to see his little girl, yeh know?"

"We know," Rob confirmed. "She helped with the soup kitchen at the local church."

"That's right." The woman had relaxed further and was opening up to them. Her whole body-language seemed less defensive as she talked. "They grabbed both of them. One of them hit Spencer with a bat."

"Did you see what they looked like? These men, did you get a good look at them?"

"They were wearing masks, like, hoods..."

"Balaclavas," Rob clarified.

"Yeah. It was dark too. They hurt them and dragged them into the back of their van. I'm just glad they didn't see me."

"A van? What kind of van?"

"A big one. It was white."

"A white van. Like a transit van?"

The woman shrugged. "I suppose so. I only saw the back edge of it."

"The number plate?" It was unlikely, but it was worth asking.

She shook her head. "No, sorry."

"That's okay. And what did they say, these men?"

"Not much. They were swearing a lot. I heard one say, 'they might as well bring her too, saves them doing this again soon.'" She sighed. "It's not the first time this has happened, not that anyone cares."

"What do you mean, not the first time?" Rob was shocked.

"It's been happening for months. I hear stories, yeh know? We talk. It's been happening all over the city. A white van appears, then men jump out and take one of us." She took a breath, fighting back her tears. "We don't hear from them again, the ones they take. I guessed they were killing them or something, but I didn't know. But, you say you found Spencer, so…"

Rob took a moment to process what he was hearing. "So, these thugs have been kidnapping homeless people across Nottingham for months?"

"See? You didn't know. Nobody cares about us. Nobody knows this is happening."

"Nobody's reported it," Rob replied, defiance in his voice. "How can we know if no one tells us?" He saw the woman's face tense and realised he was starting to alienate her. "I'm sorry, but we're here now. I want to help. I want to find out who did this. And stop them."

She gave him a solemn nod.

"Do you think you might recognise any of them if you saw them again?" Scarlett asked. "If we arrested anyone, would you try to identify them for us?"

She took a long breath and glanced out across the stretch of wasteland with its single remaining chimney, a massive, silent sentinel, standing testament to the scale and grandeur of the now destroyed mills. She seemed to be wrestling with the thought of helping the police, and given the relationship that some rough sleepers had with officers of the law—and the law in general—he wasn't surprised.

"I want to help," she said finally, turning back. "This has been going on too long, and now that they've taken Spencer... I want to help."

"What's your name?" Scarlett asked.

"Viv. Vivian Aston."

"Alright, Viv. We can bring you back to the station. You can hang out there while we look into this. We have people who can help you..."

"No!"

"Sorry?"

"I'm not staying at the station. You lot are all... I mean... Well, you two seem different, but some of you are bastards. No offence to you, you understand. I'll come in to identify someone or answer questions, but I'm not staying there."

"No offence taken," Rob replied. "But, you'd be perfectly safe."

"No. No way. I ain't staying there. If you can't help me, I won't help you. Take it or leave it."

Rob grimaced at the ultimatum, feeling like he was caught between a particularly large rock and a suitably hard place.

He could arrest her, sure, but what would that achieve, apart from confirming her worst fears and ruining any chance of her helping them. They needed her on-side.

Scarlett turned to him. "What do we do? We can't leave her here."

"No, we can't," Rob agreed. If they walked away now, she might disappear into the city, never to be seen again, or worse still, the kidnappers might come back to clean up. They needed to keep her safe and protected, in a place where they could find her and build her trust in them. Doing all four would be tough, but as long as they didn't advertise where they were keeping her, just being off the streets would likely be protection enough.

For a moment, he considered letting her sleep on his sofa but then dismissed the idea. He didn't know her or know if he could trust her, and besides, there were other, probably better options.

"How about I check you into a hotel?" Rob saw Scarlett's eyebrows climb up her forehead in his peripheral vision as he spoke. "We can put you in a room, get you some food, take your statement, and you'll be safe until we need you."

"That's…unconventional," Scarlett said.

"Needs must," Rob replied, his eyes never leaving Viv.

"Yeah, alright. That'll do."

"Good," Rob replied. "We'll make sure you have some food, and you should only need to be in there for a few days, alright?"

"Sounds like paradise," Viv replied.

"Alright, gather your things." He walked with Scarlett towards the hole in the fence so they could talk. "You wait here with her, and I'll bring the car around. We'll check her into a Travel Lodge or something cheap."

"Are you sure about this? This isn't exactly by the book. We need to bring her in."

"We will, but finding these guys could take days, or longer, and I'm not losing her as a witness. If she doesn't want to go back to the factory, that's fine, I have no issue with that. In fact, I sympathise. It's not as if I'm a massive fan of some of the people in there, either. We'll keep an eye on her, and this way, she'll be safe, off the streets, and we know where she is. If we leave her here, who knows where she'll go. We might never find her again."

"This could cost you an arm and a leg."

He shrugged, feeling sure it wouldn't be for more than a few days. "I'll claim the money back."

"You'll try."

"It'll be worth it. This is much bigger than just Lorraine and Spencer,"

"I hope she's still alive."

"She's still alive. I know it. And she's counting on us. Lorraine is still out there somewhere, desperate for someone to save her from the same fate as Spencer. I won't fail her."

"Neither will I."

Rob smiled at her conviction.

"Alright, you go get the car," she said. "I'll wait here."

21

"You've still got the receipt, I hope," Scarlett said as they walked back into the main office in Central Station. "Peter will want proof if you want your money back."

She was right. Rob pulled out his wallet and checked the main pocket. Sure enough, the paper receipt for the Mercure Nottingham Sherwood hotel was where he'd left it, along with the total payment for the room. Rob shuddered at the thought of over two hundred and fifty pounds for three nights, plus food for the witness. But all being well, he'd get that back in the next few days, and it would all be worth it. He just hoped the case didn't drag on for much longer than that.

"Yeah, I got it," he said, pulling it out of his wallet. "I'll talk to Nailer too, he'll probably share the cost if need be."

Reaching his desk, he grabbed his phone and took a quick photo of the receipt, just to be sure. Satisfied, he returned the slip of paper to his wallet, and the wallet to his pocket. "They'd better give me my money back."

"So, you want to get money out of the police? Isn't that like getting blood out of a stone?"

Rob groaned. "Harder, probably. I'm gonna call Nailer and let him know what we've found. I told him to look for a four-by-four on CCTV when he should be looking for a white transit van."

"I hate those things."

Rob frowned. "What? White vans?"

"It's not really the vans themselves, just sometimes what they carry."

"Oh, right. I'm sure the vast majority of white van owners are perfectly civil and respectful."

"Spoken like a true police officer."

"I mean it. I'm sure like, ninety-nine point nine, nine, nine, nine, percent of white van owners are adorable."

"Adorable?" Scarlett smirked. "I'm sure you'd like to think so." She didn't seem convinced, which made him wonder what bad experiences she'd had in the past.

"I would," he replied, confident in his opinion. "I take it you disagree."

"I've just had a couple of…experiences. There was a case back in Surrey before I qualified as a Detective. Some guy was driving around in a white van, kidnapping young women and killing them. He was torturing them, cutting their fingers off or something. I remember attending one of the crime scenes."

"I see. Well, I guess this isn't going to help your opinion then, is it."

Pressing her lips into a thin line, she shook her head.

"Fair enough."

"You'd better call Nick."

"Agreed." He pulled out his phone and called Nick. Two rings later, it was answered. "Aye up. It's me."

"How'd it go?" Nick asked. "Did you find anything?"

"Actually yes, we did. We've got a witness."

"You what?" Nick sounded shocked. "You're kidding. How? In fact, wait a moment, I want Nailer to hear this too." Rob heard movement on the end of the line followed by muffled voices before the sound quality changed. "I've put you on speaker, Nailer's here."

"Y'all right, Rob?" Nailer asked.

"Good thanks."

"Excellent. What's this about a witness?"

"There was a woman hiding there when Lorraine and Spencer were kidnapped," Rob explained. "She saw it happen. They were thrown into the back of a white van by several men in dark clothing."

"Damn. Who's the witness?"

"Another homeless person. Her name's Viv. We've put her up in the Mercure Sherwood, just up the road. She wasn't keen on coming into the station, but she's given us a written statement." Rob glanced at the papers that Scarlett was holding, scrawled with untidy black writing. "She's willing to testify and to try and identify anyone we bring in, or the van itself. But I was more interested in just keeping her safe. She says this isn't the first time this has happened, either. Apparently, it's been going on for months."

"Shite, this is big," Nailer said. "Okay, good call on the hotel. I'll go halves on it with you if you can't claim it back."

"Thanks, I was gonna ask."

"I bet you were," Nick said, mirth in his voice.

"No worries," Nailer reassured him. "Alright, so we're looking for a white van in Bobber's Mill. We'll start hunting."

"We'll look too. The more eyes on this, the better."

"If you find something, call me direct," Nailer said. "I'll keep Nick in the loop, but this is more your case now than his. Don't worry, though, I'll keep him busy for you."

"You're always stealing my stuff, Rob!" Nick grumbled, good naturedly.

"Miss you too." Rob smirked.

"Alright, catch you later." Nailer ended the call.

"The pathologist needs someone to witness the post-mortem," Scarlett reminded him, looking over from her desk where she'd already started transcribing the statement.

"Shit, I forgot about that." There could be even more clues coming their way.

"I'll go," Scarlett suggested. "I don't mind doing it."

"Are you sure?" He didn't want to lumber her with it, but was grateful for the offer, and it would allow her to adjust to another aspect of how things were done in their unit.

"Yeah, it's fine," Scarlett confirmed. "Gets me out of the office."

"And into a room with a cadaver," Rob added with a raised eyebrow. "I didn't realise that was your idea of a good time."

"You're criticising my idea of a good time when you listen to Genesis?"

"Hey, don't dis the Sis."

"The Sis?" Scarlett's face contorted with incredulity. "You just made that up."

"Yeah, but it sounds good, right? I should write songs. I'm wasted here." Rob mused with a smile, pleased with his accidental rhyme.

She dismissed his reply with a roll of her eyes. "I'll finish up with the statement and head on over to…um… Where do I go?"

"The Queens Medical Centre."

"Right, right. I'll find my way." She turned to face the screen, before looking back and whispering, "Incoming."

Rob looked up to see the DCI ambling over with an easy stride and a smile. Behind him, Frank followed, an undisguised sneer on his face as he glared at Rob.

"Sir," Rob said in greeting, but ignored Frank other than to glance at him.

"Loxley. Anything new?"

Rob smiled to himself. "Actually, yeah. We have a witness."

"Excuse me?" Both men looked shocked.

"Someone was watching when Lorraine and Spencer were kidnapped. They saw it happen."

Peter seemed floored by the revelation, and Frank seemed equally shocked. "Oh...that's great," Peter said. "How much did they see? Can they identify anyone?"

"She said it was dark, and they were masked, but maybe. They were put into a white van and driven away."

"That's incredible." He glanced around. "And, where is this person? Frank can process her."

"She's homeless, and she wasn't interested in staying here with us, so I put her up at a local hotel. We took a statement, and we'll bring her in when we need her."

"In a hotel?" Frank frowned. "That's not exactly procedure."

Rob directed his reply to Peter. "It was my call. But at least this way, we won't lose her."

"No, I guess not," Peter replied with apparent concern. "Not the Ritz, was it? I'm not sure Nottinghamshire Police can stretch to that if you're looking for a refund."

"No, no. She's at a Mercure. I have the receipt. I'll file it and request reimbursement."

"Make sure you do."

Rob sighed as he glanced over at Scarlett, furiously typing away on her PC before she rushed off to the mortuary. She'd be leaving Rob to trawl through hours of CCTV. "We need more people. I've got a shit tonne of footage to get through, the witness clued us in on a white van. So, we know what we're looking for, and Scarlett has to go and watch the post-mortem. We're stretched thin."

"I know." Peter sounded strained and stressed out. "We all are. You'll just have to deal with it and use the resources we have. Tony can help you again."

Rob sighed. "Sure, why not."

"Here," Frank held out his hand. "I'll take the receipt and get the thing filed, okay?"

"Um," Rob replied, unsure.

"Thanks, Frank," Peter said, before he turned back to Rob. "Every little bit helps."

"I suppose so." Rob handed the slip of paper over and watched the pair walk away, waiting until they were out of earshot before he leaned towards Scarlett. "That was easier than I thought it would be. I might get my refund."

"Don't look a gift horse in the mouth, Rob," she replied, before finishing up the statement and saving it to the system. "Right, I'm off. Don't have too much fun while I'm away."

"When the cat's away, and all that." Rob smiled. "Aaah yes, the joy-filled job of asking Tony to help me. What could go wrong?"

"Be nice. A smile goes a long way." She winked before turning on her heel and walking out of the room.

22

Feeling frustrated and annoyed, Scarlett strode along another corridor in the Queens Medical Centre, following the directions of yet another employee as she attempted to find the mortuary. She'd spoken to three separate people and ended up hopelessly turned around twice now, but finally, she seemed to be making progress, and the signs seemed to match her expectations.

It felt like she'd been searching for ages, and wasn't relishing the idea of the walk back to her car with the exhibits she'd be collecting from this procedure.

As was typical for a hospital car park, they wanted your life savings, a night with your significant other, and your firstborn for the privilege of a few hours of parking.

She hoped this would be worth it and some new and interesting details would be gleaned from Spencer's corpse. Finding Viv had confirmed so much, and they seemed to be making progress. Knowing that the gang—whoever they were—had taken both Spencer and Lorraine at the same time in a white van was gold dust but also a cause for concern.

Was Lorraine still alive, or had she already been killed, perhaps on the same night as Spencer, somewhere else?

They were on the clock and needed to find Lorraine quickly before the worst happened.

But there was another question that was nagging at the corners of Scarlett's mind.

Why?

Why did this gang kidnap Spencer and Lorraine? Why was he then killed and dumped in Sherwood? What was the reason for this? If they could find that out, it might be the key to cracking the case. There were so many unanswered questions.

Reaching some double doors labelled as Mortuary, she walked into a comfortable and relaxing waiting room with a side office, signposted as Reception. This seemed to be the public-facing section of the department, where relatives of the deceased would come to view their dearly departed, but Scarlett doubted she'd be staying in this area for long.

Walking into the office, she found a smartly dressed woman behind a desk who smiled warmly at her.

"Hello," she said in a soft, welcoming tone. "How can I help you?"

Scarlett flashed her ID. "I'm here to witness a post-mortem?"

The receptionist inspected her warrant card. "Aaah, I think you're expected. If you'd like to come through." The woman stood and led Scarlett along a corridor to a locked security door marked Staff Only. Beyond, the carpet and calming surroundings of the reception were gone, replaced by clean, scientific, no-frills rooms that smelled of disinfectant and other less savoury odours. In a large room with several desks covered in paperwork and computers, the receptionist approached a woman in PPE.

"May?" the receptionist asked.

The woman in PPE looked up. "Hmm?"

"I have someone here to see you."

"I'm Detective Stutely. I'm here for the Spencer Lawson post-mortem?"

"You're late," the woman replied, surprising Scarlett with her abrupt reply.

"Sorry, I'm new to the city, and I had trouble finding you."

The woman frowned. "I see. Well, I've got a lot to do today, so let's get started." She offered her hand. "I'm May Shephard, Home Office Pathologist. I'll be conducting the procedure today. If you'd like to follow me." She led Scarlett down another corridor. "I was expecting Rob."

"Yeah, we're working the case together, but we're stretched on this one, so I said I'd come down."

"Not squeamish, are you?"

"I've done my time on the beat. I've seen some gruesome RTCs."

"But, you've not done not of these, before?"

"I know the procedure."

"Mmm, I'm sure." She didn't sound convinced. "You'll be in a side room collecting exhibits through a window, so you're out the way. We have bags and everything you'll need."

Scarlet held up the bag she'd slung over her shoulder, which was filled with anything she'd need. "I came prepared."

Even though she'd never been to one of these before, she had spoken with several who had, and it sounded more like gruesome paperwork than anything else.

She was led into the main examination room, where a couple of other pathologists in full PPE were busying themselves. The cold, pallid corpse of Spencer lay on a metal table as if asleep but utterly immobile. To one side, she spied a small boxy room with a large window looking out over the scene of the post-mortem.

"There you go. Enjoy the show."

Scarlett snorted. "I will." In the side room, she prepared to accept the first exhibit as May finished her own prep, washing her hands and donning the last few items of PPE, before they started.

As it turned out, watching the Pathologist do her work, cutting the body open and removing organs for weighing, measuring, and examination, was quite a different experience to attending a gruesome road accident, but neither were particularly pleasant. Her time was mostly spent bagging and logging exhibits such as Spencer's clothing, as she listened to what May had to say, and made the occasional note.

After what felt like an age, May declared herself done, leaving the body for her assistants to care for. After cleaning herself up, May sat at a nearby laptop for a few minutes while Scarlett ran through some of the notes she'd taken.

Eventually, May walked into the side room. "How did you find that experience?"

"Fine. I didn't mind it," Scarlett replied.

"Good. Not everyone can handle it. Okay, let's go over the main details, shall we?"

"Please."

"In layman's terms, from what I can ascertain, Mr Lawson was killed by the stab wounds that were inflicted upon him, of which there were three. The first two, the one in the leg and the one in his arm, were nasty but certainly survivable. But it was the chest wound that killed him. The weapon pierced his heart, and he died moments later from massive internal bleeding and heart failure."

"Time of death?"

"Always difficult to work out, but I'd put it somewhere in the early hours of yesterday morning."

"Okay. So tell me about the stab wounds and the weapon."

"That's an interesting one, actually," May replied. "The weapons hit him with considerable force and passed right through the soft tissue in the case of his leg. With his arm, the weapon struck the bone and stopped, leaving a nasty chip where it hit."

"You said weapons. You think there was more than one?"

"Correct. Examination leads me to suspect that each wound was inflicted by a separate weapon. They remained in the wound for a while before being ripped out, which inflicted more damage to his soft tissue. The wounds were really quite bad, and I can think of only one weapon that fits what I saw. It's unusual actually, and ironic, given where we are. But I believe Spencer was shot with hunting arrows."

"Arrows? You mean like from a bow?"

"Correct, and not just any arrows. I did a little digging on the laptop to be sure, and I believe your killer used three bladed broadheads. These heads are big. Perhaps a two to three inches long and about one inch wide, with three equally spaced razor-sharp blades coming to a point. They're designed to inflict massive damage and open up a big wound that won't heal. Out in the wild, an animal hit with them will eventually collapse from haemorrhage and exsanguination."

"Except, the killer who did this wasn't hunting animals," Scarlett added. "They were hunting a man."

"Indeed."

"Jesus Christ, this is horrific. Poor bastard," she said, glancing out the window. "Was there anything else?"

"Oh yeah, plenty. We've already run his blood, which came back clear. No drugs in his system. There was some food in his stomach, but not much. You can see the extensive bruising all over his body. He'd been beaten up and had his wrists and ankles tied at some point in the last few days. Gagged too, I think. We also found some coarse fibres in the hair on his head, and some finer fibres under his fingernails, as well as dirt and mud. We'll get everything sent off to Forensics for analysis."

"Thank you. Right. So we're looking for a sadistic hunter using a bow and arrow, right in the middle of Robin Hood country, no less. The press will have a field day with this when they find out."

"I suspect so, detective. I hope you find the killer."

"Me too. He wasn't the only one they kidnapped, so we need to move fast. I don't want anyone else to have to go through what Spencer did."

May nodded in agreement.

"I assume I head out the way I came in?" Scarlett pointed back towards the door.

"Actually, no, come with me," she said, and led Scarlett deeper into the complex of rooms and corridors. Turning into another hallway, May approached a security door at the end and opened it. She stepped outside and held the door, revealing an outside courtyard surrounded by various wings of the Medical Centre. To her right was a wide metal roll-up garage door, with yellow warning lines painted on the tarmac before it, warning people to keep clear. She spotted car parking spaces, bins, storage crates and more scattered about. This was a back entrance into the department.

"This is where we bring the bodies in," May said, pointing to the loading door. "You can park over there next time and ring this bell." She pointed to the keypad beside the door.

"Aaah, much easier. Thank you."

"Pleasure. See you soon." May wasted no time in slamming the door shut, ending the conversation.

Scarlett said goodbye to the door, then turned to the shady courtyard and chewed on her lip. "Now, where the hell did I park?"

23

Watching through the footage from the local traffic cameras in and around Bobber's Mill was drudge work. However, their criteria had been narrowed considerably by Viv's revelations, allowing Rob to focus on specific cameras and times. Much to his delight, he soon got what he hoped was a hit. A van heading into the Bobber's Mill estate at roughly the right time. The view wasn't great, and he couldn't make out the van's plate, but it was the only white van in that area at that time.

Could it really be this easy?

Making a note of the time, Rob started looking through other cameras and directed his small team of investigators, including Tony, to do the same.

Tony had relished playing hard to get when Rob had asked for his help, offering a few choice comments before he finally got on with the job at hand. Honestly, however, it went smoother than he could have hoped for, and while the pair of them had issues, they both wanted the same result for the case.

The next two cameras didn't show anything, but Rob's darkening mood was lightened by one of the investigators picking up the van leaving the kidnapping site shortly after the first camera had picked it up. It also recorded the van heading north through the city. Using the camera and kidnap locations, they soon picked up the van twice more, including one where the image was clear enough for Rob to make out the letters and numbers.

"Yes!" Thrilled that he finally had the plate, he grabbed his phone and called Nailer while opening the app on his PC, to run the plate. The line connected, and Rob beat him to a greeting. "I got him."

"The van?" Nailer asked.

"I have the plate. I'm running it now."

"Excellent work. Nick picked up the van too, but he didn't have a clear image of the plate. So, who is it?"

Rob hit return, and within moments, a name popped up on his screen, along with a criminal record and a photo. "It looks like the van belongs to a young man called Jordan Rigby, and he's got a criminal record that makes for some interesting reading. Possession with intent to supply. Robbery. Assault and several minor car offences. He's done a little time. He's a known member of the Top Valley Boyz gang as well, which fits with the van heading north."

"Unless this is someone framing the Valley Boyz, this sounds pretty damning."

"It does," Rob agreed. In fact, we were dealing with the gang only recently. We picked up one of their number for assaulting his girlfriend and her son and putting him in intensive care. I doubt that's linked to this, though."

"You think it's a coincidence?"

"I would say so," Rob replied. "But this suggests that the gang are involved in Spencer's murder. There were at least four people that Viv saw kidnapping Spencer and Lorraine, and Rigby is unlikely to be able to do this alone. So, who better to help him than his homies?"

"I don't disagree, but why? Why would they want to kidnap and kill a homeless person and a kind local church lady? It doesn't make a lot of sense."

Rob bit the inside of his cheek. "No, you're right. It doesn't." Looking up, he saw Scarlett wander back into the office. "Scarlett's back from the autopsy. I'll speak to you later, okay?"

"Of course. Nick and I are working on things this end, so keep me updated."

"Will do, sir." He hung up and turned to Scarlett as she approached.

"You'll never believe what I discovered," she said, with fire behind her eyes.

"I've got news too, but you go first."

"Okay, well, it seems like Spencer was killed by hunting arrows."

"Arrows?" Rob felt his breath catch as the potential repercussions of this rippled through his mind. "Bollocks. Murder with a bow and arrow in Nottingham? This is getting better and better," he grouched sarcastically.

"Spencer was hit three times. In his leg, arm, and then his chest, which was the one that killed him. I've done a little hunting, pun intended, and it seems these arrows, called broadheads, are freely available online. I've seen them on Amazon and Ebay…"

"Meaning that tracing them might be a bitch," Rob concluded. "I would have thought something like that would be quite difficult to get. We do live in the UK, right? I've not been magically teleported to America, have I?"

"Not to my knowledge, no. And yeah, I found them on sale online in seconds." Scarlett pulled out her phone, tapped on it a few times, and then turned the screen to him.

Rob peered at the Amazon listing. "That's utter bollocks. They're bloody cheap, too. Fifteen pounds for six of 'em? Christ." He leaned back in his chair and bit his lip in frustration. "The last thing we need is a sadistic Robin Hood running around shooting people like a demented cupid. The press are gonna love this."

"I know. But, surely this narrows our search?"

"A little, perhaps. But this is Nottingham, and there's no shortage of archery clubs around here, and plenty of bowmen...and women, too. I know several archers on the force already."

"This is what Lorraine has to look forward to, remember," Scarlett commented, meeting Rob's eye with fire and determination.

"Yeah, I know." Rob tried to imagine himself running naked through Sherwood, pursued by a killer with a bow, shooting arrows at him. Spencer must have been utterly terrified. The thought chilled him to the bone. "And remember what Viv said, this has been going on for weeks, or maybe months. Which means this might not be our killer's first victim. It's just the first one where the team were discovered before they'd disposed of the body."

"I've been thinking about that too," Scarlett mused.

"There'll be other bodies buried in the Forest."

"But where? It's a huge area. We need to find the killer and bring him in alive. If we can get him to talk..."

"I know. I'm going to order a team to search the area where Spencer was found, just in case. We need to get the cadaver dogs up there. You never know. We might get lucky."

"A solid plan," Scarlett approved. "Now, we just need to find Lorraine."

A thought occurred to Rob as he ran through the possibilities this new information gave him, making links between bits of information or things he'd seen. "You know what I saw at Sandy and Darren's place?"

"No. What?"

"Archery trophies with Darren's name on them."

"Oh, shit." She met his eyes. "Do you think he's involved?"

"I don't know, and it doesn't fit with what *we've* just found out, either."

"And what's that?"

"We think we found the van they used to pick up Spencer and Lorraine. We've got it just a street away from Lorraine's Bobber's Mill housing estate, entering and then leaving around the time Viv mentioned. We can't be one hundred percent sure, of course, but there were no other white vans in the area at that time. We got the van's plate, too, and it belongs to a mister Jordon Rigby, who's a member of the Top Valley Boyz."

Scarlett frowned suddenly at the mention of their name. "Isn't that…?"

"The same gang that Brendon is part of? Yep."

"Coincidence, or something more?"

Rob shrugged. "No idea."

Scarlett grimaced. "I think we need to have a second little chat with Darren."

"I agree, but he's not my priority right now. Lorraine is. We need to find her, and I doubt very much she's in Darren's shed. Also, why would he go after Lorraine?"

"She was helping Spencer to see his daughter."

Rob grimaced. "Okay, yeah, that's true. I guess they could have spoken, and he took a disliking to her." It was a tenuous idea but not the craziest thing he'd ever heard. "I agree with bringing Darren in for another chat, but I don't think he's holding her anywhere. I don't know. It just doesn't fit. Also, Viv said this has been going on for months. I think we need to focus on Lorraine and the kidnappers. We have to find her and make sure she's okay."

"So, what do we do?"

"The cameras tell us that there was only one van in that area that night, a van owned by Jordan Rigby. Rigby is a ranking member of the Top Valley Boyz, and I think it's highly likely they have her."

"Alright, so what do we know about this gang? Are they well-organised?"

Rob thought back to the research he'd done while hunting for Brendon. "The gang is run by a guy called Lloyd Bristow, better known as Curby due to the legend that he likes to curb stomp his enemies."

"Sounds dreamy," Scarlett commented sarcastically.

"I know, right. The gang's territory is the Top Valley estate north of the city centre. They're known to be violent, neck-deep in the drugs game, and kidnapping is well within their wheelhouse. We've clashed with them many times, but we've yet to break their back. Their operation is big, with plenty of places where they could hide someone. Places where no one would know, or care about a prisoner."

"Like where?"

Rob turned to his PC and ran a search on the gang, bringing up what they knew about them so far. "We have a number of addresses for them on file, from home addresses to locations they frequent, businesses they use, and at least one suspected crack house they run."

"They need to keep her somewhere isolated," Scarlett said, scanning the list of addresses.

"Or where no one cares," Rob added, side eying her and wondering if she'd pick up on his hint.

"The crack house? Yeah. No one would give a shit about some middle-aged church lady in one of those."

"That's what I thought. It's the obvious place."

"So, not Rigby's place?"

"Our latest intelligence on him suggests he has a girlfriend with no significant offences on her rap sheet. So I'm assuming that she wouldn't want him keeping Lorraine there. I doubt she even knows about it."

"But you can't be sure."

"No, I can't. But, I'd be surprised if he brought that kind of work home with him."

"Yeah, true."

"Okay, good. So this is what I think we should do…"

"Do what?" a male voice said from nearby.

Rob looked up to see DCI Orleton taking the last few steps towards them. "I understand there's been some developments."

"That's right, sir. We tracked the white van, got its plates from CCTV, and know who owns it. His names Jordan Rigby. He's a gang member from Top Valley. Also, Scarlett went to the post-mortem and found out that Spencer had been shot with three arrows."

"Arrows?" Peter's eyebrow climbed up his head. "In Nottinghamshire?"

"In Sherwood Forest," Scarlett added, a knowing look on her face.

"We're aware of the cultural significance of the murder weapon," Rob remarked. "But we need to focus on finding Lorraine before she becomes the next victim."

"Agreed, so you have a plan?"

"Perhaps," Rob answered.

"Out with it, then. The Special Ops team will want to know all about this."

"Right you are, sir," Rob replied. "We have two suspects, Jordan Rigby, who owns the van, and Darren Pierson, who hated Spencer and has trophies for archery. I'm leaning towards Rigby, because of the gang link, because this has been going on for a while, and because we need to find Lorraine. But, we'll bring Darren in tomorrow, regardless. In the meantime, we've been looking at known Valley Boyz locations, and we think we need to hit this one." Rob pointed to the screen. "It's a suspected crack house and would make the perfect place to stash Lorraine."

"Because no one there would care about her," Peter mused. "Fair point. So, you want to raid it?"

"At our earliest opportunity."

"Alright. But if you want to do this, then you need manpower and the right team," Peter replied. "You don't just wander into a crack den. There'll be guns, and gang members willing to use them."

"I know," Rob replied. "We'll need a Method of Entry team."

"Ghost Busters, yes. I'll put in a call to the local Territorial Support Unit and get us booked in for later tonight. You need to do it right, so we take out the crack den as well."

"Absolutely," Rob agreed. "We'll get onto it right away."

"Good work," Peter replied and returned to his office.

"Sorry to play devil's advocate," Scarlett said once Peter had left, "but what if Lorraine or Rigby isn't there?"

"Then we move onto Rigby's house and pick him up. I'm going to have some questions for him," Rob answered. He liked that Peter seemed to be supportive of their initiative and wanted to help and give them the resources they needed. It made a welcome change, but he didn't expect it to last.

"Fair enough, and one last question. What do you mean by Ghost Busters?"

Rob smiled. "You'll see."

24

It had been another long day working through his active casework, and he'd stayed well beyond his scheduled clocking off time, but this was nothing unusual for Bill.

It wasn't as if he had much waiting for him at home, so why not further his career and show the brass how keen he was.

But, as the night closed in and the office emptied out, he finally chose to call an end to the day and head home, but not before he paid a visit to check up on his pet project.

Rob Loxley didn't have anyone at home waiting for him, so it was perfectly possible that Bill might find Rob downstairs, putting the hours in on his latest case.

The idea caused Bill to shake his head in contempt at the man's audacity and the effort he put in to prove that he was a dedicated officer when everyone knew he was corrupt. He could put in all the extra hours he liked and bring home as many cases as possible. It didn't change anything. And unfortunately, it seemed like his new partner, Scarlett, was falling under his spell. He'd tried to talk to her, to make her see sense, but it was no use. Predictably, she dismissed him and said she'd make her own mind up. In other words, she was falling for his charm and lies.

Bloody typical.

Making his way down several flights of stairs, he turned back into the building, reached a particular doorway, and peered in. The office was quiet, with just a few of the night shift at their desks. Rob and Scarlett were gone, but he could see DCI Orleton in his office, on the phone. He seemed to be in the middle of a somewhat animated discussion.

Walking over, he caught the DCI's eye through the window and gave him a curt nod. Peter raised a finger, telling him to wait one minute before he returned to his phone. He didn't catch much, but he seemed to be talking about something urgent happening later tonight.

Bill frowned, wondering what the latest developments in Rob's case were. He'd not been keeping up to date on the details, and he had the feeling that something was going down.

Moments later, Peter hung up his phone and waved him in.

"Busy night?" Bill asked as he walked into the DCI's office.

"You could say that," Peter replied as he slumped back into his chair. "Was there a reason for this visit? I'm busy."

Bill narrowed his eyes at the hostility. "I was just checking up on our boy."

Peter sighed. "He's busy on this case. We have a lead, and we're following it. I'm just trying to tie up some loose ends before we raid a crack house."

"A crack house?" This sounded interesting. "Whose?"

"A gang in north Nottingham. The Top Valley Boyz."

"I see," Bill mused as he considered this. Seeing Rob in action out in the field could be useful, watching to see how he went about his business. And not only that, he wanted to know why Rob was doing this? He already had Brendon from that gang in custody, and now he was going after the rest of them. Was there more to this? Maybe some kind of vendetta or gang warfare, and this was a way for the Valley Boyz to be weakened?

He'd learned long ago not to underestimate Rob, and what he was capable of hiding. He needed to be careful and watch this closely.

"I want in," Bill remarked.

"In? You want in? How, exactly?"

"I want to be there when the raid goes down. I'll keep a low profile, he won't even know I'm there, but I want to be close to the action."

Peter frowned and let out what sounded like an exasperated breath.

Bill knew what he was asking, that he was sticking his nose where it likely wasn't wanted, but he needed to see this.

"I won't get in your way," Bill said in an attempt to reassure the DCI. "I'll stay on the sidelines and listen in through the radio."

"Fine," Peter answered with a dramatic roll of his eyes.

Bill smiled. He knew he'd asked a lot him over the years, and Bill's near-constant presence around Rob and this unit was only allowed because he and Peter shared a mutual suspicion of DS Loxley. If Peter didn't sympathise with his cause, he would likely find his long-running investigation of Rob much more difficult, which meant that he needed to be careful and respectful.

"Thank you," Bill replied, as his phone buzzed in his pocket. Whipping it out, he saw the ID on the screen.

Mum & Dad.

Grimacing, Bill looked back up at Peter. "Sorry, I need to take this."

Peter motioned to the door. "See you early tomorrow. I'll text you the details."

"Thanks," Bill replied and left the office, heading for the stairwell before answering the call. "Hello?"

"You took your time."

It was his dad, being as blunt as ever. "I'm at work."

"You're always at bloody work, no doubt ruining some poor PC's career."

Bill sighed and bit his lip in frustration. "What do you want?"

The line was quiet for a moment as he heard his mother's voice in the distance. "Stop arguing, and get him over here," she said.

"You need to come over," his dad said, his voice tense.

"Why, what's up?"

"Just get over here, now!" His dad hung up.

Bill's heart fell as he paused on the stairs heading down, letting a long breath escape from his lungs. He didn't need this stress right now, but if his mother needed him, his hands were tied. It wouldn't be the first time he was called around to deal with something, and he doubted it would be his last, either.

Stuffing his phone into his pocket, Bill raced down the last few flights of stairs, into the garage and his car. The drive wasn't long, and the roads were quiet, allowing his mind to race. It flip-flopped between wondering what the latest crisis at home might be and his suspicions about Rob.

He tried to focus on the case and Rob, but it was basically impossible. He kept thinking back to the call and ahead to what would likely be another uncomfortable visit with his parents.

Pulling up outside his parents' place, Bill saw outward signs of trouble. Everything seemed quiet. The building was an unassuming semi in one of the city's suburbs and had been his parents' home for as long as he could remember. Pulling out his copies of their keys, he unlocked the side door and walked in.

"Hello?"

"In here, love," his mother called out.

"Hurry up," his dad added.

Bill twisted his face in frustration before rushing into the lounge at the back of the house. He found his elderly mother sprawled on the floor and his equally infirm dad sitting in his usual armchair.

"I'm sorry love. I fell over and couldn't get back up, and you know your dad can't really help much."

"Dad! Christ, you could have said," Bill complained as he raced to his mother and started to help her up. Luckily, she seemed okay, and he soon had her settled back onto the sofa.

"Thank you, love. I don't know what I'd do without you."

"I've told you to get a carer," he groused. "You can't rely on me.

"I don't want a carer," his mum replied.

"But it's not my job."

"Your job?" his dad snapped, laughing in a mocking tone. "Don't talk to me about your job. You don't work for the police. You work against us. Judas."

Bill sighed and rubbed his face as several answers ran through his mind, all of which he'd used before.

"Graham," his mother said in a warning tone. "Now's not the time."

"When I was in the police, I wasn't a bloody grass. I didn't work against my fellow officers. We were a team." He slumped back into his chair and mumbled to himself. "It's not like it was back in my day. Too much political correctness bullshit. It's a joke."

"Are you okay, mum?" Bill did his best to ignore his dad's grumbling and focus on his mother.

"I'm fine, love. I'm fine. Thank you. I just couldn't get up."

"I know."

"I'm sorry to bother you."

"It's okay," Bill reassured her. "You can call me any time."

"Have you heard from Grace recently?"

She was referring to his sister. "No, I've not seen her. You?"

"Not for a while." His mother seemed sad, but this was typical for his sister. She'd left the family home at seventeen to make her own way in the world, having had enough of their dad and his views. She'd show up from time to time and make a fleeting visit, mainly to their mum, before she'd disappear again, often for weeks or even months.

He got it. He understood his sister's opinion of their dad and shared much of it.

"She'll be out, whoring herself around, as usual," his dad snapped. "Just to spite me. Embarrass me."

"Graham!" Bill's mother snapped.

"You know I'm right." His voice was low and full of defiance. "At least she didn't join the force. I wouldn't want two embarrassments ruining my legacy."

Bill regarded the medals and commendations on the lounge's side cabinet, telling of a long and distinguished career in the Nottinghamshire Police.

"And what about you?" his mother asked. "Have you been seeing anyone recently?"

Bill sighed.

25

Rather than head south from the station that night, Rob drove north, out through the various suburbs of the city. Radford, Forest Fields, New Basford and beyond the Valley Road and Nottingham City Hospital into Bestford and finally Top Valley with its terrace blocks and semi-detached housing.

There was plenty of greenery, and despite the poverty visible on many of the roads, he could see their potential. It could be a lovely area if they could escape the grip of this crew of vandals and criminals. Their influence was everywhere, from the graffiti and tags scrawled on the walls, announcing this as Boyz or TVB territory, to the small knots of youths on their bikes, acting suspiciously, glaring at the unfamiliar car prowling the street.

These were kids. Teenagers of about fourteen or fifteen out dealing drugs to anyone willing to buy them before passing the proceeds back up the chain until it reached the likes of Curby. But he was far from the last link in the chain. He was beholden to those above him, just like these kids were to him. These links spread far out across the country to ports or transport hubs like London or Liverpool, where the gear came in. Every flight from certain countries in South America would have several mules on it with condom-wrapped cocaine in their guts, risking death from massive overdoses if the packages ruptured inside them.

Few were ever caught, and for each one that was, four, five, or even twenty others from that one flight would get through just fine to meet up with their employers here in the UK. Not to mention opioids, heroin, fentanyl and marijuana shipped in from other regions of the world.

There really was no stopping it. The trade was so massive, overwhelming, and pervasive, with so much money involved, that it was difficult to grasp its true scope. Border security and officials were paid off, corrupt law enforcement too, all to keep the wheels turning and the money rolling in.

People like him and Scarlett were never in a position to do much about it. They were there to just clean up the mess these people made, to provide a sense of safety and security to the people of their city and their county. But make no mistake, it was a false sense of security. It was a mirage and little else.

These people were out there, living amongst us, often in plain sight, but most people didn't see it. No one took any notice of the people who fell down the cracks in society into this hidden underbelly of crime, violence and addiction.

Few people really saw it, but once you did, there was no going back. It became obvious. Infuriatingly so.

Having studied the maps and chosen a spot, Rob followed his Sat Nav through the estate and parked up. He picked his spot carefully to keep his distance from his target while still giving himself a good view.

Around the corner, part way along a street was a semi sporting the usual signs of poverty and neglect, but there was more to this place for those who knew the signs.

The windows were blacked out on the ground floor. There was a hooded young man standing outside, shifting from foot to foot as he greeted each arrival with a fist bump before knocking on the door. Moments later, the door would open, and the visitor would drift inside.

And there were a lot of visitors. A new one would materialise from the surrounding streets every few moments, making a direct line towards the house before being let inside. A lesser number left the building, always looking shifty as they strode off into the night, keen to get away.

These visitors were both male and female and would arrive either in small groups or alone, and the demographic was all over the place. He saw a man in a suit who looked like he'd worked a long day in the city. Next was an overweight woman in a shabby tracksuit, followed by several skinny teen boys in hoodies and baggy jeans and a couple of rake-thin girls with drawn faces in tottering heels and skirts that barely covered anything.

They were all here for one thing, and one thing only: crack cocaine. The drug of choice for so many right now, and a crack house like this was where you got your hit. There would be a river of drugs and money running through this place.

Rob had been on his fair share of raids over the years and knew exactly what he'd find in there should he step inside. Humanity at its lowest ebb.

The high that crack gave was euphoric, and for those who tried it for the first time, almost mind-altering in its power. But each hit after the first was lessened as the user's immunity increased. But it was so incredibly addictive that one hit was often enough to hook the user, so they spent their life from that point on chasing that first high and escaping the pain of withdrawal. These users would do literally anything for that next hit, and the dealers knew it. The guys would be recruited into the gangs, becoming dealers themselves or committing any number of crimes to get that next hit. Meanwhile, the girls would debase themselves for the same thing, letting the dealers do whatever they liked to them in return for another hit of the drug. Many ended up as prostitutes, selling themselves day and night to get the money they'd then spend on crack. Then the high would be gone and the debilitating state of withdrawal was left in its place, so they'd need more money, and the downward spiral continued.

But dealing with these places was like playing whack-a-mole. Several forces had units tackling this problem. But it would depend on funding, targets, and stats as to where any given force would focus its efforts.

Such a task force would plan their raid carefully by gathering intelligence, speaking to informants, and scoping out the place to ensure their success. It could take days or even weeks to plan and get the green light, which didn't include the processing time afterwards.

But you could guarantee that within days of that crack house being removed, there would be two more just up the street. It was too profitable for them not to do it.

Rob sighed as he watched a woman in a business suit stride up and speak briefly to the guard on the door before she was let inside. Another lamb to the slaughter. She was probably an overworked office worker or personal assistant who used crack to unwind. He wondered how she'd pay for it? Money or a blow job for the dealer?

It wasn't the only thing he pondered as he sat there, watching, hoping he wouldn't be noticed by the young man standing outside the house.

Was Lorraine in there? Might she be upstairs in a room by herself, perhaps? Bound and gagged while she waited for her fate to be decided. Honestly, if they'd left her alone, Rob would consider that a blessing because the scum who ran these houses were capable of way worse.

Part of him wanted to stride over there, knock the guard out and storm inside, but that would be suicide. The guard would likely have a gun, and there would be more inside if he ever got into the house. They were usually fortified early on, often with a New York latch on the front door, and the crew that manned them would think nothing of gunning down a curious officer.

No, he needed to wait. The raid had been booked in for the early hours with a Territorial Support Unit and a Method of Entry team who were skilled at this, and would ensure they got in quick. They'd spent the afternoon planning it, sending plainclothes officers to scope the place out and report back, but Rob had wanted to see the house for himself rather than rely on intelligence. As the minutes ticked by, he started to feel like he was outstaying his welcome and needed to move on.

Reluctantly, Rob put the car into gear and drove away, heading south again back towards the city and his home on the Trent. He had a few hours to kill and was determined to try and get a little sleep before all hell broke loose tomorrow because he'd need his wits about him.

That didn't stop the creeping guilt he felt at potentially leaving Lorraine behind to spend another few hours in that house, alone, not knowing if anyone out there was looking for her or even cared. It was a tough choice to make, but it was also the right choice—the only choice.

Many recriminations later, he made it home and parked up at his apartment complex. As he walked inside, he saw Erika, his neighbour, wandering towards the main entrance. She'd been out again, judging from the short dress and heels, but she didn't seem as drunk this time and walked with poise and confidence.

"Evenin' officer," she said with a glossy lip-sticked smile that had probably looked a little neater earlier in the night. "You're back late."

"And you're out drinking again."

"Is that a crime?"

"No. Of course not. I'm just concerned that you're out, alone, late at night. There's some bad people out there, you know."

"Well, I appreciate your concern, but I've just been dropped off, so I'm fine."

He opened the door for her. "Good to hear." He ushered her inside.

"Thank you." She smiled graciously once more. "Busy night?"

"Always." If only she knew.

"I'm glad you're out there, working to keep the streets safe."

Rob gave her a wry grin. "We do our best. Where you have been?"

"Just the Lace Market." The fashionable and creative area of the city with its bars and eateries that had once been part of the industrial heart of Nottingham, producing world-class lace that had put Nottingham on the map.

"With friends?"

"No, actually, Mr Nosey. On a date." He caught a naughty look on her face as she flushed slightly.

"A date? Did it go well? I'm guessing not, given he's not here with you."

She shrugged. "Could have been better."

"I'm sorry to hear that," he replied as they reached their floor.

"Eh, no big loss. I'm in no rush to settle down."

"Mmm, I know the feeling."

They said their goodbyes before Rob wandered back into his silent apartment and emptied his pockets onto the counter. Thinking back through the day's events, he hoped their witness, Viv, was reliable. Everything she'd said had panned out so far, but this was early days, and it was certainly possible she was having them on just to get a nice bed for the night. So much relied on her testimony, including the raid in a few hours.

Speaking of which, he couldn't spot the receipt for the hotel amongst the detritus of the day he'd pulled from his pockets. Rob frowned. Where had that gone? Oh, yeah, he'd given it to Frank to process. Hopefully he hadn't lost it, accidently on purpose. It would be just the kind of stunt he'd expect Frank or Tony to do, so he would be forced into paying for the hotel.

Luckily, he had a photo of it on his phone, so he wasn't too concerned as he wandered across to the windows and looked out at the darkened city beyond the glass, its many thousands of lights glimmering in the gloom. With a meow and purr, Muffin jumped onto the nearby table, calling for his attention. He reached out and scratched behind the fluff ball's neck, much to his appreciation.

Somewhere out there, maybe in the house in Top Valley, was Lorraine. He hoped she was still alive and hanging on. They were coming for her.

26

Arriving home, John Nailer smiled when he saw the lights inside his house glowing in the evening shadows and used his key to get inside. The moment he opened his front door, delicious meaty smells from within filled his nostrils. It was an aroma that made his mouth water with anticipation.

"Hello?"

"Hiya, babe," she called back from the kitchen at the back of the house, her voice kind and welcoming. "It's just about ready if you want to come through."

"Be right there." He shed his jacket, removed his shoes, and used the cloakroom before wandering through his detached house in the heart of suburban Beeston, west of the city centre.

He found Annabel in his kitchen, pouring the cooked mince beef for a Spaghetti Bolognaise onto the steaming pasta already on his plate. Beside it sat a bubbling lager-shandy, condensation already formed on its sides from the cold drink it held.

He sipped it gratefully as she joined him at the table and smiled. "How was your day?" she asked before sipping her own drink.

"Yeah, alright. You know, the usual."

"Yeah, I know. So nothing worth mentioning then?"

"Well, we did have Rob in the office today." He put it out there as if it were nothing, but he knew she'd be interested.

"Oh? That's good. How is he?"

"He's fine. I mean, I think he's chaffing under the leadership of Peter Orleton, but otherwise, he's not too bad. He's got a new partner, apparently, although I've not met her yet."

"A woman?"

"Scarlett."

"Okay, that'll be good for him. But I thought he worked with Nick?"

"Peter transferred him to me."

"Oh, because you needed more people on your team. I remember you saying."

"Yeah, I requested more manpower, but I didn't know they'd ask Peter."

"Sod's law."

"I know. He can be a little shit when he wants. I'm convinced he's deliberately working against Rob, keeping him understaffed and isolated, only giving him enough resources to barely get the job done."

"All because of…" She didn't finish the sentence, but she didn't need to.

"Yeah, because of that."

"Why was he at HQ?" she asked.

"It seems the murder he's working on was linked to a missing person's case we were investigating. We think it's the same people and that they kidnapped two and killed one. We're trying to find the second victim before they kill her too."

"Was this the body in Sherwood? I saw it reported on the news."

"That's right. He was shot with a bow and arrow."

"Shit. A modern-day Robin Hood."

"Something like that. I think I'll be working with Rob a lot more over the coming days, so it'll be good to catch up."

"It will. That's good..."

John frowned as he took another mouthful, enjoying the taste but feeling very much like there was something that Annabel wanted to say. "Everything alright?"

"Yeah. It's just, are you not worried about working closer with Rob? He's going to find out one of these days, you know."

John swallowed as tension filled his body. "Yeah, I know. He probably has a right to know, but...not yet."

"You need to be careful."

He looked up and gave Annabel and meaning-filled glare. "I'm not the only one."

27

Racing out of the city, PC Tom Reid guided his car through the country roads north of the urban sprawl and cursed the fact that he was alone in the car. These cuts to police funding were getting ridiculous, with more and more good, hard-working officers leaving the job and finding a career elsewhere as their job became more about numbers and stats.

It was untenable and short-sighted.

But he had no plans to leave just yet. He still had hope that things would turn around. He believed in the work that he and his colleagues did on a daily basis. Their work was hard and dangerous, but he firmly stood in the camp that believed they could get a handle on the epidemic of organised crime that was threatening to overwhelm them.

He had to believe it. Otherwise, what was the point? You either fought for the things you believed in, like the rule of law, or you allowed chaos and anarchy to spread unchecked.

Ahead, in the gloom, the tell-tale flickering orange glow of fire announced the presence of just one, tiny instance of such lawlessness, and it was just where control had said it would be.

Someone had set a car on fire part way along a country road, just north of the city.

He accelerated, focusing on his driving, aiming to get there as quickly and safely as possible.

Taking another corner, Tom pulled to a stop with his lights flashing in the dark. He parked on the same side of the road as the roaring blaze and alerted control.

"Tell me that we have a fire engine en route?" he asked the woman on the other end of the radio.

"Confirmed. The fire service are on their way."

"Thanks. I'll see what I can do to secure the area, but I'm going to need some help."

"Copy that. I'll see what I can do." Tom grimaced, knowing that was code for, don't hold your breath. Getting out, he spotted a couple of people on the far side of the fire who'd parked up and were standing, watching.

"Hey, move back, please. Move back. Get out the road." He had to shout to make himself heard over the roar of the blaze, but they seemed to understand him and backed off.

Tom peered at the inferno and could make out the remains of a large vehicle. It looked like some kind of Land Rover or Range Rover. It was a four-by-four anyway, and the heat was incredible.

Moving back to his car, Tom pulled out the traffic cones and set to work.

28

The raid's timing had been planned to within an inch of its life, but as Rob sat in the van with Scarlett, surrounded by men in body armour and helmets, he couldn't help but feel a little nervous about how this might play out.

Theirs was one of several vehicles that were making their way towards the target house. All of them were taking a slightly different route and would converge in the last few moments in an effort to remain hidden from the lookouts, positioned to watch for incoming raids or attacks by rival gangs.

In one of those cars was DCI Peter Orleton, and Rob did not want to give him an excuse to take him off the case, something he would no doubt be looking for.

"I still don't understand why these guys are called Ghost Busters," Scarlett said in a low voice. Like him, she wore a police-issue bulletproof vest and seemed just as nervous about the whole thing as he did.

Rob turned to her and went to answer.

"One minute," one of the guys up front called out.

Rob lifted his radio. "We're one minute out," he repeated, relaying the information to the other units.

"Copy that," DCI Orleton replied before the other units repeated the phrase.

Dropping his hands back into his lap, he looked over at Scarlett. "These guys aren't Ghost Busters."

"So, who is?"

"You'll see," Rob confirmed with a smile that he hoped looked mysterious, but he couldn't be sure.

Outside, the familiar terrace houses and semis of the Top Valley estate passed by in the early morning gloom. It was 5 am, and Rob could almost hear his bed calling to him, telling him to go home and get some sleep. But there was no way he could do that. He needed to get in that house and hopefully find Lorraine. He'd not managed to get much in the way of sleep as he'd turned the case over and over in his head, all the while feeling guilty for not finding Lorraine sooner.

But as much as he hoped this would be the end to it, there was a creeping, nagging doubt at the back of his head that wouldn't stop clawing at his brain. Something felt off. As if this was just too easy. It was difficult to put into words or even coherent thought, but somewhere deep down, he knew this wouldn't be the end of it, no matter how this played out.

When the van pulled up, stopping as close as they dared to the house, Rob realised he was metres away from where he'd been parked just a few hours before, but they couldn't see the crack house from here.

"We're on-site, ready for deployment. Confirm when ready." Rob listened to the squawked replies from the other vehicles as they reached their final positions. Between shallow breaths, he could feel his heart hammering in his chest while nervous energy coursed through his veins, urging him to jump out and run over to the house. He needed to get in there and end this.

"It's quiet out there," an officer in the front said.

"Too quiet," Rob agreed, feeling sick with doubt.

Finally, the last van reported in. Everything was ready, and they were waiting on his order. Taking a moment to mentally run through the plan, he couldn't think of anything they'd missed or forgotten. It was time.

"Go, go, go," Rob called out over their coms and joined the members of the Territorial Support Group as they jumped out and ran around the corner towards the house. He spotted two more teams making their way in, jogging through the morning mist. "It's the house on the end," he said over the radio, ensuring no one had become mixed up for any reason. "Number seventeen."

"Oh, now I get it," Scarlett said, nodding towards the second team to their left.

They were the Method of Entry team, and several of them carried oxy-acetylene torches linked to gas tanks on their backs. Their equipment and outfits gave them a distinct look that reminded many of the Ghost Busters from the famous film.

"Ghost Busters! Funny."

"I live to please," Rob quipped as the leading officers reached the house and went to work.

They barely needed any direction having done this countless times and worked like a well-oiled machine. The Ghost Busters were there for one job and one job only, to get the officers into the house, bypassing any and all barriers, which was where the cutting torches came in.

But as it turned out, the door swung wide with just a couple of hits from their big-red-key battering ram. Rob hung back with Scarlett, letting the burly, tank-like men of the Territorial Support group, who were basically a gang of the biggest, toughest officers on the force, run in first. There was a lot of shouting and yelling, but surprisingly little in the way of resistance.

This concerned Rob.

There'd been no guard on the door, no one hanging around outside, and now the team were in, very little noise inside the house itself. Within moments shouts of 'All Clear' echoed through the house.

Shooting Scarlett a concerned frown, Rob followed the team in, striding in with Scarlett on his heels.

Just beyond the front door, attached to the wall, was a length of metal that could be braced against the front door. An infamous New York latch. It was used to keep rival gangs and police raids out while those inside made their escape or disposed of any evidence. But it had not been used today.

He added it to his list of observations that made him feel nervous.

"Guv? In here."

Rob followed the voice and marched into the front room, where two dirty, skinny guys lay on their fronts, their wrists cuffed behind their backs.

"Aye up, mate," one of them called out, looking far too happy with himself after being arrested.

"What's this?" Rob asked.

"The only two people we've found, so far," the officer replied. "They were watching TV and didn't put up a fight."

As a mounting feeling of dread built inside his gut, Rob scanned the room. The place stank of shit, piss and puke mixed with the gritty metallic smell from smoking crack and used ashtrays. The walls were stained yellow, and the boarded-up windows kept any natural light out of the room. Grubby sheets and mismatched cushions lay scattered around, along with discarded and used drugs paraphernalia. This had all the signs of a crack house, with none of the users. But they'd been here recently. Very recently. Hell, he'd seen them just a few hours ago, meaning that between then and now, the house had been cleaned out. He didn't like the implications of what this meant.

"Just the two?" Scarlett asked.

Rob turned to see her in the doorway, her nose wrinkled in disgust. "Looks that way."

"What do you want us to do with 'em?" one of the burly guys asked.

Rob sighed, walked over to the two prisoners, and crouched down, taking care to look where he was standing in case of any used needles. "Where is everyone?"

"What yeh talkin' about?"

"Where are the others? Where's the dealers?"

"No dealers in 'ere mate."

"So, is this your house?" Rob pressed.

"Nah. Dun' know whose house this is." The man's eyes wheeled around as he spoke, suggesting he was on the tail end of a high.

"What are you doing here then?"

"There was a party, ain't it. We had a few. That's all. Then everyone left." He laughed as Rob started to grind his teeth.

This was useless.

"Guv!?" The voice came from upstairs.

Walking into the hallway, he found the stairs and navigated his way up, avoiding the discarded detritus to find several of the armoured men on the landing, one of them in a doorway. He motioned inside.

"You need to see this."

Concerned and curious, he approached with a frown fixed to his forehead. "What is it?"

The officer pointed as Rob reached the door, noticing the crudely installed locks on the outside of the door. Beyond, the room was bare apart from a single chair, a radiator, and a few discarded plates of rotting food. Like the rest of the house, this room stank too, but there was something more sinister and evil about this room, and Rob had little doubt that Lorraine had been here recently.

"Bollocks!"

Moving through the room, Rob spotted a couple of discarded cable ties on the floor beside the radiator and a couple more by the chair. Crouching closer, he saw reddish-brown stains on them. Blood.

"We need Forensics in here," he said.

"They're on their way," Scarlett answered from the doorway. Rob eyed her as he considered what this all meant.

Someone had warned the gang.

Somehow, they found out about the raid. They knew when it was going to happen and used the house right up until the last minute, and then they cleared out. Someone in the station who had access to the details of the raid had tipped off the Top Valley Boyz, but who was it?

Bill would have a field day with this, and so would Peter. He could almost feel the target that was no doubt flashing neon on his back right at this moment and cringed.

As these thoughts raced through his mind, Rob eyed Scarlett, the new member of the team, as she scanned the room around him. Could he trust her? Was she somehow working for this gang? Was it a member of the team behind her, the Territorial Support Unit or the Ghost Busters, or was it one of the detectives in their office or beyond?

Nailer, maybe?

Rob turned away and rubbed his eyes in frustration. This whole thing was going sideways and fast.

"They knew," Scarlett said quietly. She'd walked into the room and was standing close. "Someone leaked the info."

"Yeah," Rob replied in hushed tones. "That was my conclusion, too. We have a mole."

"What do we do?"

"I don't know. But I know who Peter and Bill will pin it on."

Scarlett nodded slowly and whispered her reply, "You."

"You're damn right. This is fucking bollocks. Peter's outside, and he'll want to know what happened."

"This isn't your fault," Scarlett said with conviction, but he wondered if perhaps this *might* have been his fault. His visit earlier in the night was unsanctioned. No one knew about it. It was certainly possible he'd been spotted and had caused the gang to vacate the house. It sounded far-fetched and unlikely compared to them being warned, but he knew what would happen if the DCI found out he'd come up here last night. It would be just the ammunition that Bill would need to cast more doubt on him. He'd be dragged before the brass, reprimanded, and maybe suspended.

He looked up at Scarlett, who smiled back at him.

"Thank you for the vote of confidence," Rob said.

"No problem." She shrugged. "It's not exactly difficult. It wasn't you."

"Thanks. I'd better go and face the music."

"I'll come with you. I'm just as much a part of this as you are." She followed Rob out of the room and back downstairs as the officers around them griped and complained about this being a bust.

Reaching the front door, he stepped out to find the DCI waiting, and standing behind him was Bill Rainault. Peter looked pissed off, but Bill had a smug smile on his face and his arms crossed as he watched.

"What the hell happened?" Peter snapped.

"They're gone," Rob said by way of explanation.

"I can see that, you bloody idiot." Rob grimaced at the insult. "How? Why? This is a monumental fuck up, Loxley. Somehow this got out, and now we're back to square one and a bleeding laughingstock to boot. Well fucking done."

"Of course, they knew," Bill spoke up, his voice even and calm. "Why wouldn't they know?" He uncrossed his arms and took a few steps forward, looking like the cat that got the cream. "We all know about our dear friend Rob and his family connections. It makes sense that they'd find out, don't you think?"

"That's rubbish," Scarlett countered, her voice calm but forceful. "Have you seen the amount of work we've put into this? Rob's not bent, and even if he was, why on earth would he tell them about the raid? Protecting the gang's profits doesn't help solve this murder/kidnap."

"My dear sweet summer child, that's exactly my point." Bill's tone was patronising. "He doesn't want to solve this kidnap or murder. Are you that blind to this, or are you in on it too?"

Clenching his fists as hot rage bubbled up inside him, Rob glared at the DI. "Bollocks." Rob took a step toward Bill. "Shut your mouth. We had nothing to do with this."

Bill raised a disbelieving eyebrow and squared off against him. "Oh, really? I beg to differ."

"Fuck off," Rob snapped, his hands shaking with rage. He took another threatening step closer, but Peter stepped between them.

"That's enough, all of you. I want a full report asap, and I'll be referring this up the chain of command."

Scarlett took his arm gently and pulled him away. "He's not worth it."

The DCI turned to Bill. "You're done here," he said to the PSU officer. Bill backed off with a smug grin before he turned and walked away.

Rob watched him go and then addressed his DCI. "What was he doing here?"

"I authorised his attendance." His expression was defiant as if daring Rob to question him.

Rob didn't want to disappoint. "Why?"

Peter cocked his head to one side. It was a look of pity, and it made Rob feel about two feet tall. "You know why."

"This is bollocks."

"Get yourself back to the station and stay there, both of you. You and I, Rob, we need to have a chat."

"We need Forensics here," Rob stated, keen to make sure this didn't derail the investigation. "Lorraine was in the room upstairs, I know it. There's cable ties with blood on them."

"They're on their way. Now, go. I can't have you two here. Get something to eat. I'll be back soon."

"Fine," Rob sighed as Peter walked away to speak with one of the waiting patrol cars about ferrying them back to Central Station.

Rob waited with Scarlett and watched from a distance, feeling like everything was slipping away from him. He appreciated Scarlett's support, but wondered if he wasn't just dragging her down with him as he tried to fight the prejudice against him. Was this a fight he could win? "Sorry I got you into this."

"Oh, do shut up, Rob. This isn't over yet. Fight your corner. You know this wasn't you, and we now know there's a mole, a bent copper in the station. We need to get to work and finish this."

"Do you think he's here? The bent copper?"

"So what if he is? There's too many people here for him to derail the forensic investigation of this place."

"Fair point."

"You need to focus on what's important."

Taking a breath, Rob gave her a slow nod as he let her words wash over him, filling him with renewed vigour. "No, you're right. Lorraine is still out there, and she needs us."

"Damn right. And now we know there's a grass in the station, we need to move carefully. We need to find out who did this and why. We need to root them out and expose them, all while finding Lorraine."

Rob met her steely gaze and saw the conviction behind her eyes. She meant it. Her drive buoyed him up, infusing him with energy, giving him a much-needed second wind. "Right. Yes, you're right. Okay, so at best, we have someone feeding info back to the gang, but at worst, we might have an actual killer in the police force."

"Shit's fucked up," Scarlett stated.

"And then some."

29

Viv relaxed into the bed as she watched the morning news. Having finished her room service breakfast, she'd moved onto the contents of the mini bar, having forgotten this was a thing hotel rooms had until she'd gone hunting through the room in the night after waking up hungry. Finding that hidden stash of food had been glorious, and after a few seconds of hesitation on its discovery, she'd tucked in, enjoying the crisps, snack bars and nuts, as well as the selection of drinks. She didn't care. The police would pay for it all because she certainly couldn't. There was only about half of it left by now.

She'd spent much of that first day in bed, sleeping and getting some rest.

Having spent years on the streets, sleeping on cardboard, bin bags, rotting mattresses or even just plain concrete or park benches, a hotel bed was the height of luxury. Its softness seemed to envelop and wrap itself around her, lulling her to sleep. And oh, how she'd slept.

The longest stretch had been eleven hours, but that was supplemented with smaller naps before and after as she dozed while watching the TV, surfing its many channels.

She'd vacillated between mind-numbing reality shows about vacant-headed idiots working on a private yacht or copping off with each other and shows with a little more substance. Shows like the news, which she was watching right now.

That detective had called a few times to check up on her and make sure she was okay, which she'd reassured him she was. She'd also confirmed her desire to help try and catch the monsters who'd taken and killed Spencer. This needed to stop, and she would not be scared off.

Rob had seemed relieved by her conviction and reassured her he would look after her. Would that extend beyond this case, she wondered? She could get used to this kind of luxury.

A sudden knock at the door startled her. She stared at the corridor that led to the door, and after a moment, shuffled off the bed and crept over to get a better look. The door remained closed at the end of the short two or three-metre corridor along the side of the bathroom. A second later, there was a second knock.

Feeling panic rise inside, she scanned back over the room, wondering what she could do or if she could escape, but she didn't see how that would be possible. She was stuck in here. Unless... Might it be Rob?

Was he here to check on her? Should she call out and ask who it was?

She didn't feel like she had much choice and didn't want to miss Rob if it was him. "Hello?"

"Vivian Aston?" a male voice called back through the door. He knew her name, but it didn't sound like Rob. "I'm with the police. Detective Loxley sent me over to check up on you. May I come in?"

"Oh," she replied, feeling her heckles fade as she considered his words. "You mean Rob?"

"That's right. Sergeant Rob Loxley."

"Oh, okay. Then yes, I'm fine." She took a few steps closer to the door. "What's this about?"

"Just a check up. I've got some food and money for you as Rob thinks you'll be in here for a few more days."

The idea of more food was intoxicating, and the money would be handy too. "Okay. Hold on."

Closing the distance to the door, she gripped the handle and turned it, pulling it open.

It surged inward suddenly, surprising her and sending Viv stumbling back as a man rushed inside.

Viv screamed as he lunged for her.

30

Relaxing at his desk, Rob stuffed the last of his bacon roll into his mouth and glanced over at the DCI's office in the corner of the room. It was empty, and had been for the last half hour. Peter was back in the station and had appeared briefly to dump a few things in his office and shoot accusatory glares at Rob before he marched out again.

At a guess, he was dealing with the fallout from the botched raid as those further up the food chain wanted answers. Very little blowback had hit Rob yet, but he knew it wouldn't take long before he was dragging into it. Shit rolled downhill afterall, and he would be the next in line once the DCI had spoken with those higher up. He wondered if that meant Peter was answering to his usual boss, or someone in the East Midlands Special Operations Unit, given they were running the case.

He felt sure he'd find out sooner or later as he chewed on the remains of his breakfast.

Since returning to the office, he'd been racking his brain to work out exactly who knew what about the raid, but the more he thought about it, the worse it got. The list was so long and included everyone up to Superintendents and Chief Superintendents, officers like the Method of Entry team, and right down to your average PC and even civilians. Pinpointing the leak seemed like an impossible task, but it could be crucial for bringing the case to a close. It was something he was more determined than ever to do after everything that had come to light, and they were far from being at the end of their leads. For a start, they still needed to find Jordan Rigby, the owner of the white van that had been used to kidnap Spencer and Lorraine. They still had Vivian safe and sound in the hotel room, and then there was all the forensic evidence from which they were still getting results.

Rob sighed, frustrated and annoyed. Sitting and waiting for his summary judgement felt like a total waste of time when he needed to be out there, smashing heads together to find Lorraine.

To his left, Scarlett was taking a phone call, speaking with what sounded like the front desk downstairs, and as he waited for her to finish up, he noticed DCI Orleton walk back into the office. He stopped a short distance away and addressed Rob.

"Come with me." The DCI didn't wait. He just turned and started walking out.

Wiping his mouth with a napkin, Rob was getting out of his chair when Scarlett spoke up. "Rob. Darren Pierson's downstairs, waiting to be interviewed."

Rob glanced over to the DCI waiting at the door, and then turned back to Scarlett. "Okay, you're going to have to talk to him alone. I think I'm going to be a little busy. Okay?"

"Of course. I can handle Darren." She smiled while glancing between him and the waiting DCI. "Good luck."

"Thanks," Rob replied and followed Peter out of the room. They didn't go far, just a few doors up the corridor to a meeting room. Rob followed the DCI in and found two others waiting inside. Behind the table, Detective Superintendent Evelyn Landon—better known as Shorty due to her diminutive stature—sitting waiting for him, the end of her pen between her teeth as she watched him walk in. She looked annoyed, but the sight of Landon eased his nerves, as he'd always got on well with her.

"Sit," she ordered. Rob's eyes flicked to the other person in the room. He grimaced. It was Bill Rainault. Impossibly, he seemed even more smug now and sneered at Rob as he took his seat. Bill and Peter sat to either side of the table waiting for Landon to speak.

"Good morning, Robert," she began.

"Morning, Ma'am."

"Firstly, let me begin by apologising," she said. Rob felt his eyebrows shoot up in surprise before he could get them back under control.

"Apologising?" He could see similar incredulous expressions on the faces of the other two men in the room.

"I'm the Nottinghamshire regional leader of the EMSOU, and I've not been able to find a moment to come and speak to you until now, even though you're running a case for us. For that, I apologise."

For a moment, Rob wasn't sure how to handle this, and just stared at her in shock. He did eventually find his voice after a few awkward seconds. "That's okay, Ma'am. Thank you."

"Don't thank me yet," she snapped. "This morning's events are not good."

"The raid didn't go to plan, I admit, but I don't know how I could have done things any differently. This wasn't my fault." He heard Bill snort in derision.

"Given the poor result, it's a massive waste of resources and manpower that could have been used elsewhere. And for what? To arrest two druggies? It's a disgrace. I'm going to be facing questions from the DCS and above over this."

"I apologise, but we had no idea this wouldn't work. Everything seemed to be going to plan, but somehow they knew."

Landon leaned forward, placing her forearms on the table and interlocking her fingers. "Your colleagues here seem to think that the person most likely to leak such information to the gang is you." She tilted her head. "What do you say to that?"

His whole body tensed at the suggestion of his corruption. It was an old and sore wound that she was now pouring salt into.

"I would hope that you know me better," he answered. She was the one who'd assigned him to this case and deputised him into the EMSOU, so surely, she should back him up and have more trust in him than that. "I'll take the blame for the waste of resources. That's fine. But I am not corrupt."

Bill snorted, and Peter wrinkled his nose, but neither said anything.

"Actually, I blame you both for that. You and DCI Orleton."

He saw Peter shoot Landon an annoyed glance out the corner of his eye, obviously annoyed by this development.

"That's understandable, Ma'am."

"I saw the claim for expenses you put in for the hotel, by the way." Rob stiffened as he wondered where this was going and braced himself for the worst. "I hope they're credible."

"Very. They saw the whole kidnapping."

"I see. Well, they'd better impress me when I see them in court."

Rob nodded. "Me too."

Landon's voice grew serious. "You're on thin ice now, you know that, right? There can be no more screw-ups on this one. We need a result on this. We need to find this missing woman."

"Wait... you're not..." Bill stammered.

"I request that this case be reassigned," Peter cut in. "Rob has demonstrated his incompetence in controlling his team and the flow of information. I have no idea who the leak is, but I do not believe he is fit to lead this investigation from this point onwards."

"Reassigned?" Landon asked, turning to the DCI. "To whom?"

"To me. I will personally oversee the case, chase down the leads and bring it to a conclusion."

"I agree," Bill added. "DCI Orleton is a much better choice than Rob."

"No," Rob spoke up. "I'm not done. I know this case better than anyone else and given a chance, I know I can find Lorraine. I can find her and end this. I just need that chance."

"He'll just mess it up again," Bill said.

"Again? I didn't mess it up this last time, either. My one and only focus is to find the killer and kidnapper, and bring Lorraine home alive. I have no allegiance to this gang or their activities. You know this. I've passed vetting multiple times. I am not bent."

Bill slammed his hand onto the table. "We can't trust him."

"Alright, that's enough, children. My say on this is final, and I've already made my choice. I'm going to give DS Loxley one more chance. I was the one who assigned him to this role, and I still believe he can see this through. Also, we're short-staffed enough as it is without making this worse for ourselves."

"But…" Peter began, but Landon cut him off.

"You'll still be overseeing the case and reporting back to me, Peter. You have enough going on, running your unit without personally taking on a whole case alone. So no, you're better suited where you are."

"This is a mistake," Bill grumbled.

"It's also none of your business, Bill. You're in here as a courtesy, and you're overstepping your mark."

"Apologies."

"You're lucky you don't answer to me."

Rob saw Bill's mouth tense into a thin line as he held himself back from commenting further.

Landon closed the folder before her. "Right, now that that's all decided on, get back to work. Rob, I'm relying on you. Don't screw this up. Got it?"

"Yes, Ma'am." Rob got up from his seat, and Peter did the same. "Thank you."

"Go on, get out of here."

Rob gave her a final nod before following his DCI out of the meeting room. Part way up the corridor, he glanced back to see Bill stepping out of the meeting room, giving him a filthy look. He was unhappy with this development and wasn't being subtle about displaying his displeasure. Rob felt lucky. This could have gone very differently had it been up to someone else, someone who wasn't quite so favourably disposed towards him. He thanked his lucky stars, but this was far from over.

Following the DCI back into their unit, Peter turned to Rob as he made for his desk. "No, in my office, now."

Rob glanced at his and Scarlett's vacant desks. She was probably already downstairs talking to Darren. As he made to follow the DCI, he hoped she was doing okay.

He stepped into the small room and closed the office door behind him.

"Christ. You're a lucky man, Loxley. Bloody lucky. Had the choice been mine, things would be very different. This kind of failure cannot happen on cases like this. If this got out to the press, they'd eat us alive. So buck up your ideas and get control over this. I want no more fuck ups, okay? I want to know everything that goes on."

"I understand, sir."

"I hope you do because this could have ended you. We all know about your family, Rob. We know who you are. You might have charmed Landon, Nailer, and Pilgrim, but you've not fooled me. I know who you are, I know where you come from, and a leopard doesn't change its spots. You want to know who I think leaked this to the gang? Well, here's a clue, I'm looking at him, and if I can find a way to prove it, I will." Peter almost collapsed into his chair and leaned his head against his hand. "Jesus. I can't believe she's kept you on. It's madness." He looked up, staring straight into Rob's eyes. "If it were up to me, I'd have already removed you. Make no doubt about it. You'd be gone by now. So believe me when I say you're literally one wrong step away from the end of your career because if you fuck up now, I will go above Landon, and I will have you dismissed from this case and from the police as a whole. Have you got that?"

Rob continued to hold Peter's gaze throughout his rant, knowing that the man was talking utter bollocks. But this wasn't the time to protest his innocence.

"I understand, sir."

With a disgusted curl of his lip, Peter turned away. "Get out of my sight."

31

Leaving her desk moments after Rob had been taken for his interview, Scarlett walked up the corridor and passed the meeting room where Rob was being interviewed. Through the window in the door, she spotted DCI Orleton, DI Bill Rainault and a woman that she didn't recognise, who seemed to be running the show.

She didn't linger and couldn't hear what was being said as she moved toward the staircase and started to make her way downstairs. Opening her folder as she walked, Scarlett checked through the scribbled notes she'd made for this interview with Darren. They focused on the archery trophies he had and how much shooting he actually did.

This felt perfunctory, though, like a hurdle that she needed to get over rather than something which might lead to any kind of breakthrough in the case, which was annoying because they certainly needed it after this morning's circus.

The idea that there might be someone in this building who was working closely with a criminal gang like the Top Valley Boyz sent shivers down her spine. How could anyone do that, knowing they were helping these monsters ruin people's lives, or worse still, aiding a killer who thought he was some kind of twisted modern-day Robin Hood?

But the thing was, it could be even worse than that, with the killer working alongside them, somewhere in this building.

She wondered if it could somehow be Rob. She'd heard many times from several people on the force that she should not trust Rob Loxley, that he was corrupt and secretly working against the interests of the police. Was this true? Was he in league with these criminal gangs and passing them information that would save them from being raided?

It was possible, she supposed, of course, but deep down, she didn't believe it. It made no sense to her. Not with a woman's life on the line.

Despite everything these people had told her about the so-called duplicitous DS Loxley, her own experience of him was very different, and he seemed to be the most hard-working and honourable of the lot so far.

But things had progressed, and this might be the end for him.

She hoped not.

Reaching the interview rooms on the lower floor, she soon found Darren Pierson sitting in an interview room, waiting for her.

"Good morning, Darren. Thank you for coming in to see us."

"Of course. What's this about?"

"We just have a few more questions for you. This interview will be recorded, and I want to confirm that you're happy to proceed without a solicitor present? Is that right?"

"Do I need one?"

"Hopefully not."

Darren shrugged. "Then I won't bother."

"Okay," she replied and set the DIR going before introducing herself for the benefit of the recording and getting Darren to do the same.

"It's come to our attention that you are something of an archer, is that right?"

"Archer?" Darren frowned, apparently taken off guard by the question.

"You do some archery. There were a number of trophies for it in your front room with your name on them."

"Oh, I see. Well, calling them trophies is a bit of a leap. They're just little plaques, usually just for minor things, like taking part. But, yes, I've shot a few arrows in my time. It's fun and relaxing."

"Do you still shoot?"

He shrugged. "A little. It's barely a hobby at this point. Occasionally, I get my bow out and fling a few arrows down the garden. I'm always very careful, though. That's not illegal, is it?"

Preferring to keep him on his toes, she didn't answer his question. "Have you ever been hunting?"

"With my bow? No. Why?"

"So, you don't own any hunting arrows with broadheads?"

"Christ, no. Those things are dangerous. Have you ever held one? They're razor-sharp."

"No, I haven't. So you're saying you don't own any hunting arrows, and if we searched your house, we wouldn't find any?"

"Go ahead. You wouldn't find anything like that." He looked offended and crossed his arms.

"Okay, let me ask you this. Do you know anyone by the name of Lloyd Bistow, better known as Curby, or Jordan Rigby?"

"Um, no. I don't know those names. Why? Should I?"

"Absolutely not."

"Okay, then no. I don't. Who are they?"

"Very bad men," Scarlett replied.

"You still think I'm a suspect, don't you? You think I killed him, with a bow and arrow, at a guess."

"All I wanted to do was eliminate you from our investigation, that's all, and I hope you're telling me the truth."

"Like I said, search my house, please. I don't own any hunting arrows."

"I might just do that."

32

"How'd it go?"

Rob looked up to see Scarlett walking back into the office with notes and folders beneath her arm. She squinted as if expecting to hear the worst, her brows knitting together like a child waiting for a balloon to burst.

"Well…" Rob started, leaning back in his chair and stretching before Scarlett interrupted him.

"You're still here, so it can't have been too bad." She pivoted toward DCI's office where Peter was working before turning back. "Did he hang you out to dry?"

"He wanted to," Rob replied, and pressed his lips into a thin line as he thought back to the way Peter and Bill had ganged up on him during the interview. They'd clearly wanted there to be bigger consequences for him. "Bill too. But Landon wasn't having any of it."

"That was your old boss? Shorty Landon? The one you mentioned at the steak house?"

"That's the one. She said she still had faith in me and wanted to give me one last chance."

"Christ. You dodged a bullet. I bet that pissed Bill off."

"And Peter," Rob added, glancing back at the office while reliving the telling off Peter had given him. After getting off so lightly, Peter was probably just venting his frustrations. "He gave me a bollocking when we got back here."

Scarlett wandered back around to her desk and dropped the files onto it before slumping into her chair. "Well, at least you're still here. That's a good thing."

"By the skin of my teeth. How'd the interview go?"

"He admitted that he has an archery hobby but denies the rest. Says he doesn't have hunting arrows and doesn't know Curby or anyone else from that gang, and frankly, I'm inclined to believe him. I don't think he did it."

"Alright, I trust your instincts on that."

"I do want to send some officers over to have a look through his house, though, which Darren seemed happy to allow, just in case."

"Sure thing. Don't let me stop you."

She nodded and turned to her desk to make the arrangements. A short time later, Tony Darby walked over and leaned against Rob's desk.

"Still 'ere then?"

"I'm not going anywhere," Rob answered, leaning back in his chair while Tony gave him a disgruntled look. "What's up?"

Tony handed him a printed sheet of paper. "We were called out to a burning car in the early hours of this morning. Turns out it's a black Range Rover."

Rob grabbed the paper as his mind made the link. "A four-by-four."

Tony nodded. "Like the one we've been looking for on CCTV around Sherwood."

Rob read the details on the report, which said the vehicle had already been recovered and would be the subject of a forensic investigation starting later today. "Sounds like too much of a coincidence to me."

"Hmm. It's funny how things seem to work out around here, isn't it?"

There was meaning laced through his words. Rob peered up at Tony and frowned. "Got something to say?"

"An honourable person would do the right thing when their position became untenable, don't you think?" Tony smiled, but it didn't touch his eyes. "Something to ponder in your lunch break, maybe." He turned and walked away without a backward glance, and Rob watched him go, annoyed by his veiled comments.

"Ignore him," Scarlett said, leaning over. "He's just another stooge for Frank and Peter."

"I know," Rob said, gritting his teeth in annoyance before he looked back over the report of the burnt-out car. "It was found north of the city, in the countryside."

"That's close to Top Valley, right?"

"Yeah," Rob confirmed.

"So, if this is the car they used, the one that had Spencer in it, it suggests they knew we were looking for it and chose to get rid and destroy any evidence inside."

"My thoughts exactly," Rob agreed as a feeling of being watched settled over him. "And this only backs up our idea that there's someone inside the force, feeding them information. I mean, it's feasible that they would have dumped the car anyway to conceal evidence, but this just feels wrong."

"I'm inclined to agree," Scarlett replied. "So, what do we do now?"

Rob thought about this for a moment and flicked his eyes left and right. While his work life had become more unfriendly in recent years, he'd never felt like he was being watched the entire time, but things had changed, and he was starting to question everything. Rob leaned in conspiratorially. "I know what I want to do, but we need to be careful who knows."

Scarlett seemed to catch on pretty quick and shifted closer, scooting her chair over. She glanced around furtively and nodded. "Alright. Then we need a plan."

His disagreements with Peter, Bill and the others were always annoying, and he was well aware of their views regarding him and his trustworthiness. But he'd always found solace in those who believed in him. He wasn't corrupt and he wasn't working against the police. He knew the truth. So while some of his colleagues might be antagonistic toward him, they were all ultimately working towards the same goal. They were all on the same team.

But he now found himself in the weird position of questioning all that. Were they really on his side? And if not, which ones could he trust? Was the killer out there somewhere? Was he laughing as he paid off someone in the office to feed him information, keeping one step ahead of the investigation?

The office, and the entire building, felt compromised like it was enemy territory. These gangs were sophisticated, complex, and powerful. They also had money to spare, and given the current state of the defunded police, he could easily imagine vulnerable officers working in the force who might happily pass some information on in return for a little bonus.

"You've gone all paranoid," Scarlett said.

"Have I though? The gang knew about the raid, and they've burnt out the vehicle they used to transport the prisoner."

"Okay, fair point," she admitted. "But I take it you trust me?"

Rob caught her glance and smile. "I think that's obvious."

"Good, because I'm very aware that I've tied my boat to you, and I'm risking my own career in the process."

"I'll bear that in mind." She was right. Throwing her lot in with him was a risky move on her part, especially given they'd known each other for just a few days. He didn't really know much about her either, apart from a few basic details. Could he really trust her? Rob shook his head in frustration, hating that he was starting to question everything while being aware that Landon had given him a second chance and he needed to produce results. But he couldn't do that alone. He needed people around him he trusted, and for better or worse, he found he did actually trust Scarlett.

Scarlett whispered, "Right, so who else do you trust?"

Matching her volume, he whispered back, "I think the only other people I trust, for better or worse, are Nailer and Nick. Nailer's been a mentor to me for years and is about as close to a...well, a true friend as I've ever had." He'd wanted to say father figure, but he wasn't sure how that would have sounded. He trusted Scarlett, but he wasn't sure he was ready to share everything with her just yet. "And I've worked with Nick for years, there's no way he's bent. I'd have noticed."

"Are you sure about them? They knew about the raid."

"So did others around them. But yes, I trust them."

"Okay," Scarlett relented. "What do we do?"

"We go after Jordan Rigby, the van owner. We need to track him down and bring him in without anyone warning him. So, I say we keep this between you, me, Nailer and Nick. That's it. Because if Rigby knows we're coming, he might go to ground."

"He might already know we're interested in him. Our lines of enquiry aren't exactly secret in this office."

"Oh, I'm sure he does. But he doesn't know he's next on the list, and I'm betting he's a cocky shite that thinks he's untouchable."

"I think that's guaranteed," Scarlett replied. "Especially if he's a cold-blooded killer with a police officer on the take."

"Let's do this then. We'll call Nailer on the way."

"Let's roll out!"

Without a backward glance, Rob strode out the office with Scarlett in tow and made for the garage. Walking into the underground car park, he briefly eyed the pool cars but decided against them. They were fitted with trackers and could be easily traced.

Rob briefly considered his own Ford Capri, but dismissed it too. It was distinctive, and if the informant was being really clever, they could have hidden a tracker on it too. He made a mental note to give it a thorough going over when he had five minutes.

Rob turned to Scarlett. "Which is your car?"

"Mine?"

"You're new, so I trust your car more than mine."

She raised a quizzical eyebrow. "Alright. It's that one."

Rob followed her outstretched finger and spotted a brand-new purple VW Polo. "It's purple."

"I know. It's my favourite colour."

"So, it's not red, then?"

"Funny."

"I know. It's effortless, really."

Scarlett grimaced as she started out for her car. "Come on, Gramps, let's get this show on the road.

"You young whipper snappers are all the same, no respect," Rob griped good-naturedly.

Once they were on the streets, Rob called Nailer. He picked up after a couple of rings.

"Rob. Still with us then, I see," Nailer said. "I heard about the raid. That's some bad luck."

"I know. I'm convinced we've got a bent copper in our ranks."

"Probably more than one. Those gangs pay well, you know."

Nailer was something of an expert on organised crime, having spent much of his detective career hunting them down. He knew better than most the true extent of their reach.

"So I hear," Rob replied.

"What's your next move?" Nailer asked.

"Am I on speaker?" Rob wanted to be sure there was no one else listening in. "Are you alone?"

"You're taking this seriously. I'm impressed. And no, Nick's not here and you're not on speaker. I'm alone. I take it you trust me then."

"You and Nick. How can I not? You've drilled into me the influence of these gangs, and how powerful they are."

"I'm flattered, and I'm sure Nick will be too."

"So you should be," Rob quipped back. "Okay, Scarlett and I are on the road, heading for Top Valley. We need to find Jordan Rigby, the owner of the white van, and bring him in. I trust you, so I want you with us. Can you help?"

Nailer laughed. "Sure, why not. I could do with the fresh air, anyway. I'll slip out and meet you over there. I have Nick on something else, so it'll just be me. Hope that's ok? After you took his case away from him, I couldn't have him twiddling his thumbs."

"Fair enough. Yeah, that's fine."

"I take it you have Rigby's address?"

"We do. Let's meet on his street and work our way around from there, see if we can't spot him."

"Sounds good. See you soon." The line clicked off, and Rob turned to Scarlett. "He's in."

"Excellent. I take it Nailer knows what he's talking about when it comes to these gangs, then?"

"Does he ever. He's been studying and fighting them for years. He knows more than just about anyone. And has been calling for stricter vetting and security. These organisations are powerful and awash with cash, so it doesn't take much to bribe an underpaid officer."

"That's a very pessimistic view," Scarlett replied, wrinkling her nose. "It's about more than money, surely. What about integrity and self-respect? I'd never accept a bribe."

"Then you're a credit to the force. And yes, you're right, most officers wouldn't take pay-outs from criminals, but it doesn't take many to accept them before we're basically working for the gangs. Just a few well-placed corrupt officers could really screw things up."

"Fair point, but I prefer to be a little more optimistic about these things. I believe most people are inherently good, and that includes the police."

"I hope you're right. We're meeting Nailer at Rigby's, by the way."

"Way ahead of you. It's in the Sat Nav."

Scarlett sped north, following the directions the navigation app spat out. She was soon entering the Top Valley estate and making her way to where Rigby lived on the east end of it. As they drew close, Rob's phone buzzed. It was Nailer again.

"I'm here, and you'll never guess who I just saw leaving his house?"

"Rigby?" Rob answered.

"Got it in one. He's walking down the street, heading south."

"We're just about here, we'll park up and see which way he goes." Their left turn was up ahead. Scarlett navigated round it, and as the road came into view he spotted the solitary figure ambling down the path, smoking something. He didn't seem to have a care in the world.

"Pull in here," Rob said. Scarlett followed his order, swerving into a space on their left, as Rob peered up the road. "I can see him." Rob put his phone on speaker. "Where's he headed? I can't see the van."

As Rigby drew closer, Rob became aware of how conspicuous they were, with both of them staring out at Rigby. "Scarlett, face me as if you're talking to me."

She turned into the car, putting her back to Rigby. "I am talking to you."

Nailer snorted over the speaker. "Yeah, but you need to gaze longingly at Rob's handsome face. You need to admire his lustrous hair and chiselled jaw line."

Scarlett made a gagging sound before composing herself. "Sorry, I don't know what came over me."

"It's a common reaction, don't worry about it," Nailer replied.

"You two are bloody hilarious," Rob grumbled as he watched Rigby walk closer on the opposite side of the road. He glanced over once, but didn't seem to take too much interest before he turned into a side road and disappeared from view.

"Shit, I've lost sight of him."

"I'm already walking up," Nailer informed them. "He's turned into a dead-end side road, with garages on either side. Crap, I can see a white van."

"What's he doing?" Rob asked before he motioned to Scarlett. "Let's go."

They climbed out of the car and crossed the road. To his left, Rob spotted Nailer striding up. He nodded as he held his phone to his ear.

"Looks like he's opening one of the garages up."

A sudden thought occurred to him. "Lorraine might be in there. Let's go. We take him, now."

Rob clicked off his phone, stuffed it in his pocket, and started to jog. Flanked on either side by Scarlett and Nailer, they ran into the side road. They turned right into the dead-end, spotting the parked up white van and Jordan Rigby standing at the entrance to his garage. He turned to them as Rob held up his warrant card.

"Stay right there, Jordan. Let's not make this any harder than it needs to be."

Rigby froze, then glanced around as if looking for an escape. Rob tensed as he approached, ready to give chase.

"Don't you dare," Scarlett called out.

"You won't get far," Nailer added. "Give it up."

Rigby grimaced and after another futile glance around, relaxed and held his hands up. "Fine."

"Good lad," Rob said and motioned to Scarlett to cuff him while he watched. "You've done the right thing."

"Fuck you. What's this about, eh? I ain done nuthin' wrong."

"I'm arresting you on suspicion of kidnapping and the murder of Spencer Lawson. You do not have to say anything. But it may harm your defence if you do not mention when questioned, something which you later rely on in court. Anything you do say may be given in evidence. Do you understand all that?"

"I've heard it before," Rigby grumbled.

"No shit, Sherlock." He turned to Scarlett. "Call some transport in."

"On it, Guv."

"Rob," Nailer called out. He was standing inside the garage entrance, looking into the back of it. "What do you make of this?"

Squinting as he peered into the shadows, he saw what looked like a wide chest freezer that had seen better days. It was stained and covered in dirt, rust and dead leaves. Frowning, he motioned for Rigby to get on his knees. "Down."

"Yeah, alright, piggy. Fuck's sake." He dropped to his knees with Scarlett standing over him.

"I've got him," she assured him, her pepper spray in hand. "I'll call in Scene of Crime."

Rob nodded and then turned into the garage. Nailer had already moved up next to the freezer and pointed to a padlocked hasp on the outside of it.

"That's not normal."

"No, it's not." He turned back to Rigby, who was watching them keenly with an inscrutable expression. "What have you got in here?"

"Food. It's a freezer, ain't it."

"What kind of food needs locking in?" Rob frowned.

Rigby pulled a face and scoffed. "It's to keep the local scrotes out."

"You'll have to excuse me if I don't believe you." Rob glanced around the dirty garage, noting the discarded paint cans, a toolbox and blown-in leaves.

"Whatever," Rigby said. His words were flippant, but something about his tone sounded stressed or on edge.

"What do you think's in there?" Nailer asked in low tones.

"I honestly dread to think," Rob replied as he examined the outside of the freezer. It was plugged in and operational, with a worn-out sounding hum coming from inside. "I need to get in there."

"Are you thinking what I'm thinking?"

"Lorraine," Rob stated.

Nailer nodded, with meaning filling his eyes.

His mind made up, Rob pulled on a pair of latex gloves, opened the nearby toolbox and hunted for something he could use.

"Hey, that's my stuff," Rigby protested.

Rob spotted a hammer and grabbed it. "Mind if I borrow this?"

"Put that back."

"I will," Rob replied and returned to the freezer. He took a moment to position the padlock for the best possible hit.

"Don't you fuckin' dare!"

Rigby didn't seem too pleased by his actions, but Rob didn't take much notice and swung the hammer.

As the strike of the hammer echoed through the garage, Rob heard Scarlett yell.

"Oi." Rob turned as Scarlett landed on her arse with a thud. Rigby had twisted and swung his leg out, knocking her feet out from beneath her.

Rob went to charge in, but Scarlett kicked out and caught Rigby in the back of his leg as he went to get up. Rigby stumbled. Scrambling to her feet, Scarlett jumped on Rigby and flattened him, sitting on his back. Grabbing him by his collar, she held the pepper spray inches from his face and hissed through gritted teeth. "Go on, try that again. I dare you."

"Christ, she's got stones bigger than you, Rob," Nailer commented.

"Don't I know it." He turned to address Scarlett. "You got him?"

"Oh yeah, he's not going anywhere," she growled.

It took three hits to break the lock, but it eventually came loose and Nailer deftly removed it before lifting the lid.

Rob leaned over the appliance and looked inside through the fading mist to see three irregular-shaped packages. They'd been wrapped in layers of ice-encrusted cling film, but it was clear to see what was inside, and the shape of the biggest one would have given it away, anyway.

It was a chopped up, frozen human body. The biggest part was the torso and head, with the legs in another bundle and the arms in a third.

"Holy shit," Nailer cursed.

"Bollocks. Is that?" Rob shifted position to try and get a better look at the corpse, to see if it was Lorraine or not.

"No, look at the shape. That's a man, not a woman."

"What is it?" Scarlett asked from where she was standing guard over Rigby.

Rob glared at Rigby, who was looking anywhere else but not at Rob. "Care to explain why there's a dead body in your freezer?"

"Oh," Scarlett exclaimed.

Rigby shrugged. "I dunno. Got nothin' to do wi' me."

"I bet."

Nailer closed the freezer. "We'll leave it in there for now. Don't want to stink the place out before Scene of Crime get here."

"They're on their way," Scarlett said, anticipating the question, holding her phone to her ear.

"Tell them we have a body. It'll speed it up."

Scarlett did as he asked. It wasn't long before the first response units arrived, they were able to place Rigby into their care and start to secure the scene.

Scarlett walked over to where Rob was standing with Nailer, discussing their next move. She held up a couple of clear evidence bags, each holding a phone. "He had these on him," she announced as she got close. "They're locked, though, and he's refusing to give us the security codes."

"Digital Forensics will deal with those," Rob said as Scarlett handed them to one of the Scene of Crime officers that had started to arrive. "Come on. I want to have a look around Rigby's house. If he's got a body in his freezer, I think we can logically assume there's a chance that Lorraine might be in his home."

"I'm in," Scarlett stated. "Let's go."

Nailer turned to an arriving police car and waved for the two officers inside to follow him. "You two, with me. We have a house to secure."

Leaving the steadily growing chaos of the crime scene behind, Rob led them up the street, past the beginnings of a crowd of onlookers as the arriving police set up their cordon. Ahead, Rob spotted the house that Rigby called home and noted a woman standing at the door, watching the growing crowd. She saw Rob and the others approach and seemed to become steadily more uncomfortable as they got closer, and she realised they were heading for her.

The woman tensed as they turned into her front garden. "What's going on?"

Having already checked his notes, Rob smiled as he held up his ID. "Kay Hackett?"

"Yeah, who's asking?"

"You're the girlfriend of Jordan Rigby, correct?"

"What of it?" She was defensive.

"We need to have a look in the house." Rob kept to the facts.

Her expression was incredulous. "Now, hold on a moment. You can't just..."

"Miss Hackett, we have reason to believe that Jordan may be holding a hostage in this house, and under PACE, that gives us the right to enter your property in the interests of safeguarding life."

"There's no one in this house," she protested.

"Ma'am." One of the uniformed officers stepped forward and guided her to one side. "Please, just step over here."

"Fine," Kat spat in disgust. "Go on, go in. There's no one in there. He's done nothing wrong."

Rob bit his lip but said nothing as he walked into the building. He guessed she had no idea about the body in the freezer. Scarlett followed, and Nailer entered last after briefing the two constables.

The house wasn't quite as bad as he'd expected. It wasn't spotless or minimalist in the slightest, and there was a distinct smell of weed, but compared to the crack house, it was a palace. The fridge freezer was mercifully free of body parts, and so were the cupboards, cabinets and wardrobes. But there was no sign of Lorraine, or any prisoner, anywhere in the building.

They'd not been in the house long before Scarlett called out and summoned Rob to the rearmost room. She was standing beside a window and pointed outside.

Stepping over to the grubby glass, Rob spotted what had caught Scarlett's attention. Leaning up against the garden fence was an archery target.

"Scarlett, awesome work. You're the dog's bollocks."

"If it's all the same, I'd rather not be," she replied. "But at the risk of further compliments, you might want to look behind you, as well."

Rob raised an eyebrow and then attempted a French accent. "More surprises? Why madam, you're really spoiling us."

She gave him a pitying look. "Jesus."

Rob turned and saw what Scarlett wanted to show him. In the corner, tucked into a small gap between a shelving unit filled with DVDs and Playstation games and the wall, was a bow with a quiver of arrows.

"Well, shit." Rob wandered over, crouched beside them, but didn't touch. "Jordan Rigby, you little twat."

He tried to see if any of them were the hunting arrows the killer had used, but he'd need to touch them to check, and he didn't want to ruin any forensics. Besides, they'd find out soon enough. He backed away as Nailer walked into the room. Rob showed him the target and the bow.

"That's good. No Lorraine, though?"

"Nope. But this only strengthens our case. Looks like Rigby might be our man."

"We can only hope," Nailer confirmed as they walked back to the front door, summoning more officers to come and secure the house and go through it with a fine-toothed comb.

"How about I show Rigby's photo to Viv at the hotel?" Scarlett suggested as they walked out of the house. "It won't take me long, and she might recognise him."

"Good idea," Rob said. "I need to get officers out to all the locations that we know are linked to Rigby and his gang. We need to find Lorraine."

"I'll take you back to Central," Nailer suggested.

Rob nodded to the DCI. "You're coming into town?"

"I want to see how this plays out."

"Okay, thanks."

They walked back to the road. As Rob scanned the crowd, he noticed a handful of faces that he recognised. It seemed that Rigby's crew had turned up to see what the fuss was all about. Curby, the Valley Boyz top-dog, was amongst them and shuffled closer as Rob made it to the street.

"You got my bruv, ain't it," Curby stated.

"What of it?"

"He ain't who yeh want. He ain't your man."

"I'll be the judge of that," Rob said and turned away from the knot of kids and youths that surrounded Curby. He left them behind, keenly aware they were staring at his back.

Curby was sticking up for his friend and fellow gang member and didn't want him sent down. But there was a tiny part of him that wondered about what Curby had said.

33

Things seemed to be moving quickly, all of a sudden, Scarlett thought as she pulled into the Mercure hotel car park. After the balls up of the raid revealed the possibility of a leak in the force, going after Rigby seemed to have turned all that around. Now they had the van used to kidnap Spencer and Lorraine and a new body that had been kept in cold storage. The case had done a complete one-eighty, and it looked like they had their man.

It wasn't lost on Scarlett that their impromptu raid on Rigby had been successful because they'd kept it between Rob, Nailer and herself.

So, who was the corrupt cop, and who was the victim?

Once Jordan Rigby had been taken off her hands, she couldn't resist a peek in the freezer to see the remains herself. Curiously, she found herself intrigued rather than disgusted or repulsed by what she saw.

It clearly wasn't a woman, so likely not Lorraine, but that left them with several loose ends. Who was the poor bugger they'd found in the freezer, and where was Lorraine?

Having already started before Scarlett had left, Rob was likely neck-deep in arranging a general sweep of the area to try and find the missing woman while they booked Jordan in. They needed to find her, and fast.

She had no idea if Viv would recognise Jordan from the kidnap she'd witnessed. It had been dark, and the kidnappers wore masks, but it was worth a shot. There was also a chance she might recognise his voice. Besides, after everything that had happened, she felt it was about time to check up on Viv again and see how she was getting on.

The Mercure was a massive oblong of tan brick and dark brown cladding on the busy, four-lane Mansfield Road. A solid, utilitarian looking place, and crucially for their purposes, not too expensive either. The inside, with its royal blue carpets and comfy seating, was nicer than it had any right to be, and the current guests paid Scarlett no attention as she walked in.

She didn't bother with the reception and walked straight to the lifts.

Within moments, she was upstairs on the third floor, and soon found room 319, where they had left Viv.

Scarlett knocked and waited.

Seconds ticked by, but nothing happened. She frowned and looked at the door quizzically as if it might give her the answers she needed. Was Viv in here? She knocked again.

"Viv? It's Scarlett. Detective Stutely. Are you in there?"

Again, nothing. No sounds. No movement, and no reply.

Taking half a step back, she glanced up and down the corridor, but apart from a cleaning cart, she saw nothing unusual. Biting her lip in consternation, she glared reproachfully at the door. How dare it stand in her way.

Deciding to try again. Scarlett banged on the door for a third time. This time she used the base of her fist and hit hard.

"Viv! Are you in there?" she shouted.

No answer.

Scarlett grunted in annoyance.

"Can I help you, miss?" A cleaner had emerged from another room and was looking up the corridor at her suspiciously. "Everything all right?"

Scarlett glanced between the door and the middle-aged lady before pulling her ID out.

"Ma'am. I'm a Detective with the Nottinghamshire Police, and I need to get into this room."

"Oh. I don't… I don't know if I can do that. You're with the police?"

"Lady. Either you open this door, or I break it down. Call the manager if you need to, but I have to get in here. This could be a life or death situation."

"Okay, okay. Alright." The cleaner hurried up the corridor and pulled out the universal key card she had on a stretchy length of curly rubber that looked like a vintage telephone cable.

She inserted the card and unlocked the door. Scarlett turned the handle while holding her baton in her other hand, ready to extend it.

"Viv? Are you in here?"

No reply.

She pushed the door open slowly, peering through the gap, but there were no sounds or movement. Stepping in, a scene of devastation greeted her.

The bedclothes were all over the place, snack wrappers and used plates were scattered around, a chair had been upended, the desk was at a jaunty angle, and the kettle was knocked to the floor.

Easing herself into the room despite her spiking heart rate, she scanned the bathroom to her left, but it was mercifully empty. Pressing on, she approached the main room and extended her baton before jumping forward to see around the corner.

No one was in here, Viv was gone, and it looked like there'd been some kind of struggle. Either that, or she'd trashed the room and run.

"Bloody hell, what a mess!"

Scarlett turned to the cleaner. "Out, please. This could be a crime scene. I need to preserve it."

"Oh, sorry." She backed out with her hands raised in supplication.

Turning back to the room, Scarlett took a couple more steps in to get a better look at a suspicious-looking stain on the white bedclothes. There were several dried drips of something reddish-brown on the sheets.

Blood?

"Crap." She pulled out her phone, found Rob's number and hit call.

34

Rob returned to the office on an undeniable high after the disaster of the raid, thrilled with the result they'd achieved. Rigby was looking like their prime suspect, and he felt closer than ever to bringing this case home. This was especially gratifying after their raid had gone so badly. There was no way that Landon would take the case off him now, no matter how much Bill or Peter moaned at her.

Having driven him back to Central, Nailer had walked off to find something for them to eat while Rob returned to the office.

As he walked to his desk, he gazed across the office, looking to see if either Frank or Tony would say anything, but Frank didn't even look up, and Tony gave him no more than a cursory glance before returning to his work.

Yeah, stick that up your arse, he thought, sneering at them.

The DCI was in his office and spotted Rob walking in, but he didn't get up. No doubt he'd be out to hear the latest soon enough.

As he reached his desk, Rob's phone buzzed in his pocket. According to the caller ID, it was Scarlett. He answered the phone.

"What did she say?" Rob asked, curious to know if Viv might recognise Jordan.

"She's disappeared."

After a second to take in what she'd just said, Rob went to yell down the phone and then thought better of it and bit his lip. Taking his seat, Rob slid down to hide from casual view.

"What?" he hissed quietly into his phone. "What do you mean she's disappeared?"

"She's gone. Viv isn't in the hotel room anymore, and it looks like there was a struggle in there."

"How do you mean?"

"Well, I guess she could have trashed it. There's stuff everywhere. The chairs upended, the kettle's been thrown across the room, and I think there's blood on the bedsheets."

"You're sure?"

"No, but I think we need to get it tested."

"I'll call in Forensics."

"What do we do?" she asked, sounding a little desperate. Her tone matched his own racing heart as he glanced around to make sure no one was listening in. Viv had been their star witness, and now she was gone? Without her, they'd lost a key part of the case. Peter would be angry, and so would the Superintendent. Every time they got a break, something else went wrong. It was two steps forward and one back, and it was getting infuriating.

As he considered Scarlett's question, he saw the DCI's office door open, and Peter walked out. He waved at Rob and started to approach.

"Say nothing to no one," Rob hissed down the phone. "We keep this between ourselves until we know more. Lock that hotel door, and make sure the manager knows to not let anyone in. I've gotta go."

"Got it," she said and ended the call just as Peter approached.

"I hear you made a breakthrough?" He seemed hesitant and curious in equal measure as if waiting for some kind of bombshell to hit.

"We think we found our killer," Rob confirmed.

"Oh, really?" He sounded genuinely surprised. "Who?"

"Jordan Rigby. He's the owner of the white van. We went looking for him and picked him up close to his home, where he parks his van, the same one we think was used in the kidnapping. But that's not all. He was mooching about in a garage we think he owns, and in the back was a chest freezer. It was padlocked, which was suspicious. So fearing that Lorraine was in there, we opened it."

"Whose 'we'?"

"Scarlett, Nailer and myself."

"John Nailer?"

"He offered to help, so I said yes." Rob shrugged, hoping he sold the lie.

"Did he now?" Peter frowned briefly, sounding offended. "Alright, continue. What was in the freezer?"

"A body, chopped up and wrapped in cling."

He seemed surprised by this. "Oh. I see. Do we know who it is? It's not Lorraine, is it?"

"No, it's a man. We'll do the usual post-mortem and such, once he's unfrozen of course, to find out who he is. But it looks like Rigby is a killer. And given that we found a bow and arrow set in his home, and a target, I think things are starting to come together."

"But, you still haven't found Lorraine?"

"No, which is concerning. We need to find her. I've got as many units as possible working through a list of addresses we have linked to the gang, and we'll start leaning on informants too."

"I see. Well, that's good work." Peter seemed surprised at his own words, as if he didn't expect to speak to Rob like this, and he actually smiled, which was somewhat incredible. "I mean, I don't like that you went off alone, without telling anyone where you were going, but I can't deny the results. This is great work. I'm sure Landon will be pleased."

"I hope so, providing we can find Lorraine."

"And you have your witness, right?"

Rob stiffened at the mention of her but did his best to hide how uncomfortable it made him feel. "Vivian," he said by way of an answer.

"Yes. Good. So, she's safe, is she?"

"We have everything under control." He didn't want to lie, but felt very aware of how vague he was being and how suspicious it probably sounded. Was Peter picking up on that? The DCI narrowed his eyes at Rob as if he didn't really believe him, while Rob silently prayed that Peter would change the subject.

After another uncomfortable second, during which Rob felt like Peter was looking directly into his soul, the DCI smiled again, and the whole mood lightened. "What about Rigby? Is he talking?"

"No, he's not. He's clammed up tighter than a gnat's arse and will only say 'No comment' or 'I want my phone call'. As far as I know, he's downstairs now making that call."

"Calling his gang banger mates, no doubt."

Rob nodded and thought back to Curby's comment on the street outside Rigby's house that they'd arrested the wrong man. He wasn't quite sure how Curby could think that, given the mountain of evidence they had against Rigby, not least of which was the body in the man's freezer, but despite that, there was something off about all this. Something didn't quite fit, and he was sure he was missing a piece of the puzzle somewhere.

He wasn't about to announce that to the DCI, though, along with them having lost Viv. That could all come out later. For now, they needed to focus on Rigby and Lorraine.

Rob grimaced inside at the thought of what she would be going through, no doubt wondering when this would all end.

Where are you, Lorraine?

35

The coolness of the concrete soothed Lorraine as she lay on the unforgiving floor of the space she'd been dumped in. She'd hardly moved for hours, only shifting her weight when the pain in her hip, leg or shoulder became too much to bear. She longed for them to go numb, so she could feel less.

Her wrists were again bound behind her back by those horrible black cable ties. They'd wrapped several of them around her wrists where they cut into her skin, making her cry out in agony when she moved them wrong. They'd done the same thing to her ankles and wrapped tape around her face to keep the same dirty sock in her mouth.

They'd come for her in the dead of night, bursting into her room at the house. There'd been several of them in masks, and between them, they'd bound her, carried her out of the front door and thrown her into the van. She'd struggled and tried to scream past the gag, but it was little use.

It must have been the early hours, in the dead of night. No one was around, and the street was dark and empty.

A short drive later, they'd pulled her from the van, still naked, and thrown her into what she guessed was a garage. Over the last few hours, she'd heard cars, people, and other garage doors open and close. She'd tried to move to the door to bang on it, but they'd tied her to something on the back wall so she could only get halfway.

For what felt like an age, she stared at the thin gap along the bottom of the garage. She longed for the glow and warmth of the daylight she saw beyond it to hit her skin. It was morning… she guessed? She couldn't be sure.

Tiredness filled her every muscle and dragged her down into blissful naps when the pain fell away to be replaced with fitful nightmares as her imagination ran riot. She thought of her annoying but loving husband and longed for him to hold her and tell her everything would be okay. She just wanted to see him one last time before they did whatever it was they were going to do to her.

She'd long ago resigned herself to her fate. There was no escaping this. All her strength had disappeared, leaving her at the mercy of these brutes and whatever sick game they were playing.

She just wanted it to end. She was done with it and wanted to move on to whatever awaited her after this. Would God accept her into heaven? Would He grant her access to paradise? She wondered if she'd done enough, but if so, why was He punishing her like this? Why was God making her suffer?

The only explanation she could think of was that maybe He wanted her to understand the pain He'd gone through during his Passion when He'd been persecuted and crucified on the cross.

Of course, what she was going through, as bad as it was, was nothing like the horrors He'd been subjected to. But maybe if she could understand just one-tenth of the pain He'd experienced, maybe that would bring her a little closer to Him.

But, enough was enough, and now all she wanted was for these demons to end it all and let her escape this mortal realm.

As tears fell from her eyes while she contemplated her own mortality, she heard another engine draw close. Tyres crunched on the gravel outside as a vehicle drew near. She could hear voices, too.

"Alright, you're clear. Let's do this."

"Be quick, lads. We need to end this."

"Ready?"

"Yeah, do it."

The garage door swung up with a roar of metal against metal, revealing several dark shadows against the blinding daylight, walking towards her.

Had the time come?

36

Slouching in his chair, Rob faced Scarlett and Nailer in their little pit between three desks to one side of the office. But Rob's attention was drawn across the room to the DCI's office in the corner. Matilda Greenwood, the duty solicitor for Jordan Rigby, was in there with Peter and Frank.

Rob frowned, curious to know what they were discussing and why? Was it something to do with passing information up to the EMSOU leadership? This was a big case, and after the relatively recent murders of much of the Nottinghamshire branch of that unit, maybe they just wanted to keep abreast of things?

Peter had his superiors, just like Rob did, after all.

Still, it bothered him that Matilda was in there with the two people who seemed to dislike Rob the most, outside of Bill, of course. But Matilda was feisty, and he knew she'd stand up to them and whatever they were discussing with her.

Was that the issue, perhaps? Did Peter still want to take the case off Rob? Maybe conduct the interview of Rigby himself? He'd distrusted Rob's ability to handle this case from the start and always seemed keen to insert himself into his place. One of the things that Rob knew for sure about Peter was his naked ambition. From day one, he was focused on climbing that ladder and rising through the ranks. He remembered how Peter had chaffed under the leadership of DCI Pilgrim, and after Pilgrim lost his girlfriend to that Doll Killer psycho and taken time off, Peter was quick to insert himself as the logical choice as the next DCI.

The thing is, it worked. It wasn't long before Pilgrim was off down to Surrey, making a new start, and Peter was stepping into the position of Detective Chief Inspector. For Rob, it was never about rising through the ranks. He actually had little interest in becoming a DCI. Paperwork held little appeal to him, and he preferred to be out there, making a difference. He was very much like Pilgrim in that way, which was why they'd got on so well but clashed with Peter.

Rob let his upper lip curl in disgust at Peter's corporate one-up-man-ship and hoped that whatever bullshit he was feeding to Matilda about the case or him in particular, she didn't believe.

"Wakey wakey," Scarlett said, snapping her fingers at Rob to bring him back into the here and now. "Are you in there?"

"Sorry, yeah, I'm here. I was miles away."

Scarlett raised an eyebrow and glanced over to the office, where Matilda could clearly be seen. "I can see that."

"What were you talking about?" Rob asked, keen to divert Scarlett's attention.

"I was just saying," Nailer began, "how we should be happy with all this, but I just can't bring myself to feel good about bringing Rigby in."

"Yeah, I know how you feel," Rob agreed. "Rigby is a good catch. He ticks a lot of boxes, but something about him just doesn't feel right, does it?"

"I don't know," Nailer replied. "Maybe. But I think I'd feel a lot better if we had Lorraine back."

"That's it for me," Scarlett agreed. "That's the issue completely. Where the hell is she? We need to find her. Rigby can't have done this himself. Viv told us there were more guys when they took Lorraine and Spencer. He must have been working with others, but who? Was it the Valley Boyz, or someone else?"

"I agree," Rob confirmed, "but there's more to it than that. Something about this just feels wrong. Rigby is a great catch, and I'm convinced he's part of this, but we're missing something beyond finding Lorraine. I mean, who tipped the gang off about the raid, and who leaked the location of our witness?" Rob lowered his voice as he aired this last issue.

The other two nodded in agreement.

"If we can find Lorraine, I'll be happy," Scarlett said. "We can find the corrupt copper once we have her."

Rob agreed. "She's the priority, for sure."

"Don't forget the new body we discovered, either," Nailer joined in. "We need to know how *they* fit into all this too."

"The loose ends just keep on coming, don't they," Rob agreed as he heard the door to the DCI's office go. He looked up to see Matilda stride over with Peter and Frank in tow. Rob stood up and smiled. He caught Scarlett's knowing expression out the corner of his eye but ignored it.

"Sergeant Loxley, DCI Nailer," Matilda greeted them and then offered Scarlett her hand. "I don't think we've met before."

"DC Scarlett Stutely," she replied, shaking the offered hand. "It's a pleasure."

"Nice to meet you."

"I hear Rigby is waiting for you," Peter said, cutting through the courteous greetings. He sounded frustrated, and the annoyed look he was working hard to keep off his face was leaking through.

"Indeed he is," Matilda agreed.

Rob nodded. "Of course, sir... Oh, holy shit, Frank, what happened to you?" He was standing behind the DCI as if hiding what looked like scratches across his face. A couple of Steri Strips helped to seal up where the scratches had broken the skin on his cheek and forehead. One of his eyes was bright red too.

"Oh, it's nothing. Just a hostile detainee."

"No shit."

"Rob," Peter cut in, "Scarlett, please accompany Miss Greenwood down to the interview suite and see what Mr Rigby has to say for himself, will you?"

"Of course," Rob relented and picked up his notes. Scarlett did the same.

"Good luck," Nailer said.

Peter grunted in annoyance and shot Nailer a cold glare. They've never seen eye to eye over the years, most likely due to Nailer's unwavering support of Rob.

Bill was the same and didn't have much time for Nailer, unless he was grilling him for info.

"You need to bring this home, Loxley. We need to end this. The brass won't stand for any more messing about after the fuck ups of the raid, the expenses and…stuff. Find out where Lorraine is so we can tie a bow on this and send it up the river to the CPS."

"I'll do my best, sir."

"Good. Now get to it." Peter grimaced and then turned away, leading Frank back to his office.

"Ready for this?" Matilda asked.

"Rob's always ready," Scarlett said with a grin. "Aren't you."

Rob frowned, sensing a hidden meaning, but brushed it off. "Lead the way."

Leaving the office behind, they made their way along the corridor and down the wide stairway.

"How's things?" Matilda asked him.

"Oh, you know," Rob replied offhandedly. "This case is breaking my back, and I'm dealing with the usual crap, but at least we seem to be making progress now."

"That's good."

"How's Rigby?"

Matilda slowed and glanced back. "Now, now. You know I can't talk to you about that." He detected a hit of a smile in there.

"I was just curious."

"Really? Well, what I can say is that—and this pissed your DCI off no end—Rigby asked for you, specifically."

"Me?"

"Him?" Scarlett added.

Rob shot Scarlett an offended look. "Oi!"

Matilda shrugged. "I don't know why."

"Did Peter want to conduct this interview himself?" Rob asked, curious to know if his instincts were right."

"He may have been angling for that before I hit him with Rigby's request and recommended that we humour him."

"I see," Rob replied as he focused on the middle distance and considered this. Why would Jordan Rigby want to speak to him specifically? He didn't know Rigby from Adam and had no link to him that he knew of. "Do you know why?"

"Nope. I'll leave that for you to work out."

"Thanks." He glanced back to Scarlett, who shrugged, apparently as in the dark as he felt. They walked the rest of the way down to the interview suite, where Matilda led the way to Rigby's room. She didn't hesitate and walked straight in. Rob relieved the officer guarding Rigby, and they all took their seats around the table in the centre of the room, where Rigby was already sitting.

Getting right down to business, Rob got the recorder going, introduced everyone, and reminded Rigby of his rights.

"I'm going to start with the most pressing question I have, and I want you to seriously consider answering this truthfully and honestly because if you do, it will stand you in good stead when this goes to court. Where is Lorraine Winslow?"

Jordan sighed, and glanced up at him. They shared a look for a moment, with Rob searching the young man's eyes, hoping that he might find some answers there, but Rigby's eyes were dark and haunted. This was someone who'd seen more than anyone should, and the scars on his soul were clear to see. Those dark eyes seemed to stare into the depths of Rob's mind as if they could see into him and read his innermost thoughts.

But then he looked away again, back to the table, and they were no longer the pain-filled pits they had been just a moment ago. They were just sad and defeated.

He said nothing.

"You're not being very helpful, I see."

"You know where she is," Scarlett said. "We know you do. Your van was used to kidnap her and Spencer, wasn't it? You were there that night, weren't you?"

He stared at the table.

"We need to find her, Jordan," Rob said. "This will be so much worse for you if she dies."

Again, he said nothing.

"What about the body we found in the freezer? Who's that, Jordan? Would you care to shed some light on that for us? Did you kill him?"

Rigby didn't reply.

"Miss Greenwood here said you asked for me specifically. You wanted me to conduct this interview, which I'm more than happy to do. But why, and why dodge my questions? If you wanted me, surely you must have something to say to me."

Rigby smiled and spoke for the first time. The sadness was gone, replaced with cruelty and mischief. "Finally, you ask the right question. And yes, I do. My message is simple. Don't venture too far from a phone."

"A phone?"

Rigby smiled but clammed up again, saying nothing more. Rob repeated his earlier questions, wondering if he'd reveal Lorraine's location now, but he didn't do any of that. He simply remained quiet and composed and said nothing.

It was a while later when Rob's phone suddenly vibrated in his pocket. Annoyed, Rob discreetly removed it from his pocket and glanced at the caller ID. It was Nailer.

He nearly dismissed it but then thought better of it.

"One moment," he said and got up. "I'd better take this." He couldn't help but notice the smile on Rigby's face as he went to leave the room.

Once outside, with the door closed, he answered the call. "Hey, what's up?"

"Rob. We've had a phone call. It's Lloyd Bristow. Curby. He's on the line and wants to talk to you, and only you."

"Me?"

"Yes, you. Right now."

What the hell was so special about him today?

37

"Come on," Rob said as he marched away from the interview room after having made a hasty exit with a promise of return. Scarlett was with him as he hustled back to the stairwell and started up.

"What's going on?" Scarlett asked. "What happened?"

"Curby called and wants to speak to me."

She frowned for a moment. "Curby? You mean the gang leader? What the hell does he want?"

"I've no idea, but after what Rigby just said, I think there's more going on here than we know."

"Aaah, right," Scarlett mused. "So you're thinking that we play their little game for now and see where it leads." It was a statement more than a question.

"Exactly," Rob confirmed. "That gang is involved in this somehow, and I want to know how. And who knows, it might lead to Lorraine."

"That's a possibility," she agreed, nodding along. "Alright, let's do this."

He had no idea what these guys were playing at or where they were going with this, but his priority was Lorraine. He needed to focus on finding her, no matter what it took, and if that included playing Curby's little game, so be it. He felt sure that Peter or Bill would take issue with them walking out of the interview room, but he didn't care. This was more important. A woman's life was on the line, and he needed to save her.

They were back in the office in moments, striding over to where Nailer was holding the phone. Close by, Tony Darby was watching with his arms crossed and a face like a slapped arse.

"Is it one of your criminal mates on the line?" Tony asked as Rob marched to his desk.

Frustrated with the question, Rob shrugged and called his bluff. "Sounds like it."

Tony scoffed at him. Rob felt sure he heard him say the word 'scum', but he couldn't be sure as Tony walked away.

"You're sure it's Curby?" Rob asked Nailer.

"No. I'm not. But based on the voice and what he said, I think it's likely."

"Any idea what he's up to. This is a bloody circus."

"Nope. Just focus on Lorraine. It's her we need to save."

Rob gave his mentor a brief nod and took the receiver. "Are we recording this?"

"Of course. Ready?"

"Go for it."

Nailer tapped the 'hold' button.

Placing the handset to his ear, Rob took a breath and composed himself before speaking. "I'm Rob Loxley. I hear you asked for me."

"Give me your email."

Surprised by the abruptness of Curby's reply, Rob took a moment to process what the young man had said before he managed to formulate a reply. "And why would I do that?" He needed to get Curby talking and keep him on the line. If he could somehow get this gang leader on-side, even just briefly, they might find a way to save Lorraine.

"Give me your email," the voice repeated, resisting Rob's attempt to get him to talk. Tensing at the request and feeling reluctant to just let him have what he wanted, Rob decided to try and engage him a little more.

"Look, I'll give you my email address if that's what you want, but first, you have to do something for me. I need two things. First, I need to know who I'm talking to. If this is Curby, I need proof of it. And secondly, I want to know if Lorraine is okay."

The voice on the end of the line grunted. "You know who I am. I spoke to you as you left Rigby's house today and told you that you had the wrong man."

"You did, but others could have heard that. I could be speaking to any of your friends or the onlookers."

"I also know you found a bow and arrow in Rigby's house, and I saw you a few days ago when you arrested Brendon Marsh."

Rob nodded, satisfied that this was most likely to be Curby, or at least someone very close to him. "Okay, fine. It's you."

"Email."

Rob sighed, aware that Curby had probably already given him more than he wanted. It wasn't the piece of information that Rob really needed, but it was something, at least. In a show of good faith, Rob gave Curby his email, speaking clearly and spelling it out afterwards. "There, you've got my email. Now I need to know if Lorraine is okay. I need some proof."

"Two, five, eight, zero," Curby said and hung up.

"Wha…? Oh." Rob sighed. "He's gone."

"Really?" Nailer asked, a look of shock on his face. "That was quick."

"Yeah. Weird. All he wanted was my email, and then he gave me a four-digit number. Two, five, eight, zero. That was it. He said the numbers once and hung up."

"Bizarre."

"A four-digit number?" Scarlett asked, sounding curious and thoughtful. "Like a pin code?"

"That would be my guess," Rob agreed. "Some kind of security code, maybe?"

"What do we know of that needs a code?" Nailer asked.

"Well, it must be something Curby knows we have access to. Something of his, maybe?"

"Or something of Rigby's, perhaps?" Scarlett suggested. She had an idea, he could tell by the tone of her voice.

"Go on," Rob urged.

"Could it be Rigby's phones? We confiscated two of them. Maybe the code unlocks one."

"Meaning there's something on one of them that Curby wants us to see," Rob said, expanding on her thought. "Where are the phones now?"

"Exhibits," Scarlett replied.

Rob gave her a nod. "Okay, I want to do this with a minimum of fuss. Scarlett, can you head down to Exhibits and sign out those phones. Bring them to me, and we'll see if our theory holds water. You know where you're going?"

"Pretty sure, yeah. Second floor, right?"

"Right."

"I'm on it." Scarlett noted down the item numbers from her PC and strode out of the office without a backward glance.

"Do you trust her?" Nailer asked in hushed tones once she was gone.

"Scarlett?" He didn't need to think about it much. She'd already proven the strength of her character to him, and he was impressed with her ability as a detective. She also hadn't prejudged him based on the remarks of others, and that went a long way in Rob's eyes. "Yeah, I trust her. Absolutely. I miss having Nick on the team, but honestly, with the way I feel about things now, I'd want both with me going forward. They each have their strengths, and I think they'd complement each other quite well, too."

"That's a ringing endorsement."

"One hundred percent."

Nailer smiled.

38

Walking gingerly around the corner, along the glass front of the Premier Inn hotel on the corner, Viv gazed across the large roundabout. Perfectly manicured grass and shrubs covered its central island, creating a tiny shock of green in the urban sprawl, while cars swung around the junction in a constant clockwise parade.

To her right, people were waiting for the little green man to appear and give them permission to cross the road.

But it was the building on the other side she was interested in. The large L-shaped red-brick building with its darkened windows and glass topped entrance dominated her view and loomed over the passing traffic. This was Nottingham Central Police Station, where Detective Loxley supposedly worked. But was he in there, and could she trust him?

A spike of pain lanced through her side as she shifted her weight, making her tense and hiss in agony. She leaned against one of the white pillars outside the hotel and waited for the pain to subside.

Viv closed her eyes and saw flashes of the man who'd attacked her in her hotel room. That so-called detective had been trying to kill her, of that she was certain. He'd beaten her nearly senseless before she'd somehow managed to kick, claw and hurt him enough that she managed to escape his grip and run.

Those moments were a blur of hotel corridors and shocked people as she rode the wave of adrenaline to get out.

It was only later, once she was far away from the hotel and her adrenal gland had stopped pumping, that the pain set in. She'd had broken ribs before, and this felt very much like that.

Raising her head, she let her eyes sweep over the police building and nearly turned away. The comfort of the shadows and the many places she could hide sounded especially inviting against the prospect of going into that building and potentially being confronted by her attacker. Or worse, such as finding out that detective Loxley wasn't the respectable man she hoped he was.

But as she went to turn away, an image of Spencer flashed behind her eyes. She saw him smiling at her in happier times. She saw him offer her some food he'd bought with money he'd scrounged that day. Memories of laughter and friendship blossomed before her mind's eye. Then she remembered him being hit with a baseball bat and thrown into the back of the white van.

She had a chance to do the right thing here, to help her friend and stop others from suffering the same fate. With her mind made up, she set off for the station, crossing the roads until she finally turned towards the front door and walked into the reception area.

"Can I help you?" the man on the desk said as she approached.

"I need to see Detective Loxley, please."

"Loxley?"

"That's right. He works 'ere, I think. I need to see 'im. Now please."

"Okay, well, if you'd like to take a seat, I'll see if he'll come and see you. Okay?"

After a moment of hesitation, she nodded. He was probably a busy man, after all. Spotting a seat close to the corner of the lobby, she walked over and lowered herself into it as carefully as she could. Everything ached, and she was getting almost constant daggers of pain in her side, which was painful to touch. She'd need medical help soon.

With her head bowed, she sat stock still and waited, hoping that she'd see a familiar, friendly face soon.

"Miss," the receptionist called over to her. "He's coming down."

Viv gave the man a brief nod and waited, hoping it would be who she hoped.

A minute later, Detective Loxley appeared through a side door. He spotted her and strode over. "Viv. Where have you been? Are you okay? You look... You don't look great."

"I'll survive. Don't worry about me." He's already done enough for her. She didn't want to put more problems on him.

"Are you sure? What happened to you?"

"I was attacked."

He looked shocked. "What? In the hotel room?"

"He said he was a detective and that you sent him."

"I didn't send anyone other than Scarlett, but you'd disappeared when she turned up. The room had been trashed."

"I know. Sorry."

"That's okay," Rob comforted her. He was glancing around, looking suspiciously at the other officers in the room. Did he suspect that her attacker was in the building like she did? "So, he said he was a detective?"

"That's what he said, that he worked with you."

"Do you know who it was? Did he give you his name?" He sounded interested.

Viv shook her head. She had no idea who her attacker was, but his face had been seared into her mind. It wasn't something she was about to forget. "I'd recognise him if I saw him again, though."

"Good, because you might need to identify him. But I need you somewhere safe, first." He gave her an appraising look. "Are you sure you're okay?"

She put on a brave face and tried to ignore the pain. "I'm just a little stiff. I'm okay. Where are we going?"

She didn't feel in any mood to object and slowly got to her feet. Rob helped her up and guided her through a security door he opened with his ID card. They walked into what looked like a seldom used breakroom with a sofa, coffee table, and drinks facilities. Viv went directly to the sofa and started going through the process of getting herself laid down. It was a difficult and painful series of steps, but she felt exhausted and needed to lie down.

Rob helped her, and once she felt settled, he got back up. He looked at her with an appraising eye. "I'm going to get someone to come and look at you. I'll be back soon, okay?"

"Sure, take your time." She didn't feel in any mood to argue and tried her best to relax. It was a losing battle.

39

This case was getting weirder by the minute, Scarlett thought as she reached the second floor and approached the exhibits office with its attached storeroom. It felt like she was breaking the rules by coming down here and requesting the phones, even though she had every right to look at any exhibits that might help their case.

She knew this as well as any detective did, but still, the feeling persisted, and she couldn't help but imagine herself as some kind of spy or something, sneaking into the bowels of a police station to get what she wanted. Rob's conspiratorial behaviour, the games of the gang members, and the knowledge that there was a corrupt officer somewhere in the building no doubt contributed to the feeling that she was doing something she shouldn't.

Smiling at the ridiculousness of it all, she turned into the office to find one of the building's many civilian managers sitting at his desk and clicking his mouse. The man looked up, a little startled by Scarlett's entrance.

"Good morning," Scarlett began, making sure to sound bright and perky, as if this was the most normal thing in the world. But the moment she spoke, she felt like she was overdoing it and sounding even more obvious than ever.

"Oh, hello duck. Can I help?"

"Yes indeed." Settling her nerves, she dialled it down with a cough. Why was she nervous? This was crazy. "I need to check a couple of items out of storage."

"Have you got the details?"

She handed the man the slip of paper with the item numbers on. He checked it and muttered something approvingly.

"Aaah, these have only just come in." He rose from his seat and moved to the door leading into the adjoining locked storeroom.

"That's right. Sorry. I don't mean to mess you about."

"No, it's no problem. Makes it easier. I know where they are. I'll only be a minute if you just want to wait here."

"Sure." Scarlett let her eyes drift over the walls and desk while she waited for the man to reappear, noting the meticulously tidy office with everything in its place. After a few moments, the man reappeared holding two clear plastic evidence bags. He got her to sign them out before he handed the items over with a friendly smile. "There you go. Two phones. I hope they're useful."

"Me too, thanks." She eyed the two devices through the clear plastic.

"Are you new around here?"

Scarlett tensed, sensing a chat-up line. "Yeah," she answered cautiously. "I just moved to the area."

"It's the accent. You're from somewhere down south, right?"

"Surrey."

"Of course. It's the plum in your throat. Unmistakable. I like the accent, actually. It's nice. Makes us sound all common, like."

She smiled nervously, eager to get away. "Your accent's just fine. Look, I've got to get back..."

"Oh, of course. Sorry. I didn't mean to..."

"That's okay."

"I'll see you later?"

She shrugged, already walking out. "Probably."

Feeling like she'd had a lucky escape and already dreading her next trip to Exhibits, she made her way back towards the stairwell, looking at the two phones. One was a recent model of the iPhone, but the other was a cheap burner that looked like it had done the rounds, complete with a physical keypad. If she had to guess, she thought it was likely that the iPhone was Rigby's personal phone, and the cheapo was reserved for his less reputable business dealings. She started up the steps.

As she examined the pair of devices, she noticed that the keycode Curby had given them was ridiculously simple. The numbers were the middle row from top to bottom, Two, Five,

Eight, Zero. Scarlett rolled her eyes at the simplicity of the security code. They'd probably have cracked it in a matter of hours.

"Well, well, well, Miss Stutely. What have you got there?"

She looked up to see Inspector Bill Rainault above her, blocking her way.

"Evidence," she remarked bluntly. It was none of his business, after all.

He narrowed his eyes as if assessing her, sizing her up. She felt like an insect being pulled apart by a cruel kid. She felt uncomfortable under his gaze and shifted her weight.

"Do you trust Rob?"

Scarlett sighed. "This again. I thought I told you last time, I don't give a flying toss what you think my opinion should be."

"So, he's not told you why people like me hold him in a certain regard, I take it?"

"Why should he? He doesn't have to explain himself to anyone."

Bill scoffed at her statement. "I beg to differ on that point."

"I'm sure you do, but if you don't mind..." She took a step up, aiming to walk past, but Bill sidestepped into her path.

"You shouldn't trust him. His family are criminals."

Scarlett relaxed back with an exasperated sigh. "And?"

"And that doesn't give you pause? It doesn't worry you that you might be working for a corrupt copper?"

Scarlett screwed up her lips and tensed. They knew full well someone was working against them on the force, and the likes of Bill and others seemed determined to cast Rob in that role. Were they right? Was Rob the one working for the gang? She didn't think that was likely when he was the one being humiliated by the botched raid. "He's not corrupt, and if he has family members who are criminals, I very much doubt he has much to do with them."

"He says he's been estranged from them for over twenty years, but…"

"Well, there you bloody well go, then. There's no issue. If he's not had any contact with them for that long, then he's not a risk, is he?"

"Only if you believe him. He's not exactly going to advertise his links to organised crime when he's a useful pawn to them, is he? He's going to keep it to himself, remaining hidden and useful."

"I think you're reaching, frankly."

"Whose side are you on, Scarlett. That's the real question. It's the question you need to ask yourself, and you need to think carefully about your answer. Are you sure Rob didn't tip off the gang about the raid? Can you be certain of it? Okay, yeah, he got reprimanded, but he's still here. He's still working in the building."

The implications of his words staggered her. "Are you saying that Superintendent Landon is in on this too?"

Bill seemed to consider this for a moment. "In on it? No. Duped by him? Blinded by his charm, like you? Maybe."

"Charm?" Scarlett couldn't help but scoff at Bill's comment. Rob seemed kind, but he was a bit of a blunt instrument. "Yeah, right."

"We all know of Rob's family links," Bill continued. "Me, Peter, Frank and more. I think you need…"

"No!" She stepped closer, drawing up to him and standing her ground. "You listen to me, sir. I won't put up with this kind of harassment, and I'll make a formal complaint if you're not careful. I'll make my own judgements regarding Rob and will not be badgered into agreeing with you just because you think I should. I don't appreciate you spreading rumours like this, and I doubt Rob does, either. You have no proof of what you're accusing him of, and he's passed police vetting, probably several times by this point, and unless they've flagged anything up, which I doubt, then I think you need to back the fuck off and let him do his job. Now get out of my way. I have a missing woman to find. Did you forget about her, sir?" She barged past him and strode up the stairwell, seething with anger but pleased with her little rant.

It felt good to unload. But she also realised she'd been quite rude to a superior officer, which probably wasn't the best idea in the world.

She'd only been up here for a few short weeks, and already she was insulting her superiors. Not a great start, admittedly, but he'd pushed her incessantly for several days, and she'd just had enough by this point. Bill needed to hear some harsh truths and realise what he was doing was not okay, even if it was ostensibly in service of the law and the police—although she questioned that too. Corruption in the police needed to be weeded out, and she had no issue with that, but this felt more like persecution.

She hoped there wouldn't be any official pushback from this, and somehow doubted there would be.

Bill's personal convictions were obviously dear to him, and he wasn't about to let them go any time soon. Was he right about Rob and who he was? It wasn't impossible, but it also wasn't the man she'd been working with these past few days.

She was intrigued, though, and as she returned to the office, she found herself wanting to know more about Rob's past and his family.

40

This was it. This was the end, Lorraine thought as the car juddered and threw her around in the back seat. She was hemmed by someone on either side, crammed between them still with her hands tied painfully behind her back. The hood they'd thrown over her head threw her world into darkness, but did little to warm her naked body. She could only guess where they were going. All she could see through the fibres of the hood were lights and darks as they drove.

Where were they going?

Would it be the same place they had taken Spencer? It was the only explanation. This would be the end for her, and she'd leave Graham alone in the world. She remembered how they'd hooded Spencer when they'd come for him. This all felt far too similar for her to think it was anything else.

She prayed softly, reciting the Lord's prayer and mixing it with her own pleas for Him to help her and save her from all this.

If only He'd listen.

"Are you sure about this, boss?"

The others in the car with her had said hardly anything in their drive through the city streets, so when the one on her right spoke up, it was jarring.

"Course I'm fuckin' sure."

"Archer's not gonna like this."

"Like I gave a shit what Archer thinks…" The second voice was coming from the front passenger seat. The man laughed. "Archer. What a fuckin' joke."

"But…"

"Shut up. I couldn't care less what he thinks, and for fuck's sake, just say his name. I'm not calling him Archer anymore."

"But, we shouldn't. He said not to."

"Are you fuckin' deaf? I said I don't care anymore. I'm done with him. So fuckin' done."

"I thought he was useful."

The man in front of her laughed. "He's a fuckin' liability, is what he is. He's bringing too much heat on us. And all because you fucked up."

"What? No, we didn't!"

She heard the man in the front shift in his seat before shouting back at his friend. "Yes, you fuckin' did. All this shit, it's all your fault. If you'd done as you'd been asked and just picked up a homeless dude, none of this would have happened. I'd still have a Trap House, still have that car and not be dealing with all this heat from the Five-Oh. But no! You had to go and get all creative and kidnap this bitch too. She's not some homeless twat that no one would notice going missing, is she? She's a fuckin' housewife and a bloody pillar of the community or some dumb shit. Well fuckin' done, you absolute cock-womble."

"Don't forget the body they found." This new voice came from the driver's seat.

"Oh yeah, how can I forget that?" the front passenger replied. "How the hell does someone get caught out burying a body in the middle of Sherwood mother-fuckin' Forest? I mean, what the actual fuck? I'm surrounded by cock-sucking idiots, clearly."

"Sorry, boss."

"Fuck off." He sounded very upset.

"I just thought, what with him being… You know…"

"A pig?" A policeman? They work with a policeman? If they could have seen her face, they'd have seen a very shocked expression. She remained quiet, and listened.

"Yeah. I just thought…"

"But that's just it, isn't it? You didn't think, did you? You got cocky. No. Hell no. He's no longer useful to us, so I'm done. I want nothing more to do with him."

"Can we do that?"

"He doesn't own us, idiot. We own him, and I say we're done with him. Now shut up. I've got some texts to send."

Minutes passed as Lorraine processed what she'd heard. Some of it didn't make sense, but she had picked up the comment about the policeman who they apparently owned, much to her surprise. She thought that only happened in TV shows. The other thing she picked up on was the body in Sherwood Forest, which confirmed her biggest fear. That body could only be one person, as far as she was concerned.

Spencer.

She'd been right all along. They'd killed him. Would that be her fate too?

"I'm still not sure about this," the man on her right said.

"Shut up. We need to get rid of her. We're doing this."

Lorraine tensed. This was it, the time had come.

The car screeched to a stop, and she heard doors open. They grabbed her and hauled her out.

41

The First Aider was on their way to Viv with instructions to do whatever they needed to make sure she was cared for, including taking her to a hospital if need be. He had the distinct feeling that Viv was hurting more than she was letting on but was hiding it for some reason. He wasn't sure why, but was keen to get her help while he focused on the developing case.

Satisfied that Viv would be okay, Rob headed back upstairs.

Hopefully, Scarlett had retrieved the phones, so they could try the PIN code Curby had provided them. Unlocking one of them had to reveal something useful, maybe something that would lead them to Lorraine and allow them to save her life before it was too late.

Events were moving fast, and he had a feeling they were on the brink of finding something key that might just break the case wide open.

He could only hope.

As he raced back upstairs, Rob wondered who had attacked Viv? Was it the corrupt cop working in this building? If it was, how would they get Viv to identify him, and what would that mean for this case?

He didn't know the answers to this, but for now, he needed to be careful who found out Viv was in the building. If the informant heard she was here, they might try and silence her for good. He couldn't allow that and disliked leaving Viv alone, but she'd be safe for the time being. The civilian First Aider he'd tasked with checking her out was a friend and wasn't an officer of the law, so she didn't fit the profile of the corrupt cop. Viv would be fine for now until he saw where the case was going.

Reaching his floor, Rob marched back into the office on the heels of Scarlett, who'd returned with the two phones confiscated from Rigby. Both devices were still in their plastic bags as Scarlett placed them on the desk. Rob glanced between the phones as Nailer joined them.

"I'm guessing burner and personal phone," Scarlett remarked, pointing to the iPhone second.

"Undoubtedly," Rob agreed and picked up the bag containing the burner, and pressed the power button to turn it on.

"Where did you disappear off too?" Scarlett asked.

"I was about to ask the same question," Nailer joined in.

Rob leaned in close, keeping his voice low. "Viv is downstairs. She just turned up at reception."

"Holy shit," Scarlett hissed. "You're kidding. Is she okay?"

"She looks beaten up. She says she was attacked in her hotel room but managed to escape."

"Good for her."

"Who attacked her?" Nailer asked.

"Someone claiming to be a detective," Rob said as he eyed the device in his hand.

"Shit on a stick," Scarlett exclaimed.

"Does she need medical attention?"

"I've sent a First Aider down to her, someone I've known for a while and trust, but I think Viv might need hospital treatment."

"Okay, Let me know if I can do anything," Nailer replied.

"Let's keep this between us for the moment," Rob suggested. "I want to know what this PIN number does." Rob held up the phone just as it finished booting up. "Let's try it."

Rob keyed in the PIN, and the device suddenly unlocked, revealing the basic home screen of the device.

"I'm in." Scarlett and Nailer crowded around him. "What should we look at first?"

"Call logs," Nailer suggested. "Let's see who Rigby's been talking to."

Rob opened the main menu and navigated into recent calls. He found a mix of numbers, but the one that stood out was listed simply as Archer, and there were a bunch of calls between this phone and whoever Archer was.

"Let's check his messages," Rob suggested and quickly navigated into the phone's inbox, where he found Archer in the list of message threads. He clicked into it and started scrolling, skim reading the messages as he went. "Look," Rob said, pointing to one of the recent ones. "This one says, 'We've got two more targets for you. One for now, one for later.' I bet I can guess who those targets are."

"Spencer and Lorraine," Rob replied, agreeing.

"That's sick," Scarlett commented.

"So, what do we do?" Scarlett asked. "We need to find out who this Archer is."

"That's easy," Nailer said. "We call the number."

Rob considered the idea. Was it really that easy? He wanted to make the call but found himself hesitating, wondering what it might mean, depending on who answered the call.

"What's going on here?" Rob turned to see DCI Orleton walking out of his office, followed by Frank. Across the room, Tony and several of the other investigators sitting close by looked up. "Are those Rigby's phones?"

"Yeah." Rob's gaze drifted over to Frank and the scratch marks on his face. Frank glared back at him from over the DCI's shoulder. He didn't look happy.

Viv's account of being attacked and fighting back to escape flashed through his mind. The man who'd attacked her had claimed to be a detective. Was he actually a detective and knew precise details from the case? It would be a damn sight easier to convince Viv to open the door if they could say that Rob Loxley sent them, for instance.

If he was right, then the informant was closer than Rob thought.

"We were just going over something," Rob explained, trying to remain vague and calm, as his mind raced with possibilities. Was it Frank? Was he the bent officer feeding intel to the gang? Those wounds on his face were certainly fresh, and he had access to all the details of the case.

Rob felt his own phone buzz in his pocket. He plucked it out with his off hand, glad for the interruption, and glanced at Scarlett. Her face was equally guarded, but she noticed Rob checking his phone and moved to engage the DCI.

"Like what?" Peter asked.

"Well," Scarlett began as Rob opened the email that had just pinged through. It was from a generic Gmail account with a meaningless series of numbers and letters before the @.

But it was the subject line and the contents of the message that grabbed Rob's attention.

Subject: From Curby, read now!
Message: Find the killer. Call the number.

He spotted a couple of files attached to the email as he considered the suggestion from Curby.

"There might be something useful on there," Scarlett prevaricated, stalling for time.

"But you don't have the code to get in, so why bother?" Peter sounded dismissive, while behind him, Frank looked concerned, his eyes locked on Rigby's phone.

He knew.

This was it. He was sure of it. Holding Rigby's bagged phone in one hand and his own mobile in the other, Rob decided to go for it. "We have the code, and we've got into the phone, so all I need to do is hit call on this number to find out who their informant is." Rob's eyes were locked on Frank as he spoke, challenging him to protest. As the words sank in, Frank's eyes bugged with panic. The game was up. He knew it.

"Wait..." Frank exclaimed.

Rob hit call on Rigby's phone and waited for it to connect. "Why? Something wrong, Frank?"

"You don't know what you're doing," Frank pleaded.

Rob heard a buzzing coming from nearby. It took a moment for him to place the sound, but as the ringtone increased in volume, it soon became clear it was coming from Peter's office.

Confused, Rob frowned at Peter. "What?"

Peter backed off with Frank beside him, his face a mask of defiance.

"You?" Rob accused him, meeting Peter's guilty look. "What the hell?"

"It's not what you think."

"And what am I thinking, Guv?"

"Put the phone down."

Feeling intensely curious, Rob lifted his personal phone into his eye line and opened the first video attachment in Curby's email. "What will I see on this attachment from Curby?"

"Don't!" There was a warning in Peter's voice, but also fear.

The screen filled with a moving image. Someone was secretly filming a scuffle on the floor of a disused building.

"I'll kill you, I'll fucking kill you." Rob recognised the voice coming from the video.

The image zoomed in. The man doing the strangling was Peter. It was a violent and brutal attack, and Frank was standing, watching and doing nothing to stop him. "Pete! Guv! That's enough."

The noise of the recording filled the now silent room. In the video, Peter was furious as his victim fell limp before Frank pulled him off the corpse.

"That's what you get, you bastard," Peter yelled in the recording. "That's what you deserve." Ranting and swearing at the unmoving corpse, Peter raged as if he held the dead man personally responsible for what he'd done. In the video, Peter calmed, and fell silent, huffing and puffing. He pulled away from the unmoving body on the floor, and just stared at it.

"Pete, you've killed him," Frank said in the recording.

Rob looked up as the video ended. Peter and Frank had backed off towards his office.

"I know what you're thinking," Peter said. "I can explain."

"You killed someone," Rob said. "This is very clear video evidence."

"That man killed several innocent people, including children," Peter explained as he continued to back slowly away. There was very clear panic in his eyes. "He slaughtered an entire family."

Rob didn't care what the explanation was. "Someone filmed this without you knowing. So let me guess, they blackmailed you?"

"It wasn't my fault."

A sudden thought occurred to Rob. "Is this the body we found in the freezer? This man you killed? Did they keep him on ice as blackmail?"

"I can explain," Peter spluttered.

"I doubt it." Rob grimaced as he glanced back to the phone screen, and the other attached files. "Do I dare look at the other videos and images I have here?"

"Fucking bastard," Peter hissed.

Rob narrowed his eyes at the DCI, and then opened one of the attached images. It was a photo, taken out in the countryside at night. Lit up by the headlamps of several cars, a naked man knelt on the floor, bruised and cuffed. Standing above him were several other men, including one with a recurve bow, his face lit up for all to see.

It was Peter.

Rob wished he could say he was surprised, but he wasn't. "You're the Archer. You killed Spencer."

Peter tensed, pressing his lips into a thin line as he glared at Rob. His whole demeanour changed, going from pleading and trying to explain it to something more visceral. He was an injured predator, cornered and desperate, which made him dangerous.

"We can talk about this," Rob suggested, taking a non-threatening stance. "We can work this out."

"What is there to work out? I'm done for. I won't escape this. You know what happens to cops that go to prison, right?"

"Wait. Just wait," Rob pleaded, seeing the panic in the man's eyes. Frank was the same and clearly terrified. He wasn't sure what they would do. "Calm down."

Peter stared at him, then turned and ran into his office. Frank sprinted right running for his desk past a shocked Tony Darby. People yelled and screamed. Rob charged forward with Scarlett and Nailer beside him. At the door to Peter's office, Rob saw him reach into his desk and retrieve something dark and metallic. He lifted a small snub-nosed revolver and pointed it at Rob. Glancing right, Frank grabbed an X26 Taser from somewhere around his desk and aimed it at Nailer.

"I'm not going to prison," Peter said, drawing Rob's attention. "You can't make me. I'll shoot you. I've killed others. Do you think I care if I take you down with me?"

Standing his ground, Rob raised his hands in a calming gesture. "Probably not. I know you're not my biggest fan. But you will never get out of this building. You know that. Armed officers will already be on their way. Killing me will only make it worse."

"Does it matter at this point? Why not go scorched Earth and take you all with me?" With madness in his eyes, Peter walked around his desk, and across his office while Rob backed off.

"You'd really do that, Peter? You'd kill these innocent people?" Peter reached the door to his office as Rob backed away, keeping several metres between them. All around, people gasped and ducked for cover. "They have families like yours. Think of your wife, Carmen, and your kids. What about Bonnie and Ramsey. What will they think of you if you do this? You'll never see them again, I can promise you that."

"Shut up," Peter spat, his voice cracking with emotion as he took a step closer. "Shut the fuck up." Tears fell from Peter's eyes while his shaking hand rattled the gun.

"Give it up," Scarlett added. "We can talk about this. It doesn't have to be this way."

He glanced at Scarlett.

"Listen to her," Rob urged, drawing Peter's attention back to him. "She's right."

"I fucking hate you, you know. You don't deserve to be on this force."

That was a bit rich, given Peter's current actions. But Rob bit his lip to avoid voicing the smart comment on the tip of his tongue. He didn't want to enrage him any further. Instead, he needed to deescalate the situation, not send it spiralling out of control.

"I know," Rob replied, unsure what else he could really say.

"You made my life hell." Peter took another step towards him as Rob held his ground. "This should be the other way around. I should be the one arresting you."

"I doubt you're the only one that feels that way." It was a flippant reply, but maybe some humour would work? He decided to change the subject. "Where did you get the gun? The gang? It doesn't look police issue, so I'm guessing it's a reconditioned one?"

"Who the fuck cares. It'll do the same job."

"Put it down, Peter."

"You're so fucking self-righteous, Loxley. I'm going to enjoy this." He tensed. Rob ducked as the gun bucked in Peter's hand, the report of the gun filling the room, making Rob's ears ring.

Rob hit the floor. People panicked. A second later, as his hearing started to return, he became hyper-aware of his own body and any pain he felt, but there was nothing. Peter had missed. Rob turned to check on Scarlett. She'd ducked behind Rob's desk and gave him a thumbs up when he looked back.

A cry of agony drew Rob's attention back to Peter. He was sitting on the floor holding a bloodied right hand while shrieking in pain. The revolver lay on the floor, forgotten. Rob approached and kicked the gun out of Peter's reach, as Tony stepped up too. Peter's right thumb was basically gone, reduced to a mass of flesh, bone, and gristle by back-firing shrapnel. It was a common enough wound in the criminal fraternity, suffered by those who used cheap reconditioned revolvers that misfired and acted more like a bomb than a gun when they went off.

Having tackled Frank to the floor, Nailer was currently cuffing him.

Someone ran over with a first aid kit, and between them, they managed to stanch the bleeding from Peter's thumb.

Moments later, they had him laid on his back with his bandaged hand in the air. With his uninjured hand cuffed to Tony, Peter hissed and panted against the pain while occasionally asking if they'd called an ambulance.

Scarlett wandered over. "Well done."

Rob smiled. "Thanks. I'm not sure I did much."

"You confronted him. I think that qualifies as something."

"I guess. Thanks."

With Frank in cuffs beside him, Nailer walked over. Frank had a fixed frown on his face and stared at the floor, pointedly ignoring those around him.

"How is he?" Nailer nodded to Peter.

"He'll survive, I think."

"He'd better. We still need to find Lorraine."

"Shit, yeah," Scarlett said. "I'd forgotten with all this going on."

"Good point." Rob wandered over to Peter, and gently kicked his foot. "Peter. Where's Lorraine?"

Peter rolled his eyes. "How the hell should I know?"

"Don't be an idiot now. You know how this works. It's over and withholding information will not go down well in court."

"I told you, I don't know," Peter snapped as if talking to a particularly dense child. "I don't arrange that, never have. But seeing as you're best buddies with Curby now, maybe you can ask him for a favour?"

Rob grimaced. Peter was right about one thing. He could email Curby back and ask. He wanted to do this right, though, with approval from a higher rank.

As more officers entered the room, they cordoned off the DCI's office and started to take control. The situation calmed. Paramedics arrived and tended to Peter's wound before he and Frank were led away.

"Hey," DC Tony Darby said, approaching Rob. "I just want to say I'm sorry. I didn't know. I thought that you were... You know." He sighed. "I was wrong. Turns out that you weren't the corrupt officer, after all."

"Shocker, right?"

"Yeah, sorry."

"That's okay," Rob replied, impressed that Tony would come forward and apologise so quickly. "There's probably a lesson in there, somewhere. But that's for brighter people than me to work out. Go on, off you go. And thank you for your help on this case."

"Cheers. Thanks, Sarge," Tony replied and went on his way.

"Rob," Scarlett called out. She was standing with Nailer and Superintendent Landon, who'd just turned up. Scarlett waved him over.

"Ma'am," Rob said to Landon as he approached. "Hell of a morning."

"So I hear," Landon replied. "Good work on this. I'm impressed."

"Thanks," Rob replied. "This wasn't how I thought it would play out, but at least we have the killer now. Shame we still haven't found Lorraine, though."

"Actually, we have. She was dumped out front on the side of the road just a few minutes ago."

"What? By who?"

"I'm sure we'll find out details soon enough," Landon replied. "Lorraine is quite shaken up, as I'm sure you can understand. She's been taken to the hospital for shock, malnutrition and dehydration. She's been beaten up too."

"At least she's alive." Rob sighed. "That's a relief. Well, looks like we tied up most of the loose ends. I think we deserve a rest after all that."

Landon snorted. "No chance of that, Loxley."

42

Seven Years Ago.

Becoming slowly aware of his surroundings, Peter groaned. What the hell happened? He could taste blood on his lips, and his body ached. His bottom lip was swollen and felt massive, like a balloon about to pop. Opening his eyes, he squinted in the bright light. He'd taken a beating and had apparently blacked out.

His cheek and eye hurt and wouldn't open properly, reminding him of the opening punch Curby had thrown after Peter had lost his temper.

Peter rolled over, and the ground crinkled. It sounded funny. He lay on a hard surface, like concrete, but it was covered in something, like sheets of plastic, maybe?

Peter grunted. "What the hell is this?"

"Get up." It was Curby, but his voice was muffled. There was another sound in the room, too, like a shuffling and mumbling. On stiff arms, he pushed himself up and rubbed his eyes. Memories of Curby hitting him flashed in his mind's eye. It had been a hellish and brutal attack. He'd fallen to the floor, with Curby's voice ringing in his ears.

"Get up, Peter."

"Okay, fine." Snapping out of the daze he'd woken into, Peter went to stand, getting his first look at the rest of the room.

He froze on the spot.

A man was sitting, naked, bruised and bloodied, on a chair in the middle of the room. He was bound and gagged and stared at Peter with terrified eyes. The room itself was a bare, concrete box, with plastic sheeting on the floor, a small table close to the man with tools on it, and little else.

"What's going on?" Peter asked.

"You need to understand something." Curby's voice came from behind a metal door to Peter's right. "There is no getting out of this. I own you. You do everything I say, or I will destroy you. I'll make you watch while Carmen pleads for her life, and the life of her unborn child."

"You wouldn't."

"I can, and you know I will."

"They've done nothing wrong," Peter pleaded.

"Grow up. That's not how this works. I thought there was a brain in that skull of yours. You do as I say, or your loved ones will die, slowly and painfully while you watch. Do you understand?"

Peter slumped where he sat, knowing there was nothing he could do. He was a pawn for Curby to use however he wanted.

"What do you want me to do?"

"Kill him. There's a gun on the table with a single bullet in the chamber. You can end this poor man's life cleanly and quickly. Or, take your own and leave your kids without a father and your wife all alone. But if you do that, I will release the footage of you killing Joe, I will ruin you and your legacy, and then maybe I'll catch up with your pretty wife sometime. Have some fun."

"You wouldn't."

"Wanna try me?"

He didn't. Curby was scum and quite capable of everything he'd just threatened.

In a daze, Peter got to his feet and walked over to the table beside the man, where amongst the other tools, lay a gun. A Glock 17, similar to what the police used. He was familiar enough with it to know how it worked but wasn't really a big fan of guns. He preferred archery, but that was only ever shooting at targets, not people.

Peter lifted the gun, almost surprised by its weight. Gripping the slide, he pulled it back, revealing the glint of brass inside. One bullet, loaded into the chamber. Pressing a button on the side, the magazine dropped out into his other hand, revealing it to be empty. He slapped it back in and looked back down at the man. Sweat dripped from his scalp while wild eyes stared up at him. He cried and pleaded, but the duct tape across his face muffled his words, making them incomprehensible.

Rob closed his eyes, unable to look at the abject terror on the man's face. "Who is he?"

"Does it matter?" Curby replied. "Do it, or I ruin you."

Rob felt his anger and frustration build. Clenching his fist and gritting his teeth, Rob started breathing hard as he steeled his nerves. Killing Joe, the Top Valley Boyz gang member who'd killed an entire innocent family in a case of mistaken identity, was one thing. He deserved it. He got what was coming to him, and Peter didn't regret it, one iota. He only regretted all this, the consequences that followed.

He still wasn't totally sure how Curby had managed to film him killing Joe, but that didn't matter. This was how things were now, and if he wanted to continue being a DCI with an otherwise enviable family life, then certain things needed to be done.

Peter raised the gun, pressed it to the man's head, and fired.

Blood flew, his ears rang, and Peter's life was no longer his.

43

The video ended, freezing on a CCTV image of Peter standing in that small, plastic-lined room, the man he'd shot slumped in the chair, while Peter looked away, his head bowed as he dropped the gun.

Rob couldn't quite believe what he'd seen on this and the other videos and photos that Curby had sent through. The evidence was overwhelming and damning. There was no denying it, and luckily, Peter seemed to accept that.

With Nailer by his side, Rob watched the interview from the viewing room, his eyes flicking between the screens and video feeds coming from the nearby interview suites. He desperately wanted to be in there and ask the questions himself. But Peter was his superior officer, and there were rules about this kind of thing, such as bringing in an officer from another force to take the interview. Rob had been sure to fully brief the interviewing officer and give him copious notes. He wasn't about to let Peter off the hook that easily.

On the screen, Peter sat across from a Lincolnshire Detective, with his representative beside him, taking notes. Rob watched with interest as Peter explained why he'd killed the man in the video.

"The blackmail had just become too much. It had been going on for months by this point, since Joe," Peter said, his head bowed in defeat. "That night, I just lost it and had a go at Curby. But he knocked me out, and the next thing I know, I'm in that room and being forced to murder someone else. That's when I knew my life was over. It didn't belong to me anymore after that. I had to do whatever Curby said, or everything ended."

"Did you ever find out who the man you killed was?"

"No," Peter replied. He looked tired, slumped in his chair with his wrists cuffed on the table. "No idea. I never saw him again after that."

Rob would have preferred to corroborate the killing, but it looked like that would take further investigation, and it wasn't the only loose end. Lloyd 'Curby' Bristow and the Top Valley Boyz were a priority for starters. In Rob's opinion, Curby was getting a little too big for his boots and needed taking down, ideally for something big, so they could send him away for a long time. He'd been helpful with this case and returned Lorraine, but that was because doing so suited him. Make no mistake, though, the man was a monster and ruled that estate of his with an iron fist. But that was all for another day and possibly another unit. Today, they needed to deal with Peter.

"Okay," the interviewing detective replied, referring to his notes. "Let's go back to that first incident. You said the man you strangled was called Joe Moon?"

"That's him," Peter replied. "He was one of Curby's gang, one of the Top Valley Boyz. He was a piece of work too. Violent and brutal with a short fuse and not the highest intelligence. A right little hoodlum."

"Let's go over what led up to that first killing, again. You said he murdered an entire innocent family, the Tindalls, correct?"

"Yeah. We'd been looking to pin something on Joe for ages, and then he went and committed a house invasion on the wrong house. He killed everyone in there. Both parents and two children. It was a massacre. When I finally caught up to him, I was angry and lost control. I regret it to this day. None of this would have happened if Frank had just stopped me."

Rob grimaced at Peter's deflection. He hated how he refused to take responsibility for his actions.

"Or you'd stopped yourself? He might not have stopped you, but you were the one who did this, Peter. This is on you. We've spoken to Frank and others, so we know this didn't come out of the blue. This was just a long, slow escalation. You've always had a temper, and you've skirted reprimands for excessive force before, always just getting away with it, partially because Frank, your long-time partner on the force, always stood up for you. He always backed you up, didn't he? Helped with alibis and such. He's a loyal friend that you're now throwing under the bus."

Peter rolled his eyes. "Yeah, whatever. He could have helped."

Their research showed this had been a double act from the start, with Frank seeing a kindred spirit in Peter and the pair of them helping each other as they rose through the ranks.

"So, going back to Joe Moon, the man you strangled. I take it you weren't aware that you were being filmed doing this?"

"As I said before, no. I had no idea until Curby showed me the video. Joe must have been going to meet someone, and they were the ones who filmed it. I don't know. Maybe they saw me and Frank coming and hid."

"Yeah, maybe. What happened next?"

Peter looked ashamed as he replied. "We hid the body. We buried it and tried to forget about it. About a week later, Curby got in touch and sent me a clip of the video. I told him to piss off and hoped nothing would come of it. But we got a tip-off about a buried body. I was terrified, but I couldn't stop it. There were too many people involved by that point. The body was exhumed, and I was on the verge of confessing when it was discovered to be someone else entirely. Not Joe. Apparently, Curby had dug Joe up and buried some homeless person I'd never met."

"It was a warning, wasn't it? They were showing you what they could do."

"Yeah. That's when it started, the blackmail. It was relentless, with Curby asking us to turn a blind eye to this or that, make certain things disappear or run errands for them. They always loved that one, having their own personal delivery service."

"I can imagine."

Rob was shocked at the scale of the operation. Curby had always seemed like a small player, leading a gang on the streets, but this hinted at a far bigger, more complex operation. They needed to stop them or bring Curby to justice, at least. But that task might fall to others while he dealt with Peter.

Rob watched the detective as he checked his notes. "Your father, Quentin Orleton. He was a decorated officer who dedicated his life to the force, right?"

"He had a long career, yes. I remember seeing the respect and power he had. I just wanted the same." Peter sighed. "He was an amazing man."

"Your dad was an archer as well, wasn't he? He taught you to shoot a bow and arrow, and you became quite good at it, as attested by the trophies in your office."

Peter shrugged. "Anyone can buy and shoot a bow. This is Nottingham. It's hardly rare around here. Who doesn't like the idea of Robin Hood?" Peter glanced up at a camera. "Loxley clearly does."

As their eyes met through the camera, Rob sat back in his chair and crossed his arms, watching the broken man on the screen. He'd lost everything. His life as he'd known it was over.

"You've been through the wringer," the detective said.

Peter's cold, dark eyes returned to the interviewing officer. "I don't need your sympathy."

"I beg to differ, but fair enough. We've been through your house and picked up your bow and arrow set. Preliminary analysis suggests that your broadhead hunting arrow heads match the wounds found on the body of Spencer Lawson. We also have photos and videos from Curby showing you out hunting people. I'm curious because you say they made you do things, but this seems different. You actively went out and did this. Members of Curby's gang kidnapped homeless people for you to use as living targets. Right?"

"That's right."

"But, why? Why did you start doing this?"

Peter sighed, apparently resigning himself to telling this story. "The stress of doing Curby's dirty work was getting too much to bear. I was a mess, and I mean like, a few days off a nervous breakdown or suicide kind of mess. So, from what I understand, Frank spoke with Curby, and I was forcibly brought out to Sherwood, given a pistol and told at gunpoint to take out my anger on a random homeless guy...and I did. I'm not proud of it. Something inside me just snapped. I imagined it was Curby and... Well, I killed him. I felt better after that, and it didn't feel like a big deal. So when I got stressed again, they repeated the exercise. By the third time I was kind of looking forward to it, so I used my bow. What can I say? It was cathartic."

"So you've done this a lot?"

"A few times," Peter admitted. "Rigby and a few others helped. They'd go out and pick up a new victim every so often when I requested it. So that, when I was ready, when I needed to vent, I'd take them out to Sherwood."

"And you'd kill them?"

"I would," Peter admitted. "As it turned out, I actually enjoyed it. It was kind of therapeutic, in a way, to vent my anger and worries like that. I know it's not right, but I think I became addicted. I just had to do it to remain sane. I wish I hadn't, of course. I'm going to pay the price now, but without it, I would have lost my mind much sooner." He laughed. "You know, it's funny. Before I'd ever killed anyone, I'd always thought that it would change me, you know, that I'd become a different person. But that didn't happen at all. I'm still me. I still love my wife and kids and doing fun stuff with them. I just happened to find something else that I enjoyed."

Peter spoke calmly and in an honest, matter-of-fact way about what he'd done as if he knew there was no way out, and he had no option but to accept his fate.

"But your wife had no idea?"

Rob's eyes flicked to another screen.

44

"I had no idea," Carmen said, from where she sat on the opposite side of the table to Scarlett. She looked like she'd not slept all night and sported dark rings under her glassy, bloodshot eyes. She'd been crying. A partially used box of tissues and its discarded contents stood testament to that on the table between them.

Scarlett felt terrible for her. She clearly had no clue what her husband, Peter, had been up to all these years. She'd believed him to be a hard-working, respectable police officer, a pillar of the community that others respected, when the truth couldn't be more removed from that fantasy.

She'd been living with a corrupt, lying, brutal murderer who revelled in hunting and killing innocent people that had been kidnapped from the streets. As if their lives weren't hard enough for these homeless people, they had been terrorised by this gang for months.

Carmen sniffed and wiped her nose. "I don't know what to tell you. I mean, he's always had a temper, but I didn't think he could do this."

"A temper?" Scarlett asked.

"He has a short fuse, sometimes. He's never hurt me, but…" She trailed off as if suddenly aware she wasn't being loyal to him and was saying something she shouldn't.

"But? But what?"

"Well, I suppose in recent months, he's been, I guess, a little on edge? He's been getting angrier, more easily. He's scared me a few times."

"How?" Scarlett urged.

"Just in the way he shouts, you know? Getting in my face and screaming at me when things don't work out for him. Sometimes it's just simple things, silly things. Even the kids have noticed. I've been meaning to try and talk to him, but I had no idea about all this."

"I understand," Scarlett replied, feeling sad for Carmen and what this would mean for her life, marriage, and kids. Their whole world was crumbling around them, and nothing could stop it now.

"What's going to happen to him?"

"I don't know," Scarlett answered, honestly. "I don't know."

45

"Hey, come here," Scarlett said.

Rob turned as he fiddled with his tie, trying to adjust it. "Hmm?"

She stepped up to him. "Chin up," she said, reaching for his tie.

"All of them?" Rob quipped, tilting his head back.

"Absolutely, I don't want to touch your jowls. Yuk." She pulled his tie back and forth before smoothing it down once she was happy. "There you go. You're vaguely presentable, now."

"No small task, let me tell you," he replied, retaking the seat behind his desk. "I hope she doesn't keep us waiting too long. I never feel like I can get much done while I'm waiting for a meeting with the boss."

"That's silly," Scarlett replied, retaking her seat. "And lazy."

"Thanks. Still coming for that drink tonight?"

"Of course. How can I resist the idea of spending time with a bunch of old, crusty blokes in a sweaty bar serving weak beer?"

"Don't forget dodging inappropriate remarks and cringe-inducing chat-up lines. You wouldn't want to miss that."

"I know. My life wouldn't be complete without that." She smiled at the silly, yet all too true comments. Rob enjoyed her giggle until the smile suddenly fell from her face. "Oh, heads up."

Rob turned, following her gaze to the office door, and saw Inspector Bill Rainault wandering in. He wore his usual slimy smile as he approached.

"Your buddies are in custody, Bill. They don't work in here anymore," Rob remarked.

"Still with the smart comments, I see." Bill sneered at him.

"Should I not be?"

Bill seemed to bite his lip, as if he wanted to snap back but stopped himself. "Actually, I wanted to just say, well done. You did some good work. You did my job for me, in fact."

"Well, if you'd actually been doing your job, maybe you would have seen that the corrupt officers were Peter and his buddy Frank."

The somewhat friendly smile dropped from Bill's face. "I'll admit, it is annoying that I failed to spot him, that is true. But now that you've ended a DCI's career, I can take solace in knowing that you have just joined a very select club of officers who have arrested their own. You'll be hated by some for what you've done and maybe ostracised even further than you already are." Bill smiled, but Rob wasn't feeling quite so cheerful anymore, and glared back at the PSU officer.

"Are you done yet?" Rob asked.

"I'm done. And remember, I'll be watching you." He turned to Scarlett and nodded to her. "Scarlett. Good to see you."

She raised an eyebrow, but said nothing.

With a final smile, Bill turned and walked out, leaving Rob to glare at his back until he disappeared from view. With him gone, Rob leaned back in his chair, a small storm cloud gathering above him. Bill never failed to put him in a bad mood.

"He cornered me on the stairs the other day," Scarlett said, suddenly.

Taking a breath in an attempt to let the bad mood fall away, Rob turned to Scarlett. She continued to stare at the door Bill had disappeared through, running her fingers through the tail of blonde hair that fell over her shoulder.

"Oh? Warning you about me again, was he?"

"Yeah." She fixed her sapphire blue eyes on him. "He said your family are criminals."

Rob gritted his teeth for a moment. "Did he, indeed?" He'd not yet gone into much detail about his family with Scarlett. But if she was standing up for him against the likes of

Bill, she probably needed to know a little more about what she was doing by siding with him.

"Yep. He said something about you being estranged from them?"

"He's right, I left home at seventeen and never looked back. I'm from a little market town in north Nottinghamshire called Retford and lived there with my family until my mother disappeared just after my seventeenth birthday."

"Disappeared?"

"Or left. I don't know. One day she was there, and the next... The only thing I have left of hers is my car. She bought it for my birthday. I've tried looking for her, but I've not found her, yet."

"I'm so sorry."

"That's okay. I ran away too before I reached eighteen, and never went back."

"Why?"

"Because the rumours are true. They are criminals. A typical British firm. A crime family. My mother protected me from them, but when she left, I knew I had to get out before I got sucked into that world. Nailer helped. He got me out and brought me down here. I joined the police seven years later and never looked back."

"And you've not seen your family since?"

Rob sighed. "Not in any significant way, no. I've never returned to my family home or sought them out. I've got no interest in them. I've had a couple of encounters down through the years with one or two of my brothers, but that's it. I want nothing to do with them."

"You've been vetted, though?"

"Of course. I've never hidden my past from the police and was honest from day one. I'd have to be pretty stupid to hide something like that. I've passed vetting each time and never had an issue because I'm not working for my family. In fact, I don't really think of them as my family anymore. Nailer has been more of a father to me than my actual father."

"So, it's been what, twenty years since you've seen or had any contact with them?"

"Twenty-one years," Rob confirmed. "And I don't see that ending any time soon."

"So that's why Bill's got it in for you."

"Yeah. That's why. To him, it's black and white. I was born into a criminal family, so it makes sense that I must be one too." Rob shrugged. "Thanks for standing by me, by the way. I appreciate it. You didn't have to do that."

"I make a point of making my own judgements about people and not relying on the opinions of others, and that was true for you too."

"Well, thank you."

"Pleasure." She smiled brightly, her enthusiasm undimmed by Bill's appearance. He needed to take a leaf from her book and be more positive in life.

"Right then, guys," Nailer called out as he walked into the office, a big grin across his face. "Let's not keep Landon waiting, shall we?"

"Of course not," Rob agreed, standing up. The office seemed so much quieter now that Peter and Frank had left and were yet to be replaced.

Nailer walked them down the corridor and into a side room that Landon had been using as a temporary office. He walked in to find her sitting behind her desk.

"Come in Rob, Scarlett, Take a seat."

"Thank you, Ma'am," they replied and did as she asked.

"So, where are you with all this now?"

"I think there's only a few details left for us to report," Rob replied. "The burnt-out Range Rover appears to be the one used during that botched body disposal in Sherwood. We got a match from the remains of its tyres against the tracks we found at the crime scene, and we were also able to match the fibres from one of the seats to the fibres under Spencer's fingernails."

"Excellent," Landon complimented.

"We also got a match between the fibres found in in Spencer's hair and the hood that Lorraine was wearing when she was dumped outside here. It seems Spencer had worn that same hood at some point."

"Great work. And how're things going with Peter and Frank?"

"They'd in custody, waiting for trial. To the best of my knowledge, the CPS seem happy with everything and will be moving forward with the case. There's a tonne of evidence against them with the videos and photos we received. They worked with Curby and the Top Valley Boyz for years, keeping the heat off the gang in return for money and because of the massive amount of evidence they had against Peter and Frank. But as they did more work for Curby, it just got worse. They kept filming, drawing them deeper and deeper in. There was no way out for either of them, not without exploding their lives in the process. I kind of feel sorry for them in a way because they got themselves in a terrible position and couldn't get out. They'll serve time and never work in the police again."

"You feel sorry for them?" Scarlett asked, looking at him with a raised eyebrow. "After all the abuse he subjected you to?"

Rob shrugged. "He deserves everything he gets, of course."

"Good," Scarlett commented.

"What about the gang?" Landon asked.

"Curby and his crew? We're dealing with them too. We've made several arrests already, and there'll be more soon. I guess Curby was smart in handing Lorraine back and giving us his blackmail material. He'll no doubt use that to lessen any charges brought against him and deny any knowledge or involvement in Lorraine's kidnapping. I've heard talk that there is a possibility that he could be a useful informant, but that comes with massive risk, and I don't think I like that idea myself. He's a monster and an intelligent one at that."

"Why do you think Curby burnt his bridges with Peter?" Landon asked.

"Without asking him directly, I can't be sure. But I think he knew Peter was becoming more of a liability than an asset. His actions were actively damaging his gang and their businesses, so he cut his losses."

"Makes sense," Landon confirmed.

"Just to be clear, I'd love to get Curby locked up as well. He's a dangerous man, and while he's out on the streets, people won't be safe."

"I agree," Scarlett confirmed. "We'll get him."

"Noted," Landon replied. "Okay, well done. This is all excellent work. I have to say that I don't like that two of our own were corrupt and working against us. It doesn't look good to the public and damages the trust they have in us when an officer is revealed to be a criminal. But it's better they're rooted out than left to fester."

"I agree," Rob replied.

"I will warn you now, though, that you won't make any friends through this. As corrupt as he was, you have brought down a DCI, and that will make people nervous about you."

"I think I can handle a little more suspicion and less than friendly comments," Rob replied, feeling unfazed by the idea. "Bill Rainault said the same just before we came through here, actually."

"Making friends, are we?" Landon asked.

"Not quite."

"Understandable where Bill's concerned," she replied. "Well, as I said, I'm impressed, and frankly, I think you're well overdue for a promotion, so I'm going to recommend that we see about making you an Inspector in short order. Okay?"

"Of course, thank you, Ma'am." It wasn't something he had been actively aiming for, but it was a massive compliment, and he couldn't hold back the smile that broke out across his face.

"Well done to you too, Scarlett. An excellent first case with us."

"Thank you," she replied.

"And that's not all. As you are probably aware, the Nottinghamshire arm of the East Midlands Special Operations

Unit has been somewhat understaffed of late, following a recent disastrous operation, and I'd like to fix that. So, Nailer, I'm re-assigning you to the Unit, and will need for you to choose your team."

"Thank you, Ma'am."

"Might I suggest that you bring Rob and Scarlett on board as your first appointees?" She turned to Rob and Scarlett. "Providing you're open to the idea?"

Rob was shocked and thrilled in equal measure. "Of course, yes. That would be amazing."

"Absolutely Ma'am," Nailer agreed.

"It would be an honour," Scarlett added. "Thank you."

Landon turned to Nailer. "I'll expect the rest of your hand-picked list of officers on my desk as soon as possible."

Rob turned to Nailer. "Nick Miller," he suggested.

Nailer nodded.

"You'll be working out of the Sherwood Lodge Headquarters once all this is wrapped up, and you'll be covering the whole county and beyond, not just Nottingham. I'm looking forward to working with you."

"Thank you," Rob said, joining the chorus of thanks from Scarlett and Nailer.

"That's okay. Now, with all that out of the way, I think you deserve a night off."

Rob sighed. "That would be good."

"Ok, well, in that case, I have a last surprise." Landon reached for her phone and pressed a button as she held it to her ear. "Yes, send them in. Thank you."

Rob frowned as Landon replaced the receiver and smiled, waiting. Rob was about to say something, when there was a knock at the door.

"Come in," Landon said.

Being polite, Rob and the others got to their feet to welcome whoever was about to join them. The door opened, and two people walked in.

Rob took a moment to realise who he was looking at but smiled when it suddenly clicked.

"Jon? Christ, I had no idea you were here."

Jon Pilgrim smiled back at him. He was taller than Rob, but nowhere near Nailer's height and looked better than when Rob had last seen him. The dark-haired, clean-shaven man smiled back, and the pair came together in a brief embrace.

"It's good to see you, man," Jon said, while bear hugging him.

"You too." They separated. "You should have called to say you were coming up."

"And where would the surprise have been in that?"

"Yeah, fair point."

"We're just up for a visit, to see my family, and thought we'd pop in as a little surprise," Jon explained.

"Well, it's great to see you again. How long has it been?"

"About two years," Jon replied.

"And how's Surrey?" Rob glanced over at the pretty, freckled, auburn-haired woman standing beside him, wearing a fitted suit and her hair up in a ponytail. He smiled at her, and she smiled back.

"Good, thanks. This is Kate, by the way."

Kate offered her hand. "DS Kate O'Connell," she said with a slight Irish flavour to her accent. "Nice to meet you. I've heard all about you."

"Oh, shit. I hope not." Rob grinned. "This is Scarlett Stutely. She's from your neck of the woods, actually."

"Oh," Jon replied. "Surrey? Which station?"

"Mount Browne," Scarlett replied with a smile. "Maybe this is some kind of cultural exchange?"

"Don't get me started on that," Jon replied. "These southerners have some weird ways of doing things."

"Nothing compared to you northerners," Scarlett poked back.

"Girl, you said it," Kate remarked and held up her hand.

Scarlett high-fived it.

"I think this deserves a celebration," Pilgrim said.

"Drinks on you then?" Nailer asked.

"Just the first round," Jon replied. "Have you seen the cost of petrol lately? It cost us an arm and a leg to get up here."

"So generous," Rob replied with a grin and turned to the Superintendent. "Care to join us?"

She smiled. "Another time. Have fun."

"I'll hold you to that."

"Go on, get out of here."

"Will do, Ma'am. Will do."

THE END

Get 3 BONUS Chapters

Rob and Scarlett go after Curby.

Sign up to my Mailing List to get the Chapters

BookHip.com/JDKWAGT

Hell To Pay

Detective Loxley, book 2, available here;

www.amazon.co.uk/dp/B0B75FBL8G

Author Note

Thank you for reading this first book in my Detective Loxley series. I hope you enjoyed it.

The idea for this series has been hanging around in my head for a long time, and I first came up with the concept of a Detective Loxley back in the early books of my DCI Pilgrim series.

It seemed like a natural fit for me, as I was born and raised in Nottinghamshire and lived there until my twenties. I still visit regularly as my family is still based there, and it's a beautiful part of the country, filled with a rich and famous history which I felt was ripe for use in a book such as this.

If you've picked up on the many Robin Hood references in this book, feel free to reach out and let me know. Some are more subtle than others, so I'd love to know which ones you caught.

This book is personal to me in many ways, which I might well talk about more in Author notes to come (or in my face group).

But one of those ways is in Rob's cat, Muffin.

Years ago, my wife (fiancée at the time) and I got two cats, a brother and a sister, who we called Poppy and Muffin. They were lovely and got on so well. Unfortunately, Muffin got hit by a car one day, and ended up being put to sleep.

Poppy is still with us, years later (she's 14 now), but when I was writing this book, I thought I'd give Muffin another lease of life as Rob's cat.

I'm sure I can think of some adventures for Muffin in future books, and hope you will join me and Muffin on them.

If you enjoyed this and haven't read any of my other works, then you might want to read my DC O'Connell trilogy and my DCI Pilgrim series too, which do link into this book, as you can tell by the final chapter.

Thanks again.

Andrew

Come and join in the discussion about my books in my Facebook Group:
www.facebook.com/groups/alfraine.readers

Book List

www.alfraineauthor.co.uk/books

Printed in Great Britain
by Amazon